PRAISE FOR

THE FEALTY OF MONSTERS

"Grotesqueries abound in THE FEALTY OF MONSTERS—and when Ladz is the one conducting the horror, you know it's worth your time. This is one revolution best witnessed from the splash zone, so buckle up, put on your poncho, and get ready for the multiple blood baths to follow."

— **T.D. Cloud**, author of *OSSUARY*

"With the dark gothic fantasy sensibilities of *Berserk*, *Castlevania*, and *Bloodborne*, Ladz's first volume of THE FEALTY OF MONSTERS is thrilling, gory, and queer as hell. A must-read."

—**Morgan Dante**, author of
A FLAME IN THE NIGHT

"With prose as sharp and glittering as broken glass, Ladz weaves an unflinching tale of gothic gruesomeness, showing that the most danger-ous monsters live where we least expect it—in the hearts of us all."

—**K.M. Enright**, author of *MISTRESS OF LIES*

"THE FEALTY OF MONSTERS is just as sexy as it is terribly thrilling. Within a fantasy world full of political intrigue and strife, Ladz creates beautiful characters who fit inside it seamlessly. Characters who are neither good nor evil, but always keep the reader guessing, painting a fascinating air of mystery throughout the whole book. If you want horror, vampires, and alluring beasts, you need this book!"

—**S.S. Genesee**, author of the
ALL TOMORROW'S PHOTOS Duology

"you are the proletariat in petrograd for the october revolution. you go to kill the czar but—oh wait! the vampire."

—AO3 user, **jonphaedrus**

"With THE FEALTY OF MONSTERS, Ladz has built a world with foundations in Russian history but enhanced with an incredible dose of the gothic, macabre and brutally sexy. This is dark, bloody aristocratic politics with machinations so deep you won't trust a single character. A staple work of dark fantasy!"

—**Brent Lambert**, author of
A NECESSARY CHAOS

"[THE FEALTY OF MONSTERS] is a decadent and sordid novel which also asks the most urgent question of our time: what would you do to stop a war?"

—**Noah Medlock**, author of *A Botanical Daughter*

"The last days of the Russian Empire refracted through a blood-spattered, and gold-plated, lens into horror, magic, intrigue, and the best kind of scuzzy carnality. What else could you possibly need?"

—**Elijah Kinch Spector**, author of
KALYNA THE SOOTHSAYER

"Contempt for vampires, specifically the monstrous hybrids called bestiapirs, chills the air for one year after the massacre of 1917. Sasza is one such vampire working in stealth among the Odonic Empire's diplomats, alongside his father Władysław "Władek" Czarnolaski, the Imperial Magician. Their wavering political certainty begins to be tested when a retaliatory war against the Vampire States rears its noble head, and Sasza's friendship with the Crown undergoes metamorphosis into an alliance befitting beasts. An ominous, unsettling novel that knows how to scare."

—**Pom Poison**, creator of
LITTLE DEATH

THE FEALTY OF MONSTERS: VOLUME 1

ILLUSTRATED BY HÄXAN

LADZ

ROBOT DINOSAUR PRESS

Robot Dinosaur Press is a trademark of Chipped Cup Collective.
www.robotdinosaurpress.com

Publication history
First Edition: March 2024

Book Cover & Interior Illustrations by Soren Häxan (https://www.thornapple-press.com/)

No AI generated content was used in the creation of this book or its cover.

ISBN Data
eBook ISBN: 9798223465096
ASIN: B0CLKZ7JBC
Paperback ISBN: 9798989398706

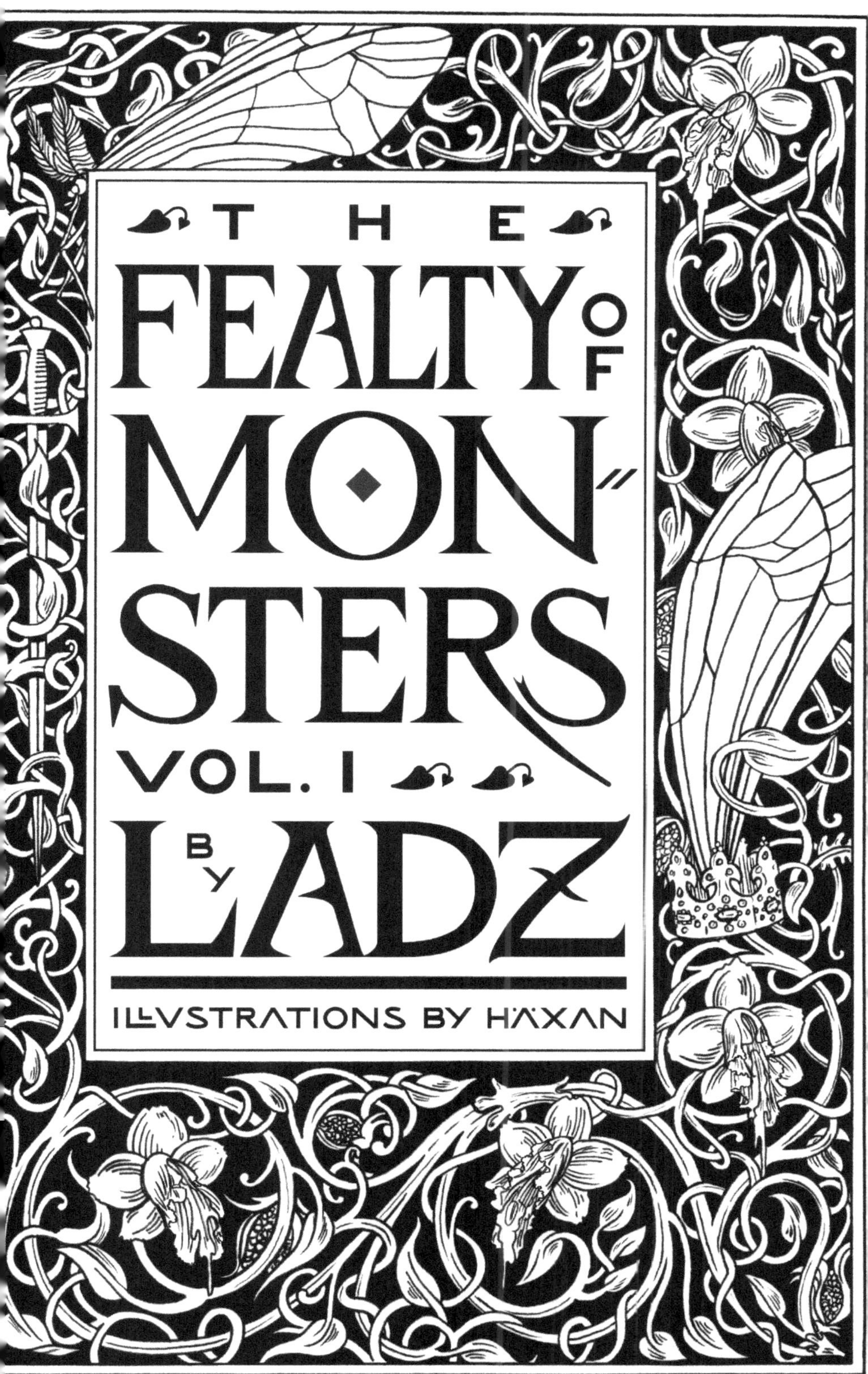
THE
FEALTY OF
MON-
STERS
VOL. I
BY LADZ
ILLVSTRATIONS BY HÄXAN

Contents

Author's Note

This is a work of fantasy heavily inspired by the history of the fall of the Russian Empire at the beginning of the Twentieth century. I use the word "inspired" because this work is not meant to be a faithful retelling of events, political or otherwise. If you want to experience the rabbit hole fell down, please see the bibliography.

There is a compendium of characters, places, and terms at the end of the work for your reference and perusal.

Trigger Warnings

Blood, gore, body horror, blood drinking, needles, emetophobia (blood), mosquitos, patricide, infidelity, explicit sexual acts and situations, dubious consent, age gap relationship between adults, urination (non-sexual), self-harm for magic use, depiction and discussion of alcoholism and drinking, depiction of a panic attack, mentions of war, mentions of sedition

To Koren –
Thank you for enabling all this

Prologue

Summer 1917

The Żyła river separates the Kingdom of Waza and the Empire of Odon with its tall, jagged cliff-like riversides and rushing waters just as sharp. The few places of safe crossing answer to either crown directly, and one such port city is known as Daszek, renowned for its scholarship, funded and ruled by House Jackiewicz.

This city of academic rigor has not one but four universities, and its population dwindles over the summer when students return to familial estates or explore more foreign affairs. Except for one week, during a celebration called the Inventors' Fair. This summer, however, the student body has expanded after the decree allowing non-aristocrats to attend institutions of higher learning, provided they can afford it or have proved their mettle with grades and auditions. While once only aristocrats studied, they are now joined by a new cohort mostly belonging to the upper classes.

To help orient these droves of new students, the Jackiewiczes put more resources into the Inventors' Fair than in a typical year. Daszek teems with craftsmen, scholars, and teachers from across the Odonic Empire arriving to show off their wares and research to their counterparts traveling in from the Kingdom. Deals are made between titans of industries, new experiments are displayed, and deeper discussion about the relationship between the workers and their technology both new and old take place at various forums and smaller conferences.

While some of the proletariat have been allowed to participate in the institutions of higher learning, those with the knowledge but not the pedigree are excluded from these conversations and presentations that might affect the future of their work. Though they know the mechanisms and technology best, some can't afford to get certifications, like Jan and his father, autocar mechanics working Daszek's outskirts.

After a long morning of tuning vehicles, they both have their shirts wrapped around their waists. Sweat cascades down Jan's father's fuzzy front like a babbling waterfall. Meanwhile, Jan's exertion pools in the grooves of undefined muscles, a body which looks soft but beneath hides work-honed strength. Hot air exchanges one stink for another—bodily odors swapping with the heavy air released from perspiring trees and the evaporating water splashing below. The iron keeping the workshop's boxy frame aloft captures this heat.

The marshlands to the south offer no reprieve, only mosquitoes, hungry and breeding.

Jan's father slaps one of the buzzing nuisances, slamming down the fifth and final autocar's hood. Its black surface glistens like tar. "Sometimes I wish these parasites would bring in their cars more than once a year."

Jan shrugs as he wipes off the insect guts and polishes the hood once again. The aristocrats who are their steady customers arrive in sleek cars which run on the conversion of self-administered magic to energy. It's a cleaner form of transport than coal, but its use confers a similar mess over time. All magic leaves a small residue, and the repetition of the vehicle activation builds up. Cleaning and exchanging the battery is a process called tuning, and it's the bulk of a mechanics' work.

For Jan and his father's rough hands, these exchanges aren't difficult. But neglect breeds problems which settle and fester unless one seeks out solutions. With autocars being the preferred mode of transportation for those who would rather not interact with the proletariat on mass transit, the work was steady. The men's informal training mattered little in terms of whether they had autocars to work on or not.

"Do you think it's stinginess or laziness?" Tata asks.

"Stinginess?" Jan knows he'll have to balance their accounts at the end of the week. But he also has a good memory for patterns and hasn't noticed anything which would warrant the question.

"See, they *could* bring their autocars more than once a year, but it's clear they never do." Sweat drips onto his thick, black mustache. "Imagine the money we could be making teaching them."

The window on their office door has empty spaces reserved for certifications they do not have. The perfect time to ask arises. "Tata, I was thinking: perhaps I could get trained in teaching and mechanics? I think it would be good for the business."

"And then what? I do all the work myself? You want to leave your father alone like that?" He throws his son a flask.

Jan takes a cautious sip. It's not water. "I'd be studying here, Tata. I can work on the weekends—"

"I'm just being a little sensitive, son. Work is drying up anyway." He takes the flask back.

"What do you mean?"

"What I mean is, we can close up shop early. That was the last of today's appointments."

Jan purses his lips to one side. "Are you sure?"

"You do our paperwork. You tell me." There had been no calls for last-minute tune ups. "I've also heard from the union that people are traveling less, but what *I* really think is that they just don't want to work with people like us anymore."

"Then let me get a certification, Tata. Then we'll get new business and—"

"If you want to waste our money on exams, so be it." Tata grunts. "As if seven generations of business isn't enough proof that we have the skills."

This is exactly like Tata. Stubborn to a fault, right for the most part, except for things like longer term planning. "I do; I truly think it'll be better for us."

"Will getting a certification fix the fact that aristocrats now take their own trains, far away from what they're calling the 'new rich' and the rats like us?"

"Where are you hearing this?"

"The union!"

Jan never knows what his father means by the union, but there have been no missives sent which suggest anything like what his father says. "You know, if I do get certified, I can probably get a job servicing those trains and keep this business afloat. I won't abandon you, Tata."

His father places a wet, meaty hand on Jan's shoulder. "Let's put this discussion away. I need a hearty dinner and some rest."

Tata speaks in an affect that's much softer than Jan is accustomed to. The last time he sweetened himself in this way, it was because Jan had just lost his best friend, as if, in his duty as a single father, it was his job to play the role of the disciplinarian and the support. He uses that same voice now, with the same promise of physical care to distract from more rooted ills.

"If that's what you want, Tata."

They would just be on time for all the other working people making their way home or out to restaurants to eat their midday meal, to get the energy required for the rest of the day. An appetite, however, abandons Jan. His heart thrums in his chest, and it's not the damp, still air of the workshop constricting his vessels. Closing early sets the next twelve months on the wrong fiscal foot.

Jan tidies up the shop, putting away their tools and oils while his father changes into cleaner, more civil clothing, leaving his soiled shirt and trousers behind on hangers in the back. To get home, they need public transit. Though they typically do not use their own autocar to get to work, Jan should have found it suspicious that in the days leading up to the Inventors' Fair, Tata would leave their schedule up to the whims of the tram. He's accustomed to late nights and the flexibility of coming and going whenever.

Luckily, the tramway stop closest to them sits across from the shop in the middle of their quiet street. The summer sun beats relentlessly across Daszek's cobbled outskirts. Maple trees line the sidewalks, shielding them in shade. There are no spaces for autocars because most of the residents cannot afford vehicles of their own, and the tramway weaving through the city provides more than enough access to most districts and neighborhoods.

After shuttering the shop for the day, Jan and his father wait for the tram, sweat mixing with the healthy layer of engineering muck still slicked across their arms.

And they wait.

And they wait.

And they wait some more.

"It seems we are walking home, son." As Jan's father says this, a tram rolls up from around the corner. Its white frame and russet brown body crawls along its rail, pulled along the electric wire suspended high above the street. It stops with a swoosh. They get on, drop the requisite coins for the fare, and home they go.

Several women off to their afternoon shifts sit next to each other, leaning into each other's fans despite the flat steel petals spinning in metal cages along the ceiling. With the windows open, air at least moves, lifting the humidity and some of the smells. The men don't dare sit on the shiny resin-coated wooden seats—the sounds of their pants unsticking and the remaining thin layer of moisture cause enough embarrassment.

Their apartment complex lies close enough to Daszek's Centrum to warrant this commute to the residential outskirts. It takes several stops, long enough to get lost in the hypnagogic hissing left behind by the moving vehicle. Jan rests his head against the thin metal pole, using his knuckles as a pillow. His father stands across from him, resting in the same position. There are those who enjoy reading or chatting on their journeys, but neither mechanic relishes in that distraction. It's the one time, Jan finds, where he has his mind all to himself, to pluck at meandering thoughts or ignore them altogether.

Despite the earlier argument with Jan's father, it's a quiet ride in Jan's mind.

The tram's halting stop throws him from his reverie. His legs stumble, and he snatches the pole. He's taken this route enough to know they're between stations. He glances at his father, who has furrowed his brows as they wait for some kind of announcement.

The conductor speaks into the public address radio. "Attention, we are being held up by tram traf—"

A mass hits the side of the tram with such force, those seated become unseated, and those standing find themselves slamming face-first into the tram's windows as the vehicle collapses onto its side. The cables feeding the vehicle energy snap. It shrieks off its rails. Jan flies, falling on top of his father, his elbows driving into the older man's back. In the cacophony of the tram derailment—the shouting, the scratching of metal against pavement—Jan doesn't see what became of his father's face. Blood stains the glass. His father does not move.

Head throbbing, Jan rolls himself off his father. The conductor emerges from his station and dashes through the tram, hopping over tangled bodies to get to the emergency hatch. He shoves it open. Passengers leave. Jan helps the conductor get others out before he secures his own exit.

He leaps off the top, only to find the other passengers lying in slaughtered heaps. Arms lay far from their crushed torsos, splayed like meat at a butcher's shop. Blood seeps into the urban streets' grooves.

Jan does not get the chance to wonder what hit the tram so hard as to cause a derailment and why he hadn't heard panicked sounds of violence. Large hands grip the top of his head and his shoulders. The vertebrae holding his skull snap. Four more hands curl around his limbs, tearing them off.

He dies before he can realize that the thing severing his head was neither human nor beast, but something else entirely.

ONE

Five Months Later; Winter 1917

I.

Her Highness Gita Iwanowicz's erotic yowling interrupts Sasza's morning coffee. He chokes on the bitter beverage, brown drops dirtying the luxurious parchment upon which the imperial aristocracy prefers to send their weeks' ignored correspondences. The bed's thudding against the ceiling had been distracting enough, but it's a sound muffled by the rest of their two-bedroom townhouse. The Czarnolaski residence is a solitary structure separated from the main structure of the Imperial Palace by several kilometers of lawns, trees, and a large pond. The only way to get into the Imperial Grounds' main boulevard is up the cobbled driveway. They have no servants or staff, so Sasza is the only other body to hear it and be bothered.

Moreover, the problem with the shouting isn't that Her Highness engages in intercourse and that she wants everyone within hearing distance to know it.

The problem is that the man groin-deep in the empress is not the emperor, but Sasza's father, Władysław Czarnolaski, the Imperial Magician.

No one quite knows what the role of Imperial Magician entails. It was a new position carved out for a man whose well-woven connections got himself and his son into the Iwanowiczes' good graces. It had been years, however, since Władysław had taken one of his allies to his bed chambers. More often than not, it had gotten him in trouble. In those earlier trysts, Władysław only had himself to worry about. It seems he doesn't worry for his offspring anymore.

Lucky for the safety of their status and security, Sasza had already been laying the groundwork for functioning as a more disciplined Imperial Magician. Most of Władysław's correspondences have already been handled by Sasza, especially after the tragedy during the summer's Inventors' Fair known as the Jackiewicz Incident. The Jackiewiczes took blame for the attack. Their defenses were unprepared; to stave off the unseen foe, they unleashed a fiery torrent upon Daszek's streets, incinerating all who got caught up in the infernal maelstrom. To their merit, they had also taken responsibility for recovery efforts, including reparations to the city itself and for those who had lost loved ones.

Sasza has been asking for weeks on their behalf if the upcoming Winter Solstice Ball can collect donations to honor lives lost and Daszek's reconstruction. He feels guilty for not having been there; he declined the invitation to attend the Inventors' Fair, but in hindsight, he might not have made it out alive. Regardless of the regret, the emperor could at least address the simple request, but he hasn't. Sasza has tried to garner support for a more thorough investigation, using Władysław's pens and the Czarnolaski seal. None came.

On his own, he gathered the phrase "Abyssal Flock" and a list of suspected dissidents, most of whom had never even been near Daszek. He suspects his father might know something, but Sasza has never mustered the courage to ask, lest it be taken as an accusation of treason.

Władysław bellows, a man gasping in the throes of that little death. Sasza drags his hands through his hair white as silver snow, hoping the silencing ward he had placed upon the house remains. Casting a spell to dampen *all* sound coming from their residence is asking a lot of Sasza.

Not only does it require a lot of magical energy, but it also requires him to reach deep into his knowledge of the protolanguage's vocabulary, which not only binds together the languages of the Vampire States, the Odonic Empire, and the Kingdom of Waza, but acts as magic's catalyst. Hardly spoken aside from contemporary cognates, its syllables and word segments are used only in casting. The more complicated the spell, the more linguistic manipulation it needs. Warding a singular room to make it silent to those beyond it, for example, takes a single thought and a snap from an experienced magician like Sasza. But entire buildings require more syllables, more gestures, and greater intention.

His third cup of coffee does not summon the focus he spent.

A third cigarette, however, might. As he lights the stick, the wooden clock hanging opposite the massive, old stove announces the top of the hour. The upstairs noises stop. Sasza sighs, but what for, he's uncertain. It's not disappointment, though that has certainly been his recent sentiment towards his father. It's not relief, though the quiet is welcome. It's a breath withheld, a promise of words to be spoken once the oxygen, nicotine, and caffeine settle into his mind's grooves. This bitter cocktail should calm his heart, which does not want to slow down.

He hopes Władysław told Empress Gita that her own daughter, Świetlana, is on her way for a breakfast time meeting with Sasza.

The last thing he wants is for his father's incompetence as the Emperor's magician to compound the incompetence of the spoiled ruler. That would make people suspicious of their roles and lead to the dissolution of the power, privilege, and comfort they had built for themselves among the Odonic elite. Some buffer exists as Władysław is quite infamous already for being a charlatan in his social spheres.

If Władysław's political foundation crumbles, people might learn the truth: two vampires have infiltrated the zenith of Odonic Imperial society. This is dangerous, especially in a climate where aristocrats still wounded from the last civil war among humans now want to start one with the vampires.

At least, that's what some of these letters from Lady Bianka Lewoński seem to suggest. It's ahistorical; the vampires have never been an enemy of the Empire, not even when they fought for their own autonomous zones and won. Sasza needs to discuss these warmongering ravings with Lady Świetlana. What he wants to avoid is having to quell the inevitable outburst at discovering her mother's infidelity.

Sasza takes a drag, the smoke pluming around him. It matches the sharp, burnt taste of most other human consumables. But unlike coffee or alcohol which require vast quantities to have the same effect on vampires, the nicotine found within the tobacco provides the right amount of clarity.

After some shuffling upstairs, Władysław Czarnolaski graces the kitchen with his presence. His gray, aged hair stands as if struck by lightning, no doubt the work of their cold-weather sheets and the dry, wintry air. Bruises pepper both sides of his neck and the bit of his chest uncovered by a loose, white shirt. Sasza barely catches a glance of Empress Gita as she sneaks out the front door, rushing to return to the palace before her husband notices her absence. He won't, for Emperor Iwan starts his days earlier than most others for unknown reasons, and the imperial mansion has plenty of servants' entrances and hidden quarters.

"Father," Sasza says, disapprovingly. At twenty-three, he's old enough to be a father himself. But without preparation or warning, he's been playing the role of disciplinary parent to a grown man over-indulging in his own infamous debauchery.

Władysław wets his hand at the sink and smooths his thinning, silvery mop against his scalp. "Sasza, I didn't think you'd be back yet."

Sasza struggles to keep his face steady. His father knows that Sasza always returns from his excursions at the work week's start, either the night before or in the early pre-dawn hours. He goes on these quarterly retreats to Castle Wanda, the nearest Vampire State, under a pseudonym, to give himself at least a few days' reprieve from hunting at night like an animal. Had his father stopped paying attention to anything that wasn't the imperial pussy?

"I returned late last night, as always," he says, tempering the annoyance with more smoke.

Władysław's amber eyes, hooded like Sasza's, catch on the pile of letters next to the coffee cup. "Did you read those already?"

"Yes."

Władysław raises a brow. "Hm, much appreciated, son. I've answered a few but didn't realize there were quite so many."

It's a lie. He knows full well the missives he receives—the way he avoids answering the Jackiewiczes or anyone else investigating the Incident is deliberate. With the clock counting down to Lady Świetlana's visit, Sasza cannot ask about it.

"More come every day, Father. I don't know if you've seen a calendar, but the solstice approaches, and it seems most aristocrats are preparing for the end of the year and its ball." This party planning has been Lady Świetlana's big project for weeks now. It's a duty more than anything; she hates attending these social gatherings, but it's the task delegated to Iwanowicz children for generations now.

"Gita tells me she's excited for what Świetlana has planned in terms of the theme. She's quite good at keeping a budget."

"Oh, I see we're referring to Her Highness by her first name." Sasza isn't even sure he's heard the emperor call his wife by her unobstructed first name, which might be part of Władysław's temptation.

"*I* am. *You* are not."

Sasza wouldn't dare. "Lady Świetlana tells me there's going to be an announcement at the ball. Has Her Highness Gita mentioned anything about it?"

Władysław pours himself some coffee from the kettle. "What would there be to announce, my dear child? That there is absolutely nothing to worry about?"

If Władysław had been reading his own correspondences, then he'd know there is plenty to be concerned with. "I suppose you're right." Sasza puts out his cigarette in the dregs of his last coffee. He grabs stamped envelopes from the side—responses ready to be sent. "After you freshen up, Father, you should bring these—"

Knocks come at the front door—the time says it's too soon for Świetlana's arrival. Sasza bristles. Someone must have seen Her Highness Gita leave the townhouse. Someone must be checking in on them, ready to arrest them as spies and beasts due to the discovery of the ill-conceived affair. Their days in the Imperial Court are numbered.

When his father doesn't move, Sasza rises from the table and goes to address the surprise visitor. Of the two of them, he's the more powerful, especially with the feeding he did while away. The Vampire States have an entire industry around blood harvesting and a thriving restaurant culture that has perfected its preparation. It doesn't have to come from the living if he doesn't want it to; the effect is the same and keeps him sated for as long. His blood tingles with restoration, sharpening his senses. As he approaches the front entrance, however, he relaxes when a familiar scent hits his nose.

"Good morning, Sasza." Her Highness Lady Świetlana has shown up uncharacteristically early. She has her black hair pulled back into a high tail, strands tucked away from her face. She's donned a blazer and trousers—the absence of a coat indicates she took an autocar, rather than trudging across the frozen imperial grounds and leaving herself vulnerable to the wintery elements. "Is it still a good time for our weekly breakfast?"

"Of course." The clock had not yet called its lesser bell for the half-hour. A sharp, icy wind kisses his cheek. The temperatures had fallen drastically overnight.

"Did you forget? You look like you have just awakened."

His trips are the kinds of holidays that require their own post-travel holiday. Sleep eludes him, as does his own schedule and any sense of time's passing. He clears his claggy throat. "Oh, it's nothing. You know how difficult it can be to return to normal life after leave. Would you like me to get changed?" He has not had a chance to change out of the unstructured, over-sized sweater and slacks he considers his house clothes.

"We have no appointments with my father today, so be as comfortable as you want to be." She shivers, and Sasza ushers her inside. Lady Świetlana notices Władysław. "Good morning, Lord Czarnolaski. And how was your weekend?"

Sasza cannot read the soft expression her gently painted lips and thick, manicured brows maintain. If she knows her mother had just been in that house, she doesn't show it.

What also helps is that Władysław had quickly changed into a sweater that covers his neck. "Oh, it was splendid, Your Highness. I was able to catch up on some work." Władysław blocks Świetlana's view of the kitchen and the papers strewn about the table where Sasza had left them.

"Since it is quite chilly outside, perhaps we can meet in the salon?" Sasza proposes as he closes the door. It's the smallest room in the house, with its windows reinforced to keep the hearth's heat in.

"I'm fine with just the kitchen, if that's alright with you." Lady Świetlana crouches to remove her boots.

"Perfectly fine with me. Did you walk over here?"

"Oh, heavens no. A valet brought me because it's cold and I woke up late."

Just as Sasza suspected. She tends to take her tardiness and transform it into punctuality regardless of the presence of time pieces.

"Speaking of autocars," Władysław says as he puts on his own thick coat and warmer shoes. "Son, I am going to bring the car in for servicing, and then I'm gone the rest of the day. Do you need anything from Centrum?"

This surprises Sasza. Though he typically cannot trust his father to maintain the errands list, Sasza is still too exhausted from his travels to make it himself, much less to execute the tasks listed. He's sure there's some novelty he might want his father to purchase at the Centrum's shops and markets, but his mind draws a blank.

"That won't be necessary, Father," he says.

"I will see you tonight, then. Have a good day." Władysław pauses. "You too, Your Highness." He throws his too-large winter coat on his lanky frame and exits with the tail trailing behind.

Świetlana gives him a tender wave as the door slams.

"Can I get you some coffee, Your Highness?" Sasza asks.

"If it's still warm, yes please. I ate breakfast before leaving."

He hadn't even considered that he would have to host her with food; it's lucky for him that it's not a relevant concern. Their scant pantry hides behind an always-closed door in the kitchen. Whenever they need to borrow a housekeeper from the palace, Sasza pays them handsomely to keep their clients' strangeness a secret.

The kitchen table with Sasza's work still on it sits pressed against the wall, beneath a window which hardly gets any sun. Despite winter's waning daylight, Sasza made sure to slather himself in the oils and lotions to protect his skin from blisters and burns.

Sasza puts the coffee opposite the seat he had claimed for his early-morning reading.

"Thank you so much; this is perfect." Świetlana places her dossier next to the mug and takes a long drink. "Sasza, I saw my mother approaching the boulevard as we turned into your driveway. I did not realize she has business with the Imperial Magician."

Her Highness Lady Świetlana does not betray her demeanor. Her face lacks any hint of concern or ulterior motive. Sasza has been studying under his father for the last eight years, learning more than just spells and diplomacy. He learned the ways people's faces change when they tell the truth and when they lie. Lady Świetlana insists she's different, but she really isn't—just an aristocratic human with the privilege of her station. Moreover, Sasza knows her quirks specifically, having recently completed four years of university together in similar classes and cohorts.

"It was nothing. She was following up on some business on behalf of His Majesty, your father." He hates to lie to her, but if she's noticing her mother's strange comings and goings, that's another problem. Discretion is abandoning Władysław, it seems. Wordlessly, Sasza makes a note to book an appointment with their family friend, Laurencja. She'll know what to do, and how to approach him.

"That's good. There's enough to worry about." Lady Świetlana coos after sipping her coffee. "Shall I start with the disappointment first?"

He raises a brow as he takes a seat across from her. "As if you could ever disappoint me, Your Highness."

"That's very sweet of you to say, but that doesn't change the fact that *I'm* disappointed. While you were gone, His Majesty, my father, decided that you cannot be my Imperial Magician as well."

"You're right, that is disappointing. Did he say why?"

"Something about me needing my own staff. And about how he admires your recent work."

"My work?" Sasza wishes he could light up another cigarette, but Lady Świetlana hates it when he smokes around her.

"You're the one who's been taking over for your father without anyone asking. There's been a lot going on. I think my father wants both of you for his advisory."

"I'll still be sharing my thornier findings with you."

"Of course, you will. I don't think that will ever change."

He gives her a little smirk. "So, will you be getting any staff? Or remain without?"

"He sent a letter to General Kwiatkowski about it. They said that the auditions for the Emperor's Chosen are underway—should any of those hopefuls not place, that person will be my Magical Advisor."

"That seems a simple solution. At least the military training will be there." The Emperor's Chosen are, as their name suggests, specifically selected to protect the emperor and his family's interests. No one truly knows of their affairs—Sasza has tried his hardest to get any intel, but found his searches rejected or coming up empty. He doesn't understand how training is enough to win loyalty. Even with his years of service to the Empire, he feels no patriotic or personal fondness.

"Indeed. I have no idea *who* is auditioning, but I suppose those surprises can be fun for someone. Speaking of the military..." She drinks more of her coffee and then jostles through her dossier. Lady Świetlana pulls out a correspondence sealed with leathery orange wax embossed with a lion entangled in vines—the seal of the Minister of the Interior, Bianka Lewońska. "I found this among my father's missives."

Sasza jaw twitches. He licks his lips and leans away as if he's going to read it aloud. The first mention of the phrases "Vermilion Envoy" and "Vampire States" makes him reconsider it. Lewoński is a house whose sum is not worthy of the scoundrels occupying its ranks, especially its most recent head. For someone who lost most of her family in the civil war not two decades ago, Lady Bianka sure has a hankering for violence in order to reverse the Odonic Empire's slow economic collapse. For someone who should respect those with the decency to stay alive, she takes every opportunity to insult every life that isn't hers, and everyone's restraint tends to be too tightly woven to show her anything resembling a consequence or accountability. Her position grants her much security, and unfortunately, the stability of the Odonic Empire rests on her shoulders.

That stability is threatened by the way she advocates for what can only be described as a war for integration. The dozens of Vampire States have been state-sized autonomous zones for centuries since the human-vampire war of vampiric secession in the early days of the Empire. They took to their own keeps and lands, taking the more monstrous vampires, the bestiapiry, along with them. There has been peace between the regions since then.

"Why would she want to integrate the Vampire States?" Sasza asks when he reaches the bottom of the letter.

Lady Świetlana pulls out more letters. "It's something she's been begging my father to consider, thinking it's related to the Jackiewicz Incident."

Sasza takes the pages from her. More slander against the vampires and bestiapiry. The violence Lady Bianka describes is in retaliation for the attack on the Jackiewicz estate over the summer, but it's not the terror of two continental powers resolving a dispute through bloodshed—she describes a genocide. She requisitions the weaponry vampires have developed against each other to be wielded by the Odonic Empire's military, its police, and, in a state of martial law, its citizens. This complete disregard for the living makes Sasaz's blood simmer.

If he ever feeds on a human again, it will be on Lewońska's blood.

"We don't have the resources for another war." The imperial coffers rely on exploitative labor, especially given the foolish number of restoration projects which have nothing to do with improving the quality of public life. Inflation crushes the working classes, despite the new decree that allows them into higher education, and further magical machination within several industries which has only made economic stability a more distant hope.

It disgusts him that some of the aristocracy see yet another civil war as the only solution, one that will decimate lives in addition to livelihoods.

"I have to talk to Ilya about this." When Lady Świetlana bristles, Sasza adds, "Not directly, of course."

"I'm impressed you two even talk about government."

Warmth spreads across Sasza's cheeks. "We do! It's not all...whatever you think it is." More so than his father, Sasza has not been so subtle about the noncommittal relationship he has with the Finance Minister, Ilya Górniak. He knew him as the peer who secured Władysław a position within Emperor Iwan's Imperial Council, but it wasn't until Sasza graduated that he realized just how charming someone who spends his days crunching numbers can be.

Most of it comes down to their shared mistrust of the aristocracy. Sasza and his father came from a Vampire State, albeit an agrarian one. Ilya had worked his way to his position over several decades of scholarship and career strategy. Sasza admires that commitment to cunning.

"I'm just teasing, Sasza." Lady Świetlana chuckles. "You can bed whoever you want. But I do think it would be good to speak to him. Lewońska will be coming for the ball, so we need to have our arguments prepared. With facts and figures."

"Of course." Such logic has rarely ever worked on aristocracy. "I don't know when I'm seeing him outside the Palace next, but I'll be sure to bring it up."

Świetlana's face lights up. "Your trust never wavers."

His left cheek twitches in an approximation of a smile. "If that is what you say, Your Highness."

"It is what I say! Whenever I ask anything of you, you are quick to oblige. I'm saying it's a good quality to have."

He nods. The quality is born from professionalism and duty, and nothing else.

They spend the remainder of their time together discussing Sasza's holiday, how nice it was to leave Korona's urban hustle and bustle to experience the countryside. How Świetlana wishes one day, she can take such lengthy sabbaticals, instead of staying behind at the Palace (though Sasza doesn't think a week is long enough a time to be considered a sabbatical).

As their time together tumbles to an end, Sasza checks the bus schedule and that of another adult whose debaucherous distractions are as raucous as his father's, but who can conduct herself in her questionable affairs and avoid political and personal devastation along the way.

II.

Iwona Ogrodnik is the last-born daughter of an aristocratic family. Because none of that aristocracy had nurtured and cared for her, she took on the last name of the gardeners who taught her the value and joy in work, the satisfaction of diligence, and the connection to the rest of the castle. But such life-giving servitude is not where her fulfillment lay. She wanted to be useful and indispensable, and there is one position in the entire Odonic Empire that guarantees such political security: the Emperor's Chosen.

In the bowels of the Imperial Military Academy, a fortress whose location is unknown to all except for its directors, Iwona enters the cavernous, torch-lit chamber where her role and fate will be decided. Its ground is recessed into a kind of arena, the floor rough and gravelly, perfect for the ridged soles of Iwona's issued boots. Iwona has her straight, brown hair tied in a low tail. Fitted armor squeezes against her well-fed muscles. Her clean underclothes—a bodysuit woven from magically-enhanced fibers—slide beneath the metal easily, allowing flexibility and movement. The thick rod of her assigned halberd feels familiar in her hands—it's been her constant companion for the last two years since she was placed into the Emperor's Chosen track.

Five years of training and excelling in her classes have granted her an invitation to audition for this elite group.

She would be incorrect in saying she did it alone. Her training partner and best friend, Ute Myśliwska, had a talent for gathering information the two of them otherwise wouldn't be privy to. She let Iwona know that they should study military strategy, espionage, and diplomacy, in addition to the training regimen. These were the classes of the Emperor's Chosen track, something kept a secret in the earlier years, but it transforms into an assigned track for the third year and beyond. Iwona only ever focused on herself, improving without seeking help from anyone. It was Ute the social butterfly who used her name and influence as leverage. It wasn't always necessary—Ute is not so cruel and cunning. In fact, she's incredibly reliable, and free with her knowledge to those she holds dear.

Ute is how Iwona learned the opponent to be fought—a bestiapir, the other vampire species that doesn't look human. What they gleaned in their cramming was of the beasts' agility and their scant regard for their own well-being when fighting. If there was an opposite to the military's strict discipline and demands for honor, this should be it.

It makes sense to Iwona. The halberd she wields is not one of wood, steel, or some other metal. It is an undead blade crafted out of the remains of bestiapiry, carved with magic to give the wielder the upper hand. It's a vampiric weapon used to fight other vampires, either human or bestiapir. Typically, vampires regardless of type are defeated via beheading or staking through the heart. In the right hands, however, these weapons can kill any vampire as if human.

If Iwona needs to dispatch a bestiapir to earn her deserved role, so be it.

Her instructor greets Iwona, but her attention lies with Teodora Łukasiewicz, the woman newly appointed the captain of the Ninety-Second Regiment of the Emperor's Chosen. She wears her sparrow-brown hair coifed up in a wave. The midnight-blue captain's uniform with its high collar and various patches and medals signifies her rank and accomplishments. She's not particularly tall, but the heeled, black boots give her the illusion of height and authority. Pink facial scars shine against her pale skin in the low light.

She's judging this trial, which also makes sense.

Iwona tries not to think how observation will ruin her form—when it comes to battle, aesthetic performance and elegance have not always been her strongest suit. She prefers mechanical efficiency and success in execution, and it's the preference that has earned high marks in all her classes and trainings. May it serve her in this trial.

She takes a deep breath and watches the two esteemed members of the Empire's Military climb the stone stairs to the balcony—perfect for spectating, ideal for staying out of danger.

Her instructor shouts a command and twin panels on the opposite side of the arena slide apart. From the chasm rises a cage sized perfectly for the monstrosity held within. Behind those magically-enforced iron bars is a bestiapir. This one has the fluffy, brown fur of a well-groomed, overly large bat. The fan-like ears make it easier to see with sound, while a smushed nose makes it easy with which to smell. Bulging reticulated arms connect to skin flaps perfect for flight, and tiny legs tuck away easily in the air. But it's more grotesque than simply an enlarged aerial mammal. Its exposed chest has the planes and grooves of a human's, complete with small, exposed breasts, embraced by stiff human arms. Beneath its pteropine snout is a woman's elegant jaw. The human parts are the same brown as the bestiapir's fur.

The horror is within comprehension and is one the Academy only exposes to students they believe can conduct themselves accordingly in its presence. It's the other common form of bestiapir—the insectoid one

Iwona has only ever seen sketches and anatomical charts of—that has her withering in fear.

The bestiapir hums a growl that makes the blood drop into Iwona's groin. Her stomach clenches with desire, though she tries her best to hide it—some natural urges and reactions cannot be eliminated through training and rigor. She knew that the calls and pheromones cast something like a spell on humans. She never expected it to specifically have this seductive effect on her.

Too late, she pulls her mask over her face. The filtering fabric will not do much for the poisoning already present, but it will prevent further enchantment.

A snap echoes against the chamber's walls. The iron bars clatter against the ground, freeing the bestiapir. Its large, webbed wings unfurl. They pulse red with the rivers of blood flowing through webbed vessels, growing brighter and more furious with each flap. Winds whip and howl within the room. Iwona raises her halberd, but it does nothing to spare the tender skin around her eyes nor stop her heels from grinding against the stone floor.

The bestiapir shuffles toward her on its uneven limbs, its sharp claws digging up the sand along the arena. Iwona needs that space to fight as well. Hands gripped around her halberd, she dashes towards the bestiapir. A wide arc carries the blade, priming it to slash at the monster's feet. Iwona hopes to perforate its wings. She fails. It leaps over her, carrying dust and debris which patter against her head. It irritates her throat, but she can't stop to cough. Years of training taught her the dangers of stillness. Stillness leaves room for error; stillness invites death.

She spins and faces it. The bestiapir opens its human jaw and shrieks, casting that spell. She regrets not taking up Ute's offer to procure wax which protects the ears from excess noise and auditory magic. There's no time to dwell on error.

Iwona crouches, holding her weapon at her side. She knows her blood can activate the true potential of her undead halberd. There is no time, not with the beast's panic and hysteria. Instead, she steps one foot over the other, building up momentum and careening herself into a dervish whirl. The bestiapir stomps over to her. But it gets caught in her blade. Her movements flow like water, splashing against the monster as blood spurts around her. Hunts like these will be messy, but it's the smell that prods at her focus. The mask does little to protect her. Unctuous and enticing, confusing in its temptation, Iwona does not let it distract her, even with the wetness growing between her legs and the way her tight clothes press against her cunt.

There will be an opportunity to relieve herself later.

It shrieks again, and Iwona trips, losing her breath. Her mouth hangs open. Her tongue goes dry. But she won't let herself be eliminated.

The beast launches itself above her. She drops low, her halberd poised to strike. With a grunt as fierce as any creature's, she pushes the halberd into its feminine chest, slicing through muscle, crunching through bone. Her arms tremble from this first time attacking with the intention of taking a life. She pushes it forward, cutting though the bestiapir's stomach.

Blood slops from the wound, falling thick like uncooked black pudding. The smell of rot and manure makes Iwona gag. To spare herself from vomiting, she shuffles away from the mess. She hops back on her feet and crouches, ready to attack again. But the creature likely won't be picking itself up anytime soon.

The wound unsettles the compact arrangement of organs kept within its skin. Despite not staking its heart and not activating the blade, Iwona has frozen the bestiapir in death. Its unfurled intestines bathe the air in shit's humid stench.

The mask does nothing to protect her from that olfactory assault. It makes her head spin and stomach lurch as if to vomit, but she remains composed. The arousal has also abated, leaving her with only a mess and none of the desire.

"Iwona!" Captain Teodora's crisp voice punctures the disorientation.

Iwona cranes her neck and gives a nod. She's alive. Exhausted, but alive.

"We'll have the results for you shortly."

Deliberation comes quickly. "Teodora and I have reached a verdict," her instructor shouts. "You, Iwona Ogrodnik, are invited to join the Emperor's Chosen, for showing prowess with a vampiric weapon and holding your own against a bestiapir. Congratulations!"

Her body holds too much pressure for her to express her excitement. She captures it carefully in her heart, proud in the knowledge that she now outranks the family who functionally abandoned her. She will no longer be beholden to their scrutiny because of her work. She will not be able to divulge any details either. Communication with them is no longer necessary. It's wonderful.

It's something like freedom.

But she doesn't want it just for herself. As the instructors come down from their perch, she approaches them and asks, "What of Ute Myśliwska? Is she also one of the Chosen?"

Captain Teodora knits her thick brows together and defers to the instructor.

"Unclear. There are no details at this time."

Disappointment and confusion sting Iwona's heart. If all the Chosen auditions are against a bestiapir, of course there's a chance one might not survive. But Ute proved herself time and again to be as good as Iwona at weapon arts.

Her instructor didn't declare Ute dead, so Iwona drowns that potential sorrow with the immense pride in winning the only prize she's ever wanted.

III.

A chance to try out for the Ninety-Second regiment of the Emperor's Chosen is a dream for all students of the Imperial Military Academy, except for Ute Myśliwska. She holds her large rapier close to her chest. It had been crafted from bestiapir-harvested materials, a necessity for defeating a monster much like its source.

Fear of a different kind has Ute hyperventilating outside the trial chambers. Not the terror of beasts but the psyche-shattering uncertainty of reaching the end of the long road of proving herself on her own terms.

Except such self-validation is not the real reason she had used her family name and their renowned military pedigree to get into the Academy.

Spite against her family's name had been Iwona's motivation for her own excellence, and the strict training regimen Ute's dearest friend maintained infected her own reasoning. In the routine of morning runs followed by classes and ending with evening sparring, the reasoning behind their pursuit of a spot in the Emperor's Chosen had coalesced into something of a partnership.

Ute's success also came in a form of cheating. She kept her ears to the ground, catching every possible rumor to help her with exams and trials alike. This one was no exception. The last bit of information she collected suggested that the next round of Emperor's Chosen missions are happening at such an accelerated timeline that the Ninety-Second Regiment—which Ute should qualify for—won't even get a private audience with Emperor Iwan Iwanowicz and his family.

She won't get to see Świetlana again, and this sends her spiraling. The evening before, she sleeps poorly, feeling foolish and crumbling under self-betrayal. Ute doesn't make mistakes like this, but she also couldn't confess to Iwona her true intentions with the Chosen. In contrast to Ute's desire for upward social mobility, Iwona's has all to do with her own esteem and general dislike of the aristocracy.

Ute put herself through five years of strenuous training and transformation into a perfect imperial weapon for a chance to elevate her social graces and be in Świetlana's company in the same way the two had been close in lyceum. That second goal now hangs in a balance.

The only way Ute thought she could reclaim that proximity had been via the Military. The weight of the delusion squeezes her heart in a vice. The Emperor's Chosen is held in high regard for the clandestine way they keep the imperial family safe, but that often means risking their lives on dangerous tasks far away from polite company. If they survive, gratitude comes in the form of private salons and festivities.

But if they die, no one gets to learn why. No thanks. No honor.

Ute would rather risk her life now in the name of a path not isolated from the rest of imperial society than be a casualty to clandestine operations.

She takes a deep breath and straightens. She will not meet the winning conditions of this trial. Despite her collateral achievement of rising above her family's station, it's not worth it if her skills mean her exclusion from the imperial inner circle.

Guilt pinches her conscience: she *had* promised Iwona that they would be in the Chosen together. But Iwona's pursuit of excellence has such a simple outcome. It does not match the outcome Ute envisions for herself. If she had known sooner, she would have dropped out. But if she dropped out without telling Iwona, Ute wouldn't be sure if her friend would ever forgive her—the disappointment would be worse than this crushing anxiety.

Given that Iwona likely completed the trial already and only a closed door stands between Ute and her own career progression, there's no time to confess her real intentions. They can reconnect after the auditions. Ute can apologize then.

The stone doors open, revealing the audition hall. With her body alight with nervousness and ulterior motives, Ute steps inside the familiar space. She bribed other students to get her in because without that preparation, she wouldn't be able to prove herself. Though nepotism got her into the Academy, she wasn't going to leave on its coattails. That's not how these final trials work, and that might be in Ute's favor, now that she wants nothing to do with the Chosen at all.

The instructor introduces her to the captain of the Ninety-Second Regiment. Ute is polite, but distant. She cannot risk impressing them. After a handshake, they go up some side stairs to a viewing balcony.

She takes a spot on the closest end of the fake arena. To obscure the uncertainty in her face in addition to shielding it, she pulls up the kerchief attached to her armor. Pulling her finger around the seam, she frees her lavender-gray hair from pressing into her cheeks. She breathes in the fresh fabric as the ground on the opposite side of the room comes apart.

A cage carrying what must be a bestiapir emerges from the ground. She got that intel from a bribe several nights prior—it's no less horrifying in real life. The creature reminds Ute of a bat with its shining ivory fur and membranous wings. Its chest is a human torso, with round, lactating tits dripping creamy milk onto the cage's floor. Ute can smell the savory, moldy cheese flavor from her side of the room. It disgusts her. She doesn't want to think of how or why it was captured, but she wants it out of her shared space.

Round, brown humanoid eyes are bloodshot and full of something akin to rage, if such beasts can even feel discrete emotions. Saliva drips from the lower, human half of its face.

Its breaths come heavy, accompanied by mist-like spit. She can sense its negative countenance. What she learned in her hasty research is that people react to bestiapir pheromones differently. It curdles her blood and nausea bubbles up the back of her throat. Ute swallows hard.

Whatever the other reactions are, Ute can manage this one.

Ute's weapon—called an undead blade—needs fresh blood to activate its full potential. In its crafting, weaponsmiths infuse steel with bestiapir parts in a largely secret procedure. For Ute, this is fine; she has never needed to know the history behind the weapon's engineering. Her only concern had been its mechanics and the foibles of wielding it.

A hollow, sharpened finger bone jutting from the hilt alongside the blade demands feeding. Ute pierces the softer meat of her left hand's forearm, thick with scars and calluses. Her blood rolls down the rivulets, entering miniscule chambers along the hilt's heel, still half-full from the previous night's final practice session.

With this feeding, the blade's bone hisses. Its silver-white surface changes to a fierce glow red as a harvest moon. It's an inhuman weapon meant for monsters, despite being made with human hands.

The bestiapir roars. It punches its clawed hands against the cage's bars. Though it might be humanizing to think it recognizes its kindred in Ute's weapon, the more likely reaction is that it hungers for the sustenance bubbling from Ute's newest wound.

Whether they're human like the vampire nobility or beastly like this creature, all blood drinkers crave the same thing.

The chains restraining the creature clatter against its enclosure. The cage walls fall, freeing it. The bestiapir bursts forth, limbs flailing and a shriek piercing Ute's wax-stuffed ears—another preparation tip she gathered as part of her intel. There had been no announcement that the audition had begun.

In its haste, the bestiapir's claws pull apart the tiles, smashing it to dust. The only defense she has is the speed of her dodging and how well she controls her own body. She sidesteps out of the way. It falls onto its fat belly. The bestiapir's human arms do nothing to brace the fall.

She takes its distraction and dashes towards the discarded iron grates. Thoughts don't come fast to her. This ferocity has overwhelmed her rationality and preparedness. Metrics and descriptions can only go so far; nothing she learned on paper made her pulse rush in her ears and her muscle fibers tremble as they do now. Her knuckles strain, holding onto her blade, despite her familiarity and self-made expertise.

The bestiapir hops into the air and turns back to face Ute. It charges again. Ute leaps and slashes her sword in a three-count spell to activate the undead blade's full ability. These patterned swings unleash a spiral of nigh-invisible tendrils woven from blood—her own blood. Each one whips frenetically at the beast, interrupting its advance and streaking its white fur red. The more successful of the attacks yield plumes of fetid stench.

Ute lands softly on the balls of her feet at the end of the attack sequences. The bestiapir screeches and thrashes, blood popping in chunks from torn wounds like mud. It's disgusting. It's the antithesis of natural. It stands in opposition to the tastes of the aristocracy. They don't perform such violence.

For a brief moment, Ute wonders if she can put it out of its misery. Another sequence of bloody hacks, and the bestiapir would rest forever. Such a succinct execution, however, would guarantee her success, and thus personal disappointment. Iwona's likely disappointment, however, does not even cross Ute's mind.

All she cares about is how to fail this audition. She's shown prowess with the blade, and death might not be necessary for passing.

She thinks about how she can throw this audition. The first thing that comes to mind is an injury, but not one so grievous that the Academy risks the scandal of dead aristocracy. Should she survive, it will be considered a freak accident, not self-sabotage. The perfect cover-up.

The bestiapir swipes a sinewy arm at Ute. She blocks the attack with her narrow sword, using it like a shield. The impact pushes her backward and sends a shudder through her body.

The creature flares its upturned pink nose. It sniffs Ute's sweat and darts its tongue to taste the rich scent of blood. Its angry eyes identify Ute.

With a gaping mouth of triangular teeth, it dives towards her. She raises her sword again, shuffling to the side to attempt a decapitation. Her arm comes up high enough to reach its maw. She miscalculated the distance.

Fangs and canines tear through her armor, slicing deep into her flesh. Her severed nerves keep a tight grip on her undead blade. The pain is unlike anything she's experienced, somehow a dull ache and immense pressure stretching her muscles and bones apart. It blocks all thought from her brain, blocking her from accessing the protolanguage and casting a spell—any spell—to free herself.

Perhaps she didn't deserve to join the Emperor's Chosen to begin with.

The bestiapir flings its head and body back and forth, dragging Ute's body through the air with all the structural integrity of a rag doll. Bones within her arm crack and joints snap with each violent throw. The pain and lashing heave vomit up her throat, adding to the streaks of various bodily fluids flying through the air. The keening noise ripping through her ears might belong to her, but she's unsure.

Other hollow shouts ring through the hall, but they're far away. Her instructor and the representative from the Emperor's Chosen might put the beast down to save her. It'd be in their best interests, socially and politically. But the outcome is not for her to determine.

Darkness swallows Ute when her body slams against the ground, snuffing out the pain and the sickness.

TWO

There are two people in Sasza's immediate sphere of influence who would have counsel regarding Władysław's imperial affair. He first visits Laurencja Wielkodomska, a fellow stealth vampire whose primary profession is that of a doctor to all, but first and foremost, to the Czarnolaskis. She's followed them all across the Empire as a favor to his vampire mother, Zofia, almost taking her place in most functions. Truthfully, Sasza assumed Laurencja wanted to swap places with Władysław as his second parent. Any inquiry about the nature of Laurencja and Zofia's relationship had been met with a no-nonsense glare. It's something they had never discussed.

After getting off at the main autobus station in Korona's Centrum, Sasza walks to the clinic, his only companions the stars above and the intricate lanterns brightening the wide, stone streets. Laurencja's clinic is off the main boulevard at the end of an alley with bent over trees casting eerie shadows against stacked bricks. As he approaches, the door swings open. A person runs out, checking Sasza's shoulder. At this late hour and during these days of longer night, Laurencja should not be having any appointments.

Sasza backs off respectfully. He only catches their short-shorn scarlet hair before they throw a hood over their face. He leaves a wide berth for them to make their way back to Korona's empty streets. The desire for anonymity doesn't surprise Sasza, even though with just that glance, he recognized the young person as Lady Bianka Lewońska's only remaining child. It makes sense that they would seek Laurencja—when she's not performing radical acts of medicine with the special healing factors found in vampire blood, she provides gender affirming care. It's none of his business to pursue why that fellow young person would seek it out for themself.

There was a time when Sasza considered pursuing a transition of his own, but the more time he spent around the humans and their still-regimented ideas of gender, the more he accepted his own indifference to being referred to as a "boy" and a "young man." It neither bothered nor endeared him. He'd much prefer to be referred to as "vampire," but that's not possible given his current duplicity.

The aristocrat scurries off into the night, leaving Sasza behind and likely hoping no one else discovers their secret. Without saying a word, Sasza agrees to keep it to himself with a nod they can't see.

Sasza pulls open the wooden door with its frosted glass and enters the clinic. Unlike most hospitals, dense wooden furniture yields a more homely and less sterile feel, if one ignores the cabinets upon cabinets of glass jars and flasks stationed behind a heavy desk used to display wares like monoculars, bifocal glasses, and canes, but also the occasional scalpel and metal dish.

Laurencja sits on the far side of the room, in front of a pair of double doors behind which lays the infirmary. She organizes the files on the reception desk, making sure they're ready for the attendant arriving in the morning. Her curly, blond tresses come together in a bun at the nape of her neck. She no longer wears the black habit which protects her hair from bodily fluids and protects the bodies from errant golden strands. The matching black dress goes well below her knees, though it's anything but modest on her curvy figure. The green x emblazoned on her sternum bends under her plump breasts.

"Oh, hello Sasza." Laurencja's voice trills like a bell. Before her work in medicine, she pursued a career in theater. Not anymore—the dramas both scripted and work-related were not worth her stress.

He shuts the door and removes his scarf and coat. "I had called reception earlier and they said you had no more appointments until tomorrow."

"That's correct. I do not." She rolls her pale orange eyes when Sasza raises a brow. "If it weren't for the Oath, I'd tell you all about my last patient for the evening." All doctors swear an oath of confidentiality as part of their practice, and it surprises Sasza how closely she keeps it.

He exhales through his nose. "You can take the gossip out of the theater, but you can't take the theater out of the gossip."

"Oh, don't be rude. It's not becoming of you." If not for the distance, Laurencja would have swatted him with the folder in her hands. "It's good you came though; I have something I need to tell you. Actually, can we take this elsewhere? I'm quite famished." There's no jest in her voice.

"I would prefer the privacy of the infirmary." A groan like a death rattle crawls from behind the door leading to the ward of sick beds. "Never mind, it seems we're not alone."

She shrugs. "That patient is the only one here and on his literal last breath. There's not much else that can be done for him."

"But you're a doctor." Sasza cups his chin.

"Yes, which means I can heal ailments but not reverse the inevitable. In fact, there are some illnesses that cannot be cured, only managed. Even among our own, medicine only goes so far. Which for me means we can feed later, and that's always fun."

"Is this how you keep yourself sated?"

She flashes him a smile. "A proper woman never tells her secrets. I don't prey on all my patients; that's absurd. I'd be investigated immediately and no one needs that mess on their hands. Especially not you and Mr. Imperial Magician."

"Funny you should mention him, that's exactly what I came here to discuss."

"For such a young person, you're so serious, Sasza. Come, let off some steam by having supper with your favorite healer." Laurencja gestures for him to follow her into the sick ward.

Though Sasza fed just a few days before, another blood meal has never not cleared his mind.

He follows her through the doors to the cavernous infirmary. Dozens of beds with fresh-pressed clean sheets line the walls all the way as the eye can see. Each station has its own light and only one glows through the cold, barren hall. Sasza would assume that the clinic runs warm, to keep the patients comfortable. But then he remembers that so often, many pass in the night. Perhaps keeping the temperature low preserves the bodies and spares bedfellows and staff alike from the stench.

They approach the patient. A white sheet already covers most of his body, as if Laurencja had accepted his passing as a matter of when, not if. She kicks a stool over to Sasza, the legs screeching over the sleek wooden floors. The shrill sound doesn't bother the patient at all. They keep breathing, though the inhales and exhales pass more infrequently with each cycle.

Even though the man won't be around much longer, neither vampire dares to speak. They sit in silence, with the only sounds being that death rattle. Sasza simply stares at the way the patient's chest rises and falls, sometimes shuddering at air's entrance and exit. He threads his fingers together in his lap, warming them despite the chill.

As a child growing up in Castle Dytryk, the Vampire State in the Empire's northeastern corridor, Sasza had never experienced peaceful death—only violence in retaliation for perceived slights or the slaughter that followed the myriad scandals which chased Władysław out of several towns, dragging Sasza along with him. Those conflicts always ended in spilled blood and interminable trials. There was a whole year where Władysław had been under judiciary examination because the wardens of that Castle couldn't prove that the recovered bodies had been killed under a motivation of anything other than self-defense. Whenever enemies went after Władysław, more often than not, they sought Sasza as well. They caught rumors of his being an aberration—neither vampire nor bestiapir, but a hybrid. Born a vampire like all others except for the blood curse that allows him to change forms.

This man's death rattle reminds Sasza of that blood-drenched transformation. Especially how he recalls sucking on a cut and suddenly hearing his own wet breathing as his body shattered and reconstructed into another form. Sasza had been alone, running through the copse of trees by their little hut when he had skinned his palm after tripping. He lapped at the wound, just as he had seen so many others do. Something painful like death had happened, and the next thing Sasza remembered was coming home with his clothing soiled in his own blood and torn apart by the corruption of his flesh.

At first, Władysław didn't believe Sasza. Being a hybrid is such a rare occurrence that no midwife thinks to check for it. To prove his father wrong, Sasza mustered the audacity of his single digit age and bit into the meat of his palm, slurping the crimson that spurt. He painted the walls of their hut red, but somehow spared his mother from the filth. Władysław made Sasza swear to never do it again because of how much it scared him as a father. Zofia, on the other hand, made him promise her that he would never share that ability for his own safety. He doesn't think she even told Laurencja. There hasn't been a need to. It's quite easy not to drink one's own blood.

With all this secrecy around the vampirism and the hybrid transformation, Sasza wonders how anyone had learned about his bestial truth back during their Vampire State days. Perhaps Władysław had trusted too easily, despite being a charlatan himself. Now they keep even fewer friends. It also helps that being in the Imperial Court proffered both of them much protection. An attack on the Czarnolaskis—or anyone in the Emperor's Imperial Council—is an attack on Emperor Iwan Iwanowicz himself. Since he passes so well for a human aristocrat, Sasza keeps the secret even closer to his chest. There's no reason for anyone to attack him and no reason for anyone to find out the truth of his condition. It's a myth that no humans know and only a few vampires believe.

The mental wounds of seeing his father fight back ferociously, more like an animal than a man, have left scars. How could a rumor inspire so much vitriol? The only one Sasza had ever hurt with his hybrid transformation is himself. He doesn't know if he can consider it a violent death, but it tore his limbs apart similarly.

Thus, it comforts him to know that people can pass peacefully. It isn't all metal rending flesh or magic tearing through bone and muscle. He and Laurencja sit in serene vigil. When the inhales come almost infrequently, Laurencja gets up to go through the back doors. She holds a hand up so Sasza doesn't follow her. He isn't left alone long, as she returns quickly with a rolling cart full of tall, glass decanters, many clear tubes, and needles.

"What's that for?" Sasza asks.

"I'm draining him." The man's breath doesn't respond in a way that would suggest he heard and understood Laurencja. He's no longer in the room.

"Is this how you normally feed, Laurencja?" He tries his hardest to keep the disgust off his face.

"Unfortunately. I have the tools. I have the sources—and this is my clinic. I have no one to report to. Even if I did, I keep my own logs to stop the death rate from getting excessive, if you can believe that." He does. "How do you feed? How does Władek take care of you?"

She's the only one allowed to use that diminutive for him.

"If I can afford the time off, I go to Castle Wanda. Otherwise, I feed on small animals. It's not much, but it's better than fasting."

Castle Wanda—named for its central keep like every other Vampire State—is a few hours by train from Korona. Vampires have an entire segment of the citizenry called thralls who have sworn their lives in service of the State. They live in the lap of comfort and care because their blood is so essential to the entire infrastructure of the Vampire States. From the restaurants to the cafes, it all looks awfully similar to human food culture. It is an affront to ethics, sanitation, and propriety to be feeding off corpses. It is offensive to Sasza's preferences as well, as he prefers fresh blood from warm flesh. Certain venues offer living offerings, such as the anonymous finch parties he developed a taste for during his university years. It's not something he would want to share or attend with someone charged with his care. It's not something he has even told Świetlana about, while she shares everything about her romantic and sexual proclivities with him. His depravity is his own.

Laurencja nods her head sagely, curls bouncing with each movement. "That makes sense to me. And you feel...lucid?"

"My focus improves for a few weeks upon my return, yes."

"And here I assumed he found a way to at least get you pig's blood more often than on your birthday. Well, please, enjoy this meal with me."

As they had talked, Laurencja prepared the butterfly needles. The sharp point pricks the skin. A small bead of crimson bubbles out, then spills into the tube, tumbling into the bottom of the narrow-necked flask. Blood hits the bottom, splashing against the sides, leaving legs like stains.

The man breathes his last, shallow and slow. The flask catches his passing.

Despite how quickly the thick liquid enters the flask, it takes a while to fill the flask halfway. They wait until the blood slows its flow considerably. Once drops come in infrequent intervals, Laurencja pops the needle out. She drips some tincture—likely an anticoagulant—into the bottle and mixes it up with the clinic's stale air. Into the two mini beakers, she pours about a shot for each of them.

"I'll need to prod some of the other veins, but first." She hands him one. "Zdrowie."

"Zdrowie," Sasza replies. The blood tastes bad. Not expired, but terrible. Most animal blood tastes the same to Sasza. Most human blood he had supped on, likewise. This stuff, despite being fresh and from the source, is acidic and thick, clinging to the sides of his mouth. If Sasza had anything resembling a gag reflex, it'd be activated. The aperitif is enough to stave off hunger, but not enough to satisfy him, not that he wants to be sated by something so foul.

Laurencja, on the other hand, relishes it like a dessert wine, daintily smacking her lips.

"Why didn't you tell me that you had been hunting like an animal this whole time? I could have had you over more often like this."

Pursing his lips, Sasza finishes his shot of the diseased blood. No amount of tincture can quell that taste. "You're a certifiable mad woman, Laurencja. How can you drink that?"

"I hate to say it, but you get used to the taste. I can tell you the flavors of most terminal illnesses. Would you like me to tell you about them?"

"Perhaps another time." He carefully places the empty vial among the graveyard of other pieces of glass. "You said you had something to tell me?"

"I wanted to tell you that I've taken a position at the Institute of Manners, as their head clinician."

Sasza whistles. "Congratulations. That's quite the prestigious offer."

"They had an opening, so I took it. Have you gotten your acceptance yet?"

"Laurencja, I've only just applied for the graduate program." He put it off by a year to get his footing in court. He missed the deadline once. It wasn't happening again. All he knows is he'll get a response in the new year.

She scoffs. "Yes, as if the Imperial Magician's son will be rejected as part of their class roster."

This makes him bristle. At university, Sasza achieved among the highest marks and earned recognition for his proficiency in magic and contemporary political studies, all on his own merit. To have his acceptance into the top program in the entire continent of Mokosza be attributed to his proximity to the emperor stings. Sasza brushes off the perceived insult.

"I suppose you're right." He exhales, ham-fisting his way into talking about his father. "It will be nice to get far, far away from the capital for at least a year, though I do worry what the condition of the imperial inner circle will be in my absence."

"Oh no, is Władek being negligent again?"

"Completely, and that's before my week at Castle Wanda. He hasn't been keeping up his responsibilities and has barely been present at the meetings. Someone has to keep inquisitive minds at bay, so I've taken on his duties."

She rubs her temples. "Of course, you've taken this responsibility on. What's been distracting him?"

Despite the dead man between them, Sasza lowers his voice. "He's having an affair."

Laurencja bursts out laughing. "Your father? Having an affair? Next thing you'll tell me the stones in the Pewter Square are gray." She can't stop, inhaling sharply to pause. "Please, Sasza, tell me something new."

He exhales, exasperated with the older adults in his life. "It's with the empress."

"Oh." She covers her mouth, brows raised in shock. "Oh my, that is serious. And you're certain of this?"

Sasza wishes he could erase the sound of the empress's ecstasy from between his ears. "I would not have believed it myself if I didn't see her leaving our home with my own eyes."

"I'm assuming Emperor Iwan has no idea?"

"*I'm* certainly not telling him." He raises his brows. "And you better speak of this to no one."

She fans her fingers against her chest, offended. "How little discretion do you think I have? It's been what? Almost a decade since we left Castle Dytryk, and no one suspects a thing about us."

"I'm worried if he continues, none of us will be safe. I doubt Father will take relationship advice from his twenty-three-year-old offspring. So, I need you to speak with him. Tell him to call the affair off."

"You think he's going to tell her about us?"

Sasza groans. He doesn't know what he thinks. This scandal feels too much like shitting in the bed Władysław spent almost a decade making. "I'm worried he's going to be so negligent it'll launch an inquiry."

He cannot tell her about the unification rumors. There's nothing she can do about it to help, and it's a conversation for Ilya, not Laurencja. Trying to lead with the tenderness of the relationship instead of with the political and economic strategy.

"You just said you've been acting as Imperial Magician? People might just see it as ambition instead of overcompensation."

"I don't want it to be taken as treason."

"Treason?" Laurencja snorts a laugh. "People are attacking entire cities, and you think you doing too good a job is going to be seen as treason?" She puts the needle in the dead man's neck, collecting more blood. "Please, we all go through phases where we put in our professional bare minimum. Perhaps the change in seasons is affecting him."

Sasza knows this is different, but he can't place why. Władysław Czarnolaski is infamous for failing up, for causing a scandal and having someone in a higher position of power to bail him out or offer an even more lucrative opportunity. With the imperial family, however, there is nowhere higher to go. Something isn't right, and it frustrates Sasza that Laurencja can't see a potential problem.

"Laurencja, I'm not sure my Father has attended *any* meetings when I myself was absent. I'm normally the one for whom attendance is optional. But the emperor has since insisted I be there."

"That's a good thing, Sasza. It means he trusts you, and he's noticed your work ethic. You haven't even had to advocate for yourself. I wish my own advancement were so lucky."

"Please, Laurencja, just...talk to him." He rubs his temples. "You're an expert on these matters."

"And what matters might those be? Relationships? It sounds like your father is doing well for himself. It's no secret that he got to his station through more clandestine relations. Unless...you somehow had no idea." She tilts her head, lips pursed, preparing to offer pity and disappointment.

"As you said yourself, it's no secret." Sasza had not been old enough to understand when Władysław first mentioned his half-sister, Sylwia, but the two had maintained a steady correspondence during the itinerant years of the Czarnolaskis. When their father wouldn't tell him why he left her behind in Castle Otto, a state on the opposite side of the Empire from Korona, she did. He wanted to support her ambitions within the Vampire States, instead of interrupting her schooling and other progress by having her traipse around the Empire with him. Despite her perceived cunning, she honored the tacit agreement between the humans and the vampires that one does not infiltrate the other in a way Władysław never respected. Sylwia warned him of his predisposition towards scandal and to not to be surprised if he abandons Sasza in a political den of wolves for his own gain.

Perhaps this is it.

"Please, don't worry so much, Sasza. Perhaps I can tell you about the different flavor profiles of the various diseases?" She picks up a vial. "Could be a distraction that doesn't involve interrupting other people's lives."

Laurencja is giddy and enjoys the sound of her own voice. She starts her presentation off with the wasting disease she and Sasza sampled and how it differs from other wasting diseases. After so many years of these scraps, she can now diagnose several illnesses by taste, licking samples from blood draws. Of course, she keeps this "gross habit" a secret.

Laurencja tells him about the different ways food-poisoned blood tastes. All afflictions carry their own flavor profiles. Like the viruses carrying her favorite bitter, biting, and almost salty palate. But the ones that leave her with an excitement almost sensual, however, are the blood samples carrying activations against those same viruses. Instead of boiled eggs, the flavor mellows out to spices and vanilla. It's almost a dessert for her, rather than a proper meal. This recently deceased patient's blood gets its bitter taste from a longer-term illness.

She wishes to return to school at some point to study virology and biochemistry in earnest. Sasza agrees with her that she would be good at it, and it's a shame that the Institute of Manners has no such track.

Laurencja offers him another shot of the diseased blood. He declines.

A distant clock bongs across the hall. Sasza checks the time on his wristwatch. "I have to go." He needs Ilya's counsel, and the autobuses will stop running soon. The Finance Minister would know how what to say to his father to save Władysław from his own impulses.

Sasza doesn't think Laurencja will actually talk to Władysław. She's good at keeping secrets, but she's absent when responding to problems that aren't hers.

"Thank you for indulging me," Laurencja says. "Telling you not to worry isn't going to yield anything, but don't lose yourself to baseless concerns."

Easier said than done. He leaves her to her drinking and gets his coat. Sasza scrounges around his pockets as he makes his way down the nighttime Korona streets and lights a cigarette, hoping the smell of smoke is enough to mask the taste of blood.

"YOU'RE A LONG WAY from home, young man," Ilya says by way of welcoming Sasza into his one-bedroom apartment on the opposite side of Korona's Centrum from the Palace.

Having settled in for the night, a plush robe wraps around his meaty frame, leaving a window from his neck to his sternum, revealing a patch of gray and black hairs on his plump chest.

"And it is far too late for you to still be up, old man." Sasza kisses his cheek as a greeting and bends forward to remove his shoes. He catches the glint of melted ice dyed soft amber in a glass. "You're still drinking at this hour? How youthful of you."

"An elder needs to wind down at the end of the week." He goes to have a seat in the high-backed armchair tucked into a corner with stacks of books piled beneath it. All around his feet are notebooks with pages hanging out from them, a veritable archive of Ilya's scattered thought process. Sasza's been in this apartment before, and the man keeps it the epitome of clean but the nadir of tidy.

"Indulge me, Sasza." Ilya takes a sip of his drink. "What's a handsome lad like yourself doing out so late at night? I'm imagining you went to the bars, talked to a young man who struck your fancy about Odonic classics and the metaphors found within the great symphonies."

Sasza snorts. "Please, I barely did that when I was in university."

"Ah yes, that bygone era of six months ago." Ilya smiles, revealing a dimple before taking a sip. "I'm kidding; I know it's been far longer than that."

"Far longer than I intended." Sasza thought he'd be pursuing advanced education immediately after university. Politics got in the way of those plans. As did Ilya, to a certain extent, but Sasza did not at all mind that interruption.

"Anyway, I imagine that you've had one too many drinks, but he wouldn't take you home upon realizing who you are, so you find yourself at *my* doorstep because you know I'll always make time for you. And space in my bed."

Sasza shudders at the clenching in his stomach. "That does sound like an evening I'd experience. But, no, alas, I was visiting a family friend and did not feel like going back to the townhouse."

"This location is nowhere near that townhouse." Ilya gasps and rises. "I'm being a terrible host. Would you like me to pour you some samogon? I fermented it myself with a recipe from my home village."

"I would enjoy that, thank you." It won't taste much different from the other alcohols he consumes to maintain a human veneer, but the blood coursing through his digestive system might open him to subtler tastes. Sasza has never tried human food or drink so soon after his own vampiric meal.

Ilya leads Sasza deeper into the living room. The floor can scarcely be seen underneath the personal mail both answered and untouched. Upon a wooden bureau dark against the cream-colored walls sits the red beverage with its glasses made of crystal. For a man so dedicated to improving the lives of the proletariat and supporting measures like increased schooling, Ilya has some subtle ways of conveying his higher rank.

Sasza does not mention this when he receives the glass, cold in his hand. They take seats beside each other in front of the coffee table also smothered by papers.

"If you must know, Sasza, I too did not spend my university years with the same frivolity as my peers. I made a good word with them, of course, but I had to be better than them all if I were to achieve anything resembling advancement."

"I'm sure that's how you become Finance Minister to the emperor without an aristocratic last name."

Ilya sits beside Sasza on the couch, angling so that they can face each other. "Exactly."

This makes Sasza reflect on his and his father's sudden appearance and ascension into Emperor Iwan's Imperial Council and inner circle. They had no merits that would guarantee them an entry without the status, but then Ilya had vouched for them. On what basis Sasza never asked and his father never elaborated, despite sharing more obscure and minute details from all their scheming. Perhaps there is a limit for how much and for how long Władysław can trust someone, even if that person is his own offspring.

"Come now, Sasza, you're not one to come visit without a reason, though I suppose a nightcap would be considered reason enough. You seem distracted."

"Things have been busy since I returned. The work seems to increase, and if anyone is distracted, it's my father. I did not agree to take on his work as Imperial Magician, but here I am."

"Sometimes, in order to seek advancement, it's what one must do."

Sasza takes a sip, relishing in the brief interruption of warmth as the astringent liquid goes down to his stomach. "It's not about that at all.

If that were my goal, I'd tell my father about it. But this…is something else."

"Oh? Do tell."

Sasza inhales deep before answering, "I think he's having another affair. And I'm not sure with whom." The second statement is a lie, of course, but he doesn't want anyone beyond the Czarnolaski household to bear that truth.

"You are right, he *has* been distracted. But I've known Władysław for most of our shared political career. He's only ever pursued those who can offer him a leg up. And I'm not sure there's any higher to go…" He scratches his bearded chin. "Unless he is sleeping with an Iwanowicz, which could be any of them."

Sasza swallows the bile that rose at the incorrect and lewd thought that his father might be bedding Świetlana. It has nothing to do with the age difference between them; Sasza would be a hypocrite for that judgment. It's more that he knows full well that she harbors no attraction to men. "It is an Iwanowicz, but I cannot say which one."

"Do you not know, or do you not want to tell me?"

"I'll keep some secrets to myself, if that is all right."

"Please, when have I ever disrespected your secrets?" He smirks and takes a sip of his drink.

Sasza copies him. "I can't say you have, that's true. And of that, I am appreciative."

Ilya settles into the couch, resting his elbow along the back, cradling his beverage. "Now, I'm not going to share this in order to coax out your hidden truths, but there is something I'd like to tell you about your father, if that's all right."

There is nothing Sasza can do to prepare for whatever might come from Ilya's seasoned mouth. He already knows of his father's charlatan past, how they both came up from backwater villages in the far northeast of the Empire. He settles deeper into the couch. The sleeves of his sweater cover his knuckles, and he tucks his long legs under himself. The roaring fire bathes them in warmth.

"Your father and I had worked together long before he even told me about you and his interest in bringing you both to Korona. He was a researcher with a group I am still involved with. Because, if I'm to make a confession, my motives for empowering the proletariat are not entirely altruistic, but I'm sure that comes to you as no surprise."

Sasza shakes his head. No one at their tier of government does anything from the goodness of their heart, only in pursuits of their own ends.

"It's something I've been meaning to talk to you about, actually, given your affinity for the non-aristocracy. It's so difficult to find someone who shares a more opportunistic view of eliminating the harsh differences between classes." He slurps, loudly. "And there are many more like us. We call ourselves the Order of the Flock."

Sasza halts a change in expression before it comes to fruition. He's heard most of the name before—his research referred to an *Abyssal* Flock. But it's likely that Ilya refers to something adjacent, in the same way the police and the imperial police are technically similar entities with several key differences. He wants Ilya to lead; he doesn't interrupt and continues listening.

"Much like the way birds travel together and protect themselves from larger threats in one well-oiled machine of a group, so do we believe that humanity can achieve something resembling this unity. Empower the great throng of people who statistically cannot be part of the aristocracy and redistribute the wealth. Now, I know we haven't made many strides in that, but there are attempts being made."

"This would be news to me, Ilya."

"Of course. Now, I deliberately say 'attempts.' No one is going to be willing to part with their generational wealth or hard-won riches, but they can with some persuasion."

The number of dead aristocrats at the incident at Daszek raises the question of the exact nature of this persuasion. Of those dead, it was mostly aristocracy. Butchered in ways that cannot be excused by simple dissatisfaction with a lack of privilege or perceived oppression. Sasza had seen that kind of ravenous rage before, in the reports from the previous civil war and in the histories of why the Vampire States sought their own autonomy.

"Is that what my father researched? Ways to persuade the aristocracy to part with their money?"

"No, he did more scientific research, preparing little advancements to prove his worth to those above him. It worked, didn't it? It endeared the Iwanowiczes to pull you into their council, advising them on magic in all places where technology intersects with society."

There is no denying that Sasza's father definitely had someone else pulling strings, but the fact that Sasza's father might have also had a hand in the Daszek attack seems impossible. He's read all his father's missives, checked his ledger. There is no involvement. Moreover, such recruitment should have come up sooner. Perhaps Władysław plans on bringing Sasza into that fold, at his own slow pace.

Sasza will only mention it to his father if Władysław brings it up first.

"And the Flock's governance, is it centralized?" This answer solves so much of the mystery behind the assault in Daszek. If Sasza had been putting his mouth on its architect for the many months since the incident, it's a disappointment he can outgrow in the same way a scar forms around a wound. The immediate approval of the emperor for quelling one aggressor would guarantee him and his father more freedom and safety.

"It is not, no. I'm not even sure who leads the other factions. We all have our different agendas. It makes us stronger, in fact, this fealty among us. It grants us more faith and power than fanatical belief in singular rule.

As I said earlier, much like the mechanism of birds traveling for changing seasons, we are stronger together."

Sasza finishes his beverage and sets it off to the scant space allowed for a coaster. He leans against the back of the couch, with his cheek resting against his fist and an arm folded under his elbow. All this information, aside from the name of the group, is new to him. His father had never shared his work with him, only that which Sasza could feasibly take over come adulthood, after proper schooling. But Sasza had never thought of either himself or his father as scientists. Władysław worked with magic, yes, and even recommended spells, but the nature of those advancements had always eluded him.

Perhaps he too should have been keeping a closer eye on Ilya, whose interests lay far beyond the Empire's immediate economic policy. If Ilya truly had been involved in orchestrating the Jackiewicz Incident—especially at this kind of debut of the new learned proletariat—why would he have allowed it? This summer had been the first Inventors' Fair where proletarian academics could attend in addition to their aristocratic counterparts. To attack it would have undermined his own labor. It would make Sasza regret ever having opened up to him about his own affinity towards non-aristocrats. Ilya would have betrayed Sasza's values and vulnerability.

With his own glass half-empty, Ilya lets the robe slide off a shoulder demurely, this small bear of a man playing the part of a courtesan. "Perhaps, Sasza Czarnolaski, I can give you a small taste of that very faith and that very power."

Sasza's heart skips a beat. "I'd very much like to see what you have to offer."

"Of course." Ilya leans in and presses a loud, mouthy kiss against the point in Sasza's neck where his heart thuds.

Letting the robe fall, the much older council member slides off the couch and onto his knees. He rubs his nose against Sasza's crotch, carefully unbuttoning his trousers. Such teasing generally has no effect on Sasza, but it's the novelty of the deliberateness that makes Sasza rock hard, despite the lack of urgency and sense of danger. Their ruttings had always taken place between meetings, in clandestine spaces in the hopes that no one would catch them. The thrill of almost getting caught got Sasza off almost as quickly as the coitus itself.

This care, these agonizingly slow caresses are new, despite the familiarity of the location. And this excites him.

Ilya frees Sasza's cock and wraps his pouty lips around his head, the length of it slipping easily down his throat. A once-broken nose presses into the softness of Sasza's snow white pubic hair. Soft grunts like choking echo from deep within Ilya's throat as his head bobs.

Sasza closes his eyes, one hand running through Ilya's wavy, salt-and-pepper hair, mussing the thick strands. With the same soft reverence, Ilya palms Sasza's scrotum, pressing up against his taint. It pulls a groan out from the heat in his stomach.

As much as he wants to lose himself to the wetness around his prick, Sasza turns over the facts in his mind. Though not immediately affiliated, Ilya has something to do with the true enemy. His agenda is not fulfilled with violence—it's with political manipulation Sasza aided in unfolding. Both of them have been recognized for that work. Regardless of his personal gratitude, that political mentorship put forth agency for the proletariat in a way unknown to the Empire. It is a positive gain that has not fully paid its price yet. And there will be a transaction, the nature of which eludes him.

Sasza realizes he is not safe as long as Ilya serves the emperor and his council, manipulating them and his own faction to meet his own gains. Moreover, he wants Sasza as a recruit or an acolyte, not as a lover or a compatriot.

Sasza's dick slackens. Ilya slides off, holding Sasza's base with his large hand. "Is this not to your liking?"

Desire burns like Ilya's hearth. "I..." Sasza swallows. "I need your other hole, my apologies. My head is simply too full."

Ilya smirks. "As you wish." He gives the tip of Sasza's head a loud, sloppy kiss.

He leads Sasza through the cream-colored expanse into the tidy, sparse bedroom, unbesmirched by work. Most of its space is filled by a four-poster bed with a lush berylline duvet and several layers of sheets. Across from it is a mirror, which makes Sasza squirm. It's the closest he can get to being watched while fucking. The unkind thoughts he reserves for himself while viewing his own erotic abandon only enhances the experience. It's a show for himself in the absence of an audience. It helps him remember the truth of what he is: an animal who feasts on blood rather than a being who sees food as something to be celebrated and enjoyed.

Ilya drops the underwear, leaving nothing hidden. The thick meat around his stomach and hips beg to be clawed while a cock fills that fat ass. Sasza's dick hardens again as he throws his sweater and shirt off his frame. He left his pants and underwear behind in the living room.

Without asking, Ilya gets on his elbows and knees, hole facing the bronze-framed mirror. Sasza gets behind him, and the reflection hides nothing. Sasza sees his long, lanky body looming over the shorter, squatter man. He lowers himself to a seated position, his face level with the fuzz and musk emanating from Ilya's seam. Long fingers expose the pink entrance. Sasza mashes his tongue against it, gliding up and down, tracing the grooves, relaxing the muscles. Ilya grinds into Sasza's face. He flits his tongue as if his hole is a different kind of man's cunt. It opens up similarly as well, gaping and eager.

Sasza knows where to find the oil—he's convinced Ilya keeps a vial in every drawer in his vicinity. He spills a little bit onto his hands and makes eye contact with himself in the mirror as he tugs on his cock, moistening it from root to tip. Sasza cannot see Ilya's expression but hears the older man whimpering.

Much like Ilya's careful attention earlier, Sasza takes his time lining up his own weeping head against the entrance. He inserts the tip and slowly pulls it out, gently pistoning like this while Ilya begs. Eventually the amusement abates, and Sasza rolls his hips inside the Finance Minister, pulling his cock out and inserting it a bit more than with the previous thrust. He wishes he could watch himself fuck Ilya. His heart pounds at the imagined sight of his youthfulness mounting a man old enough to be his father.

Sasza drags his fingertips down Ilya's back, alongside the fur crawling up the older man's spine. He allows his nails to catch, leaving pale, pink scars in the skin of this man who made something of himself rather than have a name associated with destined greatness. There's a lot to admire about Ilya.

But false promises of faith and power are not becoming of him. The rhythmic slapping of Sasza's sack against Ilya's makes it clear that what's going on between them is fornication. Flesh teasing and pleasing other flesh. Electrifying currents of orgasms more like waves upon a shore than a maelstrom shaking foundations. One person sinking into another, laying claim to each other's composure like generals on a battlefield.

Sasza tires of Ilya's skin being so far from his own. With a grunt like a yell, Sasza hooks an arm under Ilya's shoulder, snatching his soft breast to pull him up against his chest. He grabs the man by the throat, pressing gently against the arteries leading to his head. Ilya lets out a laugh. Sasza doesn't understand the joke.

How easy it would be to just tear into the meat. Sasza would eliminate a recruiter of a potential enemy, coat that beautiful bedding in fresh blood for Sasza to sup on. Emperor Iwan would reward him handsomely, for one threat within his inner circle had been eliminated.

Ilya, however, is not for Sasza to dispatch.

Despite the promises of utopia, it cannot come to pass without cooperation between the ruling classes and the working classes, the aristocracy and the proletariat. Ilya is the only one other than Świetlana that sees the folly in a war of unification. He's the only one that sees the populace as more than a means to profit and increased luxury. More than just tools of war and violent whims. More than merely servants. After all, it had been Ilya's motion to open the universities to the proletariat in order to challenge the aristocracy's stagnant order.

He meant it in more ways than one, Sasza now realizes.

Skin slaps against skin, and it's not loud enough to quiet Sasza's racing mind. He cannot take on new allegiances. The only one who will have his side as a vampire playing an aristocrat is himself, as long as he keeps his own secret.

Spilling aristocratic blood for his own tasting goes against that vow of self-preservation.

One final thrust has him emptying deep into Ilya's guts. It doesn't take long for Ilya to follow, aided by Sasza using his waning strength to pump Ilya's cock. The older man slides onto his stomach, skin pressing against the soiled sheet. In a practiced display of tenderness, Sasza kisses Ilya's neck and the tops of his shoulders.

"And what say you to that, dear Sasza?" Ilya says into the bedspread with ragged breaths.

"I'll consider it," he lies.

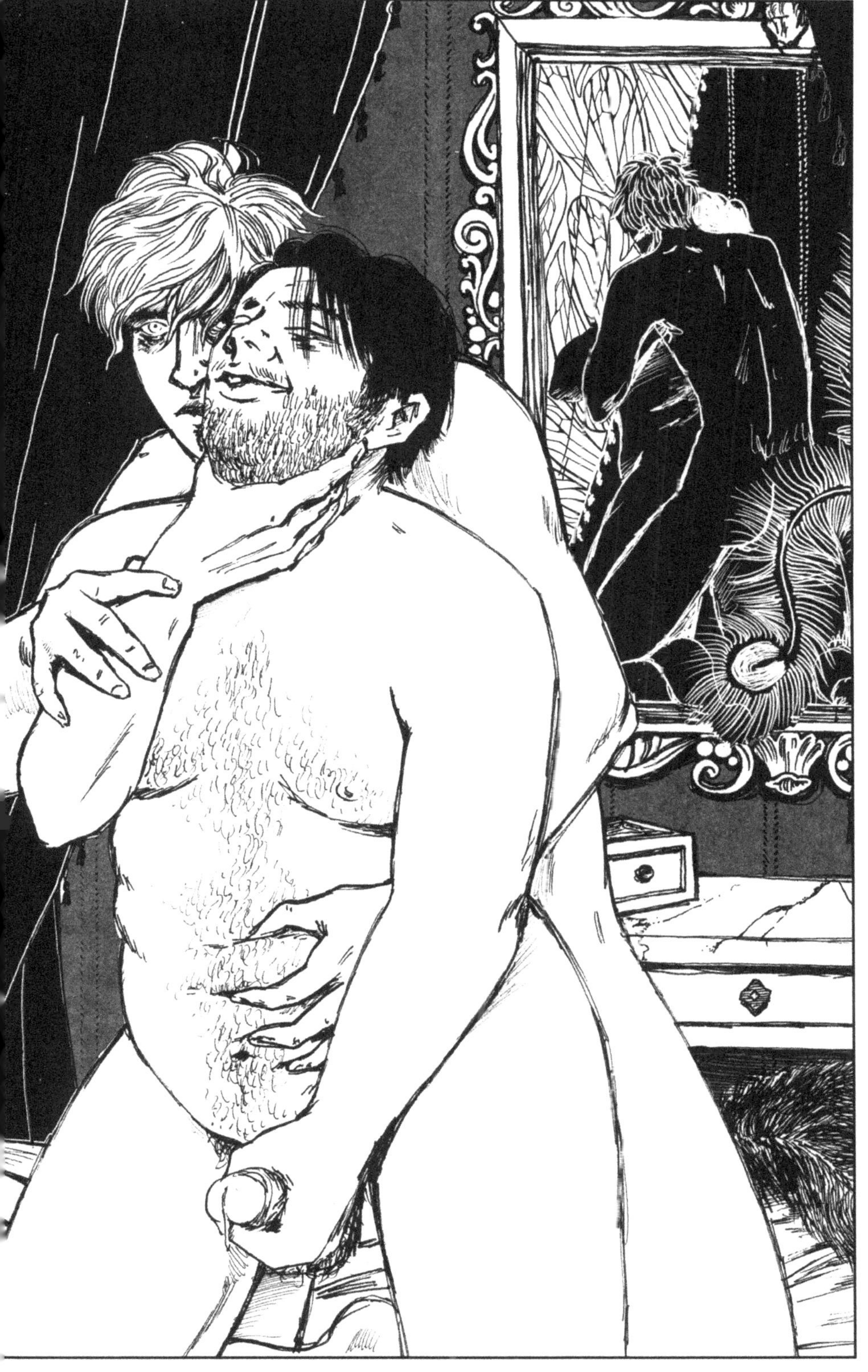

THREE

I.

The graduation ceremony's closing bloviation about pride, tradition, and love of the Empire marks the end of Iwona's schooling and her return to society. The students bound for the Academy are whisked away to its secret keep deep in the woods at the base of a mountain—only the highest echelon of the Military knows the school's exact location. The commitment comes in the punishingly long travels in windowless autocarriages, and Iwona didn't realize how much she missed comforts like fine garb designed to keep winter's embrace at bay or the freedom to choose her own meals until she found herself in the reception hall within the Military's Korona Headquarters.

Each table has a wide variety of appetizers and snacks forbidden to those honing their bodies as instruments of wars not yet declared. Stacked trays of pies and galettes, glistening with syrup and melted fat. They bulge from within their casings, golden surfaces smooth but brittle. Tiny herbs artfully decorate servers' trays. It activates some primal spirit within Iwona, one that cannot reject the impulses that come with decadence and foods designed to provide entertainment with little satiety in mind. Despite their savory flavors, these samples are more dessert than fuel.

Iwona weaves her way through the small crowd of fellow Chosen and their families. Hers had not come to celebrate her that evening—they wouldn't have cared, and if they did, their jealousy got in the way of congratulations. She doesn't deserve their last name, and they don't deserve her bearing it.

She stops at a table and loads her small plate up with enough treats such that it's no longer possible to hold with one hand unless she starts eating. Rough, flaky pastry hits her tongue and tears prick her eyes. She might as well have been starving during her studies. She's not sure her solitary heavy pettings in the dead of night provided as much instant gratification as this small parcel of culinary magic.

The longer-term validation comes in the pride that she made it. Not everyone qualifies for the chance to join the Emperor's Chosen. It takes a level of dedication that has abandoned most people. It takes a love of country and discipline. And it allows Iwona to enter rooms such as this reception hall, designed to be beautiful and not much else. The tiled, marble floor glistens in the warm, chartreuse torchlight. High above, a clear, indigo wintry night sky shimmers with stars; the ceiling's glass keeps the frost at bay. Thick, red velvet curtains cover some of the windows to keep out the chill like an unwanted guest. The capital has already been blanketed with snow, its rooftops hidden until spring comes in earnest, unless it submits to summer much like autumn does to winter year after year.

"Aren't the treats at Military events simply divine?"

Iwona nearly spits up crumbs in her mouth, startled by Captain Łukasiewicz's sudden appearance. The captain's cropped sparrow-brown hair cascades over her ears like a wave. She dons the midnight-blue Military formal uniform with its high collar. An assortment of patches and medals decorate her biceps and breast, each one signifying her rank and accomplishments. Other tassels and adornments in gold and silver are mostly to her own taste. There are a few other captains in attendance and none of them have the same accessories.

It surprises Iwona that she didn't hear the captain's heels clacking on the pristine floors. "They are quite delightful, Captain." The title bursts like candy in Iwona's mouth.

"Please, call me Teodora. Reserve 'captain' for when we're on assignment and must be coy in our communications."

Iwona nods politely and eats another tiny tartlet, swallowing down a moan alongside its salty filling of mushrooms and onions. For the first time, she understands how food can be better than intimacy.

"If I recall correctly, your name is Iwona Ogrodnik." Captain Łukasiewicz grips her wineglass by its bulb instead of the stem.

Iwona nods again, pride bubbling once more. The captain *knows* her by name—it makes sense, as she oversaw the audition.

"It's an interesting name for an aristocrat girl. If you don't want to tell me the story behind that, please: you don't have to. But if you think holding such a secret will be a distraction on the field or in preparations, then do tell me." She sips the maroon sparkling wine. "A party like this is the best venue for discussion that borders on gossip."

Words fail to connect between Iwona's brain and her mouth. She wonders how much slander against her family she can get away with. They've never hurt her; it's just been a vague disinterest in her that had her seeking attention and praise elsewhere. It feels to Iwona as if it would hurt *her* more than cause any kind of reputational harm.

It's not just this indecision around vulnerability that holds her tongue. It's been so long since she had socialized and talked to other people about anything other than training that she forgot that people could have genuine interest in each other. That people in and of themselves can be of interest. They are more than their personal records and misunderstandings of the day's lessons or week's home-work.

And Iwona finds herself deliberately charmed by the captain, robbing her of the ability to summon any appropriate response. The lively string music filling the room from floor to vaulted ceiling drowns out the scant thoughts that do cross her mind.

"Are you alright?" Captain Łukasiewicz asks. "I can't say I know anything about you, but you seem distant."

Ute. The fear that some terrible misfortune had befallen her rears its ugly head. If she had placed in the Emperor's Chosen, she would have been at the ceremony right beside Iwona (or somewhere close, as their last name's first letters are nowhere near each other in the alphabet). If she hadn't, she'd have attended the induction ceremony as a guest.

Moreover, Ute made parties like these bearable. Neither of them were for dancing, but they would sway on each other as if the music lent itself to that sort of ruckus. It's that shawl of loneliness and absence which hangs on her like another heavy cloak, one that confers darkness instead of warmth. It steals the comfort conferred by this opportunity for a new connection.

"I wouldn't be here tonight if not for one of my classmates. We're not family, so I understand if I'm not entitled to information, however…"

"Oh, I understand entirely. They say no news is good news, but I understand how difficult being in the dark can be." Captain Łukasiewicz's casual tone does not match the melancholy in her words. "Let me reach out to General Kwiatkowski. They would know best."

"I would very much appreciate that."

"I hope she gets back to us before we're gone."

"Gone?" Communications about missions would come after this elaborate inauguration, but this casual mention makes Iwona suspect that it's coming sooner than expected.

"*Fuck.*" Captain Łukasiewicz throws back her drink. The splotches on her pale, freckled face suggest it wasn't her first drink of the evening.

Her reaching for another flute as a waiter waltzes by suggests that it won't be her last either.

"I can forget you mentioned anything." Otherwise, Iwona has no idea how to handle a situation when a superior seems to have little agency and needs someone else to be responsible.

"No, no. It's important you don't. I might as well slowly tell you now." She steps closer to Iwona, alcohol-soured breath filling her nose as Captain Łukasiewicz's voice infiltrates her ear. "On New Year's Day, the Ninety-Second Regiment is departing for our first assignment. I'm still working on the transport detail, but I recommend conducting yourself as if you know nothing." She pulls away to throw back the booze.

Iwona expected their first assignment to be well past winter, months into the future, not *weeks*. This kind of mobilization reminds Iwona of the stories the Ogrodniks would tell her of the last civil war, which had been resolved when she was a toddler, much like her newly graduated peers. Captain Łukasiewicz might be old enough to remember that bloody conflict whose destabilization still echoes in the rumors of current economic and social decline. The Chosen are mobilizing to protect the Empire, but from what, Iwona isn't sure.

The last thing she heard had been the aristocrats' excesses and inexperience ruling a country to be the last real threat. That's not something that can be resolved with the military's force.

"It is the way of the Emperor's Chosen after all." The captain hiccups. "Excuse me! No one is really supposed to know what we're up to. It's for His Majesty's safety. Probably better for everyone else to think we do nothing than to know the truth of the danger we're constantly in."

All she can muster to show Captain Łukasiewicz that she'd been somewhat listening is, "That's very soon."

"It is, it is." Captain Łukasiewicz clasps Iwona's shoulder with her free hand. "I hope you get to see your friend before we depart." Her glazed, brown eyes scan the crowd for the other Chosen. "I should tell the others at least this little bit of information."

"You should," agrees Iwona.

"I'm sorry this is how you found out."

Before Iwona can say anything to accept or decline the apology, the captain slinks away like a specter.

II.

The first true blizzard of the year hits Korona something fierce, shutting down most of the roads while service workers brave the tempestuous winds and wet flakes tear through the streets. Sasza debated canceling his dinner with Świetlana. It was her proposition, but he insisted they meet privately. He scoured his father's appointments for a free evening but hadn't considered the volatility of the weather. In Korona, however, once snow starts falling, its intensity only varies, and it stays for several months, teasing an exit.

Unlike the Czarnolaskis' dinky autocar, however, the Palace has vehicles equipped for the gathering snow and packing ice. Świetlana arrives, snow piling on her stiff, woolen hat and shoulders. She holds a steaming parcel close to her chest as she ducks under Sasza's arm to enter the warm townhouse. He takes the food from her and unpacks the savory meal he cannot taste.

"How does eating in the kitchen work for you?" He calls while she removes her winter gear.

"The kitchen is great." Fire crackles in the wood-burning stove, more for warmth than for food prep.

The orange glow catches on the dark bottles of the wine rack Władysław keeps for human guests. "Can I get you anything to drink?"

"Red is fine!"

"I can make that happen." Sasza approaches the rack and several labels in, he arrives at a loss. He doesn't know how any of it tastes, and the grape names mean nothing to him. Władysław wasted his memory on tasting notes, while Sasza committed them to a notebook he should probably keep in the kitchen. Władysław spared every effort to maintain his role of a human aristocrat, proving even more convincing than the people raised in those circles. Sasza mastered only some of the tricks—he wants to blend in true to himself.

He selects the middle bottle and pours each of them a glass. He hopes it will satisfy Her Highness despite his inability to tell her about the wine as he's seen other servers do.

Lady Świetlana takes a seat close to the stove, legs crossed in the seat as if settling in for a lazy conversation. He grabs the bulbous glass too wide for his long fingers and takes a sip. No taste, no flavor. No complexity of which humans speak so reverently.

He hands her the second glass. Lady Świetlana holds it in her smaller hands, bringing the rim to her lips like a child. "This is most excellent. It will definitely warm me up."

Sasza takes a seat. He wonders if he should have gotten more dressed up, aside from the sweater he stole from Ilya and his own silk house pants. Despite their camaraderie, Lady Świetlana is polite company, and he should have considered an outfit more formal. It makes him feel immature.

At the same time, Lady Świetlana seems content in her girlishness, wearing a large, black sweater with her hair loosely tied in a bun. It's endearing and reminds him that though previous emperors took the crown at her age, she's not yet enslaved to tradition or a maturity she hasn't yet embodied.

Her eyes dance along the wine as it sluices down the smooth glass. "How did your visit with Ilya go?"

Sasza sips his own drink to stall. He doesn't know how to tell Lady Świetlana about his visit to Ilya. He had every intention of discussing economics and finding evidence against obliterating the Vampire States' autonomy. Ilya telling Sasza about the Flock derailed all that, and the knot created in his brain has still not been untangled. How could the man who did the most for Daszek's recovery also be behind the disaster? Sasza doesn't know if he should bring up the existence of the Flock to Lady Świetlana at all. She is a proxy to her father's rule; her position is not one of decision-making.

Neither is Sasza's, but no one dares tell him. He would refuse to believe it.

"Unproductive," he eventually says.

"Not surprising."

He snorts. "Not like that, Your Highness." (It was exactly like that.) "He did say he'd do some research into what can be done to quell the unrest among the proletariat. He's working on getting them councils like those Emperor Iwanowicz rules with."

Lady Świetlana raises a brow; she knows it's old news. Instead, she takes a long drink. "I've snooped around my father's study. It's not sealed yet—he wants to discuss it at the meeting where even Lewońska will be in attendance, but, it might as well be official: Next year is the year the Vampire States come under the Empire's fold."

Sasza's jaw twitches. "Are you for certain?"

"I might not be sleeping because of all the research I've been doing but trust me, I reread the scheming over and over again. I even checked older correspondences and, Sasza, this is going to be a disaster. In general, I understand that innovation seems to be getting in the way of employment and that the Empire still hasn't recovered from the last war. People are hungry and on the verge of something terrible." She cradles her wine glass, stopping herself from worrying on her nails.

"But why the Vampire States? It's the aristocracy who don't do enough with the wealth they've amassed." Trade and commercial exchange happen between the Odonic Empire and the autonomous zones, but one isn't financially beholden to the other. The people's frustration has nothing to do with the vampires.

"His logic is taking tithes from the Vampire States." She laughs at the glare Sasza gives her. "I know, I also refuse to believe him to be that stupid."

Given the litany of nonsense plaguing that clan, Emperor Iwan being an idiot is not far out of the realm of possibility. "Someone must see the profit in it."

"They're ordering weapons, ones that I hadn't heard of before." She extends her hand. "Can you pass me my dinner?"

In her parcel, there is only one meal, not two. Sasza keeps his face neutral; given the hour, it's safe to assume Sasza had already eaten, even though he never took these meetings on what looked like an empty stomach.

He hands over the foil-wrapped meal, and Lady Świetlana unpacks the crusty bread buried underneath cheese, mushrooms, and preserved tomato sauce.

"Thank you." The loud crunch echoes off the wall as she bites into it. "It's...it's terrible, Sasza. I feel like they've been itching for a conflict since it leaked that only vampires survived the Jackiewicz Incident."

"That's not true," Sasza interjects. He never interrupts her.

"I *know,* but tell that to Lady Bianka. She's convinced that their survival means some kind of collusion. But it's worse than that—our Military swore to only train the Emperor's Chosen on weapons capable of killing vampires made from bestiapir parts. Except they now want the whole Military to have access to those blades. I couldn't stomach reading about it, but I tried. The engineering and smithing are almost as gruesome as the butchery required. It's absolutely abhorrent...fuck."

She presses her hand into her eye socket, as if trying to scrub away the image. "I don't think humans ever made weapons *out of other people* in order to eradicate them. It's awful, Sasza."

Sasza lets out a measured exhale and tries his best not to correct her. This tool-making is more the equivalent of humans making tools out of the bones of other animals. Undead blades, as these weapons are called, can be used to kill vampires in more ways than decapitation or damaging the heart. When fed the wielder's blood, they become magical items, capable of so much more.

"Is there any mention of how this harvest happens?" Sasza speaks calmly. He's not distraught, not like Lady Świetlana. The typical collection process is a scavenging and grave-robbing operation. The bestiapiry have no elaborate rituals or rites for when one of their own passes, at least, not in the same way humans and vampires do. They simply leave their corpses behind for others to do as they will. Smaller predators snack on the meat while vampires take the bones, skin, and sinew. Their blacksmiths and tanneries make weapons and armor. And then they can kill each other.

"I'm worried that's what they're using the Emperor's Chosen for—to kill bestiapiry to make more weapons. Not even my father knows what they do, anyway, but I don't think it's beyond the realm of possibility. For all we know, they could just be fulfilling their duty to protect the Empire." She pauses to catch her breath. "I don't understand how you're so calm about this, Sasza. Because why *I'm* worried is that if something can kill a bestiapir, there's no doubt it can also kill a vampire such as yourself."

Fear and a need to scream strike him at once. The shock almost makes him drop his wine glass. He cannot commit violence against Her Highness for her knowledge. It would raise more questions than answers, and absolutely invoke some kind of investigation into his origins.

It'd be a scandal no one, not even Władysław Czarnolaski, would be able to talk himself out of.

He loudly sets his glass down and leans back in his seat with his arms crossed. "How did you figure it out?" This lack of discretion ignites a hypocritical anger—his father is the same kind of sloppy, and Sasza is more mad at himself than he ever has been at Władysław. The anger simmers; a father should maintain the secrets that keep himself and his offspring safe, not the other way around.

"You do a great job of covering it up, if that's your concern. It took me a while to notice that every time you return from your trips, you smell a little coppery. Or you use perfumes to cover it up, but it lingers. And your demeanor completely changes, you just look healthy." She drinks from her wine glass. "Oh, and there is that one time I snooped around your bathroom and the creams confirmed all that I suspected."

Sasza pinches the bridge of his nose. "This is why we never have anyone over."

"That's not fair, I think we enjoy each other's company."

A groan like a snarl simmers within his throat. "What's next, Your Highness? Are you going to turn me in? Tell the council who want to wage war against vampire kind how there is a vampire in their midst?"

She glares at him like he's stupid. "I have been nothing but forthright with you about the war brewing against your kind. There's no circumstance under which telling them you're a vampire makes sense."

"How can we be certain that the Imperial Council hasn't also figured out about the vampires among them?"

Lady Świetlana shakes her head. "Unless you've been inviting them all here, there's no reason for anyone to be suspicious. I only figured out the blood smell thing because of how much time we spend together in close quarters."

He tries to take her words at face value, but he wonders if his veil of deception has already fallen. Father has been the antithesis of careful.

Empress Gita has spent considerable time in close quarters with Father. Others have as well, though his father wears his cologne much heavier than Sasza does. But as Świetlana demonstrated, the scents lack the strength to fully mask blood's musk.

If the discovery of Władysław's affair with Gita sparks a civil war anyway due to aristocratic rage over the vampires interfering in their government, Sasza is not sure he'll take his father with him on their next escape. In fact, he might be the reason his father never makes it out of Korona at all.

"If that's what you believe." Sasza grunts. There's also the matter of Ilya and the intimate moments he spent in even tighter quarters with the Finance Minister. Ilya must know of Sasza's inhumanity, but simply not said anything because now Sasza carries his secret of the Flock. One cannot out the other without sacrificing their status and security.

"It is what I believe," Lady Świetlana replies. "It's what I know, anyway. But I think, what I want to know most is about you, Sasza. I hate phrasing it this way, but: who are you?"

Sasza should have assumed the time for telling his truth would come.

"I'm not going to judge you, Sasza. I'm here as your friend, not as the emperor's heir."

Her honesty makes him soft, almost endeared, though the suspicion remains. "Very well. I do warn you that it's a bit of a long story."

It starts when Aleksander Czarnolaski is born to a field-working woman in a village belonging to the lands of Castle Dytryk. He had barely known his father— Władysław stayed out of his life for months at a time. Sasza omits the part where he transforms into a bestiapir as a hybrid. He conveys to Świetlana that, yes, he is a vampire, just like his father and mother.

In his early adulthood, Władysław got into some terrible business with a furtive group, the kind of trouble that could only be solved by faking one's death and changing one's name. He had allies in several

Vampire States who agreed to host him not as a vampire, but as a human mystic with a special proficiency in magic who could serve as advisor to the courts. The name Sasza's father gave himself is the incredibly provincial Władysław Czarnolaski. It's his mother's maiden name, and it's one connected to a place, not a role or a person. No one would suspect a thing.

And so, he took Sasza around, bouncing from Castle to Castle, among different noble courts, until he got into the cultural graces of a certain Emperor Iwan Iwanowicz. In fact, his father wanted his last stop to be in Korona, to get protection both social and political from the elite in the entire continent of Mokosza.

"What did he need protection from?" Świetlana asks.

"Himself," Sasza answers too quickly. "He made many enemies. But Father also mentioned that if he's playing his cards correctly, then I would never need to find out what he's been on the run from."

"And you've never tried to find out?"

"Believe me, I've tried. But my father has never once mentioned it since we settled in Korona, in relative safety. But he's making some choices that might mean we have to shed our current identities and disappear again."

"I'm not letting that happen," Lady Świetlana blurts out with un-characteristic desperation. "We'll figure it out."

The door to the Czarnolaski home opens and slams shut. Sasza immediately recognizes his father's gait, though it's unsteady, as if he's drunk in the way humans are. Władysław grunts and bumps into the furniture as he wrestles his winter gear off. A pair of wet thuds hit the wall. Sasza and Lady Świetlana exchange concerned glances when he enters the kitchen.

Władysław's hair hangs down his shoulders in gray ropes damp from snow, exertion, and his own rapture. His robes are dry, so at least he wore a coat out in the storm. Judging from the bright redness in his eyes rather than on his pale cheeks, Władysław's drunkenness is a product of blood, not alcohol. If his father is feeding with such little regard for getting caught, the end of their tenure in Korona is coming sooner rather than later.

It might be too late for Sasza to do anything about it.

"Good evening, Father. Forgive me for having Her Highness over, I didn't know when to expect you home." Sasza swallows. "Are you hungry? I can cook something up."

"How sweet of you to offer. But as wisdom suggests, sometimes an empty stomach is the key to a full mind. I'm quite all right for this evening."

"Would you at least like a seat?" Sasza prepares to move.

His father waves at him and leans against the wall. "You're too good to me, my boy." He bows dramatically to Lady Świetlana. "Good evening, Your Highness. As much as I'd love to offer my pleasantries, I will be off to bed."

Her Highness Lady Świetlana meets Sasza's amber eyes with her dark purple gaze. Neither knows how to proceed, which is unusual for them. She gives him the smallest nod.

"Have a good night, Father." Sasza's voice comes out even keeled, despite his heart thundering in his chest and unequivocal metallic stench of blood following Władysław like a tail. He stomps upstairs, tripping over himself.

When the door to Władysław's bedroom thumps to a close, Lady Świetlana tips her glass towards Sasza. "Perhaps this will help?"

"No, it will not."

She lowers her voice and leans towards him. "Oh, does it not have an effect?"

"Ha! In fact, it does, but the amount required would be enough to pickle a person like a summer cucumber. Can't taste it either, which is a shame."

Lady Świetlana throws down the remaining wine in a single swig. "We cannot trust him."

Sasza wants to laugh. His father generally hides his debauchery from his live-in child, but to not even perform as a sober person in front of someone as influential as Lady Świetlana makes Sasza nervous. "I'm sorry you had to witness that. He usually keeps it to himself."

"That must be really hard, I'm sorry." If she thinks Father is an alcoholic, Sasza will take it.

He didn't mention in his story that Władysław had little reservation with his blood gluttony. When people did not think him a secret thrall to one of the vampire nobles, they thought he had a blood kink. Far too often, he would gorge, the comedown from which showed cracks in the facade of being a human Magical Advisor. He lacked control over his magic when he could summon it. Halfway through casting, he would switch from the human dialect of the protolanguage to the vampiric one, impeding spells and making him look more a fraud than necessary. A polyglot suddenly clumsy across several languages. And as a teenager, Sasza would take it upon himself to cover up the errors, make it look like his father's magic worked fine.

Since gaining the title of Imperial Magician, Władysław has had far fewer opportunities to make a fool of himself. But now that he has been drinking from Empress Gita steadily, though when is a mystery, Sasza worries that it's becoming obvious that Władysław's wobbly movements and strange sayings are because of excess blood, not booze. Especially if even Świetlana can detect the smell, despite his careful perfuming and presentation.

Something is unraveling within Władysław. As much as Sasza wants to pity his father, his patience grows thin. Father's inability to process his own negative emotions and unfettered impulses is going to get them both executed.

"It is hard," Sasza says finally. "But it's nothing I haven't dealt with before, unfortunately."

"Is there any way I can help?" She scrunches her brows in concern.

Sasza doesn't feel worthy of it. "Why are you giving me this much attention?" He points to the ceiling. "Do you see what's advising your father?"

She gives him that impatient glare again. "You're my dearest friend, regardless of the roles and duties you perform. I care about you, not as a political ally, but as a person. Your happiness doesn't necessarily influence mine, but I do not like seeing you in this kind of stress. I *want* to help."

"I appreciate it." Sasza lifts his mouth in a half-grin. "I don't think there's any help for Władysław Czarnolaski that can be externally provided, I'm afraid. He needs to work on himself."

Lady Świetlana nods. "We cannot trust him."

"You said that already."

"It bears repeating." She hastily finishes her dinner. "Do you want me to stay the night?"

The thought of her being under the same roof as the man with whom her mother is cheating on the emperor makes him shudder. "And what? Start more rumors? Let's see what the snow is like."

Sasza rises and goes to the window, pulling back the curtain. The world is a sepia-toned wonderland of light reflecting off ice like shattered glass. Clouds remain, but no new precipitation falls. The snow on the ground is fresh and soft, best for driving over as it hasn't had a chance to pack upon itself, even if no one will be able to clear the roads until the morning.

"Are you good to drive?"

Lady Świetlana softly places the glass on the table. "Please, one glass is not enough to incapacitate me." She stands. "Thank you, Aleksander Czarnolaski, for the company and the counsel."

He rises and gives her a deep, wholly serious bow. "There's nothing else I would rather be doing."

FOUR

I.

LIGHT PUSHES AGAINST UTE'S eyes, prying her lids open when she comes to. Air forces its way into her lungs. It smells fresh and vaguely alcoholic. Her lavender gray hair clings to the grimy skin on her neck and shoulders. Familiarity makes itself known immediately—she's at the Military Academy's infirmary.

A medic in her white habit stands over her, taking notes on a board, while the red X crossing her chest glows in the lamp light. Her wrinkled face does not betray her disposition towards Ute. No relief that her patient woke up, but also no frustration that her work of observation and medical ministrations continues. The real work of health care begins now, where healing turns to recovery.

The pristine infirmary chamber with its white walls and clean sheets is not where Ute expected to find herself, not after getting caught in the maw of a giant bestiapir.

She wills herself to sit up in the uncomfortable cot, but her body won't listen. It feels limp and heavy, like a slab of meat purchased from a butcher. No rigor, no structural integrity; only muscle and bone held loosely together with skin. Not all of it is there either.

She stretches her left arm forward, expecting her right palm to meet her hand. Nothing comes. She feels no movement in her right arm not because of disorientation, but because there is nothing to move. The hand is gone. There is no wrist where the stump should be. The absence crawls up her forearm, her elbow—all those segments are missing.

All that remains is a bandage capping her right shoulder.

Ute takes a deep, shuddering breath. Her scream comes hollow, barely a noise at all. Not enough liquid moistens her mouth for any proper sounds. This must be a nightmare. Like the progression of most terrible dreams, she knows exactly how she got to this space and the last events before the darkness. But from what she understands of the Military's handling of aristocratic children and offspring, they come out how they entered. Some have scars, sure, but none of them return ruined. Most of them graduate whole. They don't come out with parts of them missing.

"The patient is lucid," the medic says out loud. There's an unsettling rigidity in their speech that even during her Academy training, Ute had not gotten used to.

Ute's voice comes out in a rasp, and the medic brings her over some water from the sink tucked into the corner. It tastes chalky, likely due to the nutrients and pain killers added. The soreness where her arm should be throbs like a headache, though there is no muscle to feel pain.

"What is the meaning of this?" Ute tries not to shout, but she tries to siphon all the domineering energy appropriate for a woman of her status. She hasn't spoken to another person in an untold amount of time. Her head swivels from looking at the medic to glancing at her missing arm. "Where did it go?"

"Down the gullet of a bestiapir." A stern, deep voice echoes within the small room.

Ute peers past the medic at the figure who walked in. She recognizes the regalia of the higher officers: the double-breasted coat with the stars and badges denoting significant contributions and their rank—a general. Their close-cropped black coif and precise chinstrap beard communicate a serious severity appropriate for one of such high status.

"My name is General Oktawia Kwiatkowski, Director of the Emperor's Secret Service and Overseer of the Emperor's Chosen. I'm here to discuss your career options after your unfortunate…" They search for the right word. "Accident."

This person reports directly to the Emperor. They are the one who determines if Ute belongs in the Emperor's Chosen. Does she? Fear and uncertainty rob her of any response. Every aborted question blossoms from her own paranoia and vulnerability. Is she going to be investigated for her duplicity? How much audacity and hubris would one need to perform as one worthy of the distinction, but to throw it all away because…

This further tunnels her vision. The Emperor? So many other aristocrats do things for the Iwanowicz family, either with transactions or with charity. Ute, however, wanted proximity to Świetlana—who likely doesn't even remember her. They had so many classmates in Lyceum, but she had been a consistent member of the carousel of friends circling Her Highness.

Ute should have thought to consult with Iwona beforehand. Iwona would likely have told her not to throw her final trial. Unlike most aristocrats who had their roles handed to them and assumed, Iwona had been one to keep her work ethic aligned with her goals. If only Ute hadn't gotten so easily distracted.

The mistakes she's made and the opportunity squandered swirl in her head, making her a bit light-headed as she waits for General Kwiatkowski to speak again.

"The results of your audition for the Ninety-Second Regiment of the Emperor's Chosen are inconclusive. Though you survived, you failed to execute the task presented. I will be honest about that. The next action we should take is to administer another audition, but in your current state, that is not possible. Moreover, projects are already underway that cannot wait for your full recovery. I will give you a moment to process that disappointment." They clasp their hands behind their back.

Ute does need a minute to process. She suffered five years of proving herself and overcoming the allegations that her name and not much else got her into the Military's most exclusive academy. On the other hand—she succeeded in not getting into the Emperor's Chosen with her head still attached to her shoulders. The guilt starts nibbling at her relief—she had promised Iwona that they both would make it. Iwona would take time out of her own training rituals and rigorous extracurriculars to help Ute train, only for Ute to throw it all away on what looks like a whim.

Up until that morning of her trial, she wanted nothing more than to be in the Emperor's Chosen, especially given the fact that she had a friend helping her get there. And Ute abandoned her. There are no laws in the Odonic Empire declaring such a dangerous change of heart a crime. But if Iwona finds out, it will feel like a transgression and a rejection of their friendship.

She sips some more water and nods. Normally right-handed, the glass feels strange in the clumsiness of her left hand.

"If the medic would please leave, I have an opportunity I would like to personally offer you."

Without so much as a twitch of a brow, the medic gives a curt bow and leaves the two in privacy. The darkness of the room lends an air of conspiracy. Sunlight barely makes it through the clouds. Through the window cracked open, a brisk autumnal breeze blows. Only Ute's left arm shudders, and it's not a result of the slight difference in temperature.

General Kwiatkowski looks upon Ute with brown eyes rimmed with an exhaustion no amount of sleep can remedy. "I have come to invite you to an appointment that I feel befits someone of your training.

According to your school records, you did pass the requisite courses in the Emperor's Chosen track, but, as I have stated, the results of your exam are inconclusive. As such, my offer is this: an advisory role with the Secret Service, directly observing Her Highness Świetlana Iwanowicz."

Ute suppresses a laugh, and manages to say, "I'm sorry, repeat that?"

"You are to be Her Highness Świetlana Iwanowicz's Magical Advisor, a kind of personal aide but constant companion. Similar to the position of Emperor Iwanowicz's Imperial Magician, a role held by Władysław Czarnolaski. They're both largely ceremonial, and the conclusion my office had come to is that while it would make some sense to have someone who would have qualified for the Chosen to go into the regular rank and file, it poses too much of a threat. A waste of talent, if you will. Instead of granting you undue membership in the Ninety-Second Regiment of the Emperor's Chosen, you would be acting in the service and protection of the imperial family in the most direct of circumstances."

Ute wants to vomit the entire contents of her torso in appreciation. The risk she took in turning her back on a promise made to Iwona in search of her own esteem and status paid off. If she knew that on the opposite side of a failed audition was a place by Świetlana's side, she might have cut off her own arm with the undead blade before the audition even started.

"I..." She is so giddy and so freshly awakened that the words struggle to meet her lips. "I accept."

"That was quick." General Kwiatkowski raises their manicured eyebrows. "Are you sure you don't need more time to consider?"

Ute shakes her head. If given more time, she might have some realization that will cause her to change her mind. At least she'll be under the Military's employ and protected by her proximity to the crown. She found her way back to Her Highness, a devotion stemming from within her own feminine desires. The friendship she had with Iwona was mutually beneficial in its own way, but it mostly reaped benefits for Ute. Iwona's goal had singularly been a position among the Emperor's Chosen. She'd have taken it regardless of Ute's absence, even if Ute had backed off less impulsively.

"The one thing, I suppose, that I really want to know, is what I'm supposed to do about this." She shrugs the incomplete shoulder.

"Well, now that you're awake, the staff here can get you your measurements and fit with a new limb right away. With practice and skill, it can replace some of the proficiency of what was lost. It will take time, and it will take much training to strengthen your left arm. Even with magical enhancement, unfortunately, full replacement of what had been lost is not possible. We can have someone on staff at the Palace for the hours you're there, and perhaps another doctor on call for when you're elsewhere."

"That..." Ute considers it. She wouldn't have to leave Świetlana's side if she didn't want to. "I'd very much like that, yes."

"I will make those arrangements. Congratulations on your new post, Ute Myśliwska."

Ute's heart pounds in her chest. She takes another sip, and the water's coolness does nothing to slake the dryness in her throat or drown the nerves. The impulse of wanting nothing more than to return to the proximity of the crown paid off. A post with the Emperor's Chosen would have taken her too far away from the member of the imperial family she would have wanted to serve most.

General Kwiatkowski leaves before Ute can decide how to bring up her connection to the current Chosen cohort. She wants to get a message out to Iwona that she is fine, a little battered, but will ultimately be in a better place, though no longer at her side.

II.

The salon is the one room in that house which belongs to the Czarnolaskis. Sasza and his father keep its oak door shut, away from the prying eyes of occasional guests who do not deserve to see the gallery untouched by the grime of their everyday routines. In the over-large credenza stand several tiny porcelain dolls of soldiers and winged beings, often in conflict, which are to Władysław's tastes, while the ones enraptured are to Sasza's. These delicate pieces of décor defend plates intricately painted with flowers which even humans wouldn't use for their daily meals. On birthdays, however, Sasza, his father, and Laurencja would enjoy some kaszanka and blood cakes prepared by the imperial kitchens to be served from these fine dishes. The humans assumed it was their favorite foods and special treats, not sustenance essential to their survival. It amused Sasza that humans enjoyed such primal foods at all.

The eating experience must differ between them, but now that Lady Świetlana knows of Sasza's condition, perhaps he can ask her what she thinks of such fare. Is it taboo or distasteful? Is it one of those acquired tastes he's heard so much about but lacks the palate to understand? It's only one of many inquiries he has about the human condition, his curiosity about what it's like to be human, but the opportunity for that conversation lies in a time of less-dire politics.

His father's affair leaves him with pangs of jealousy. Sasza has never been intimate with someone within his own four walls. With Ilya, it had always either been the office or his apartment. Because he didn't want a scandal, but he liked the company Sasza provided. Not without ulterior motives.

Even if Sasza had the indecency to take Ilya home to his own bed chambers, it wouldn't be the same as fucking anonymously in the Vampire States. Such entanglements have only ever taken place at finch parties where human guests offer their blood in exchange for carnal favors while other pairings do the same.

His mouth goes dry at the memory of soft, broken skin spilling blood down his throat while a wet mouth bobs up and down on his length, and the muscular squish of boypussy squeezes his curled fingers sunk deep inside. So many men, so much to feast on with others watching. His cock swells at the memory.

What Sasza wants, more than anything, is that post-orgasm serenity. The evening's loneliness grants him the isolation with which to take care of himself. No one except the salon furniture and the flames dancing in the hearth will know any better of his transgression.

Sasza slides his nighttime trousers to his ankles, leaning back on the plush, maroon, velvet couch, careful not to put his bare feet on the silver-and-glass coffee table in the room's center. His knee-length robe protects the furniture from his bare skin. His cock rises stiff and red with want. He smooths a hand up and down its length, taut and perfect for plunging deep into someone's throat. A small bead of cum glistens in the fire light, perfect for someone to lick while gently nibbling on the tip. He spits on that palm and clutches the base, dragging it up and pulling it down as he has to himself and others so many times before. Much time has passed since he's indulged, typically so tired that sleep pulls him under as soon as he hits his own mattress. The hunger also keeps thoughts of other satisfaction and satiety at bay. But for one evening, he can steal a small moment of self-intimacy.

It's well over a week since he emptied himself in Ilya; he's not sure if he could do it again, not with the little regard he has for both their safety. Sasza pushes aside all thoughts of the Finance Minister as he grips and pumps himself, the veins in his arm forming web-like ridges as the pressure builds and builds. The slapping of skin against skin echoes as he strokes himself.

The small gasps he lets leave his lips remind him of the melodies heard from the throats of other men he's enjoyed. He goes faster and faster as he remembers their humming while he gorged on the blood trickling down their necks and chests.

Despite the solitude, Sasza shoves the back of his wrist between his teeth to muffle his own groans. They're not as arousing to him, but it's the closest he can get to that delectable sound.

His balls tighten, and Sasza knows better than to leave his mess like an inexperienced teenager. His left hand hunts his robe's pocket for the white kerchief he carries on him. Freshly laundered and unblemished, the pristine fabric catches the sticky ropes spurting from his uncut head. His chest unclenches from his own tension, pulling air deep into his lungs.

Sasza sinks further into the couch, relishing in the high that simmers through his veins and envelopes his mind—bubbly and effervescent, cutting a refined focus that blocks out most extraneous thoughts. It's not quite the same as post-feeding, but he'll take the approximation. With another proper meal several weeks away into the new year, it's all he can go off of unless he takes Laurencja up on inheriting her menagerie of diseased blood. He hasn't committed—the foul, complex tastes have him reconsidering. Is he so desperate for sustenance that he will debase himself with such meager morsels of vile tastes? A few weeks remain before he must decide.

The crackling, pale fire lulls him into something like sleep as he puts away his slackened cock and pulls his trousers back up. Before he can fall into complete unconsciousness, the stench of blood and alcohol sours his peace.

Sasza smells his father before he hears the door slam, heaving boots stumbling against the entryway. Władysław Czarnolaski should not be feeding enough to be smelled by others, especially not his offspring with his heightened senses. Father hasn't fed like that in years—why is he starting now and with whom?

"Father?" Sasza calls from his shattered comfort. When Władysław doesn't respond, he gets up and greets him by the door. "It's awfully late for you to be coming home."

His father is a disaster. Red and brown flecks stain his cheeks and chin. Some had gotten on the flaxen wool of the sweater under his undone cloak. His amber eyes are pink and lustrous, much like the evening when he interrupted Sasza and Lady Świetlana's last dinner. Władysław Czarnolaski is blood drunk, again. It's only been a few evenings—much like the human condition of alcoholism, such excess consumption wreaks havoc on the psyche and physiology in ways both reparable and not.

Władysław kicks his boots off. One slams into the wall. At least he remembered to close the door before making such a scene. "Can I ask what's wrong, my sweet child?"

Sasza clenches his jaw. "We're taking this to the salon." It's the inner sanctum of their shared home. The evidence of his indulgence sits squished in Sasza's pocket.

"Oh, I love that room. Let me follow you."

His father tries to walk steadily behind Sasza but winds up stumbling like a newborn fawn rather than an aristocrat of grace and decorum. His clumsiness will break the facade of sophistication, but at least there is no one else to see it.

"I see you already got the fire going," Władysław says, before falling onto the loveseat opposite the couch. It is black with large pink, red, and white flowers.

Sasza tosses a fresh log. It catches a small flame which dances along the bark's grooves. He glares at the controlled destruction because he cannot look at his father. He's witnessed his father's debauchery before. He's observed Laurencja's attempts at shielding a younger Sasza from it in the name of maintaining his innocence. There is nothing innocent about ripping a vampire child from the town he grew up in because of a threat that has never been explained.

It is good that he relieved himself earlier. Instead of a torrent of incomplete and inconsistent thoughts firing through his mind, there is a single stream of focus: betrayal.

Władysław pats the empty space beside him. "Come, my son, have a seat."

Sasza obeys, wrapping the robe tighter around his bare torso. His father should go upstairs to his study as he always had once his day ended but letting him sleep off the blood drinking seems foolish. Władysław will dismiss the suggestion with his own manic energy, putting off a confrontation until later, and then get blood drunk a third time in succession, and Sasza cannot allow it to go unaddressed. Feeding upon humans has never been allowed in the Czarnolaski household. Why now?

When Sasza sits, his father puts a hand on Sasza's head, mussing his hair. "I'm so, so grateful for you, Aleksander."

Sasza shudders at the use of his full name—he hasn't heard it from his father in a non-introduction in several years. "Thank...you?" He tries to mask his scorn.

"I'm sure you want to know the reason behind my tardiness, and my absence. And you have been nothing but patient and gracious while I have been working on my own projects. For that, I thank you."

It surprises Sasza to hear the word "working," but he masks his skepticism. "I did it to protect us."

His father's hand moves to his shoulder, resting heavily on it as if he were limping. "Of course. I've trained you well in the art of survival among humans and their courts." Władysław closes his eyes and smiles wide.

The smell of stale, curdled blood twists Sasza's stomach. "Father, may I ask who you've been feeding on?"

"That's exactly what I needed to speak to you about, my boy. But I won't be getting there yet." He opens his bloodshot eyes wide. With red-stained lips, Władysław is the perfect image of a vampire in satiety. "First, I have to tell you why we came to Korona in the first place. The full tale. With what's going on around our Empire, it's important to me that you also know what the emperor doesn't."

Sasza braces himself, squirming on the couch so that he faces his father, and the fire burns brightly behind him. The warmth suffocates. He has never pried into the minutiae of his father's past; security by way of ignorance is often the path of least resistance.

But Sasza doesn't understand what fight his father prepares him for.

"Sylwia's mother and I have no softness for the way the Vampire States are run or for the existence of the Empire itself. This was before Zofia, of course. We both met at a gathering for those who also shared that mistrust, who wanted a third option in terms of coexistence and leadership. It started all right at first. Civilized discussions over petite meals and strong drinks. I loved those salons, where humans and vampires mingled without the rigidity of the institution of thralls or the fear of becoming prey. But while the ideas of what life could be without either oppressor sounded fine, the execution proved...violent. Biological experimentation, commanded by leaders who made themselves invisible to their constituents. As the director of research, I knew exactly the mutilation they sought." Władysław coughs, blood or spit falls down the wrong tube. He bends forward and beats his chest with a firm fist. "Apologies, it makes me sick to think about. They seek immortality and knowledge, at whatever cost."

The Jackiewicz lineage are renowned for their science as much as they are for their diplomacy. "So, the massacre at Daszek, ruled by the Jackiewiczes, that was—?"

"Them! Yes, the Flock."

Sasza swallows back disdain for Ilya and his lying. "What knowledge were they seeking?"

His father stares straight into the pristine glass surface of the coffee table that occupies the room's center.

Sasza clears his throat. "Father?"

Władysław remains unmoving like a statue.

"Father." Not by blood, but Sasza has experienced such inebriation before—the kind where the mind simply stops and serenity befalls the body. There is nothing peaceful, however, in the way Władysław's cheeks quiver and small spots of blood prick the wrinkled perimeter around his eyes.

With a ragged breath, Władysław spits up a crimson bolus. It bounces across the coffee table's surface, leaving a trail of scarlet wetness and gore. "I apologize, Aleksander." He shoves a finger into his mouth, his wrist bending and extending as he searches his throat for the next discharge.

Sasza sits away from him, unsure how to help. "Father, how can I—?"

Another one of the gory balls launches from his father's maw. Between coughs, he manages, "That is how they ensure their secrecy. Through spells more ancient and fearsome than anything taught by even the most learned magicians in all Mokosza, they ensure silence. It's painful enough to silence, but—"

"Stop telling me about obscure curses, and get to the point, Father."

"I know you've been looking into the Jackiewicz Incident, Sasza." He lets out a single roaring cough. "The reason I haven't been able to help with that is because I cannot have *them* catching up to me. To us. Because they figured out a method for creating dhampiry." His cheeks puff but he swallows loudly. "It involves the transfusion of hybrid blood to bring a human back from the brink of death."

"Transfusion?" In Laurencja's clinic, her own vampire blood is often used in the mixing of potions and medicines to accelerate the recuperation of those who can be saved. But that is a small sip of liquid from between the lips. Not infusing foreign vampire blood into a human body as a replacement therapy for healing. "That's…has that been attempted?"

Before the words can be uttered, Władysław chokes, sputtering red, wheezing. Wind whistles as the space in his air hole constricts. He claws at it as if choked by an unseen force.

Sasza cannot watch his father suffer. He wants Władysław to experience true, lasting consequences, not momentary physical pain like this as punishment. The kind of consequences that make it hard to trust anyone and leave him unable to sleep for days on end. He scoots forward and grasps his father's face between his hands. His skin is feverish and pale in a way a vampire's should not be after feeding. Sasza wedges his thumb between his father's uneven teeth and pries his mouth open. No air gets through; the head of an unbirthed mass peeks from the root of Władysław's tongue.

Shivering with disgust, Sasza pushes his long index and middle fingers into his father's mouth. Władysław's throat contracts and loosens under this new intrusion. The thing squishes and squelches beneath the pads of Sasza's fingers, yielding to his ministrations, sticky muscles slipping away from the dry digits. It reminds him of removing offal from a fowl to prepare it for roasting, rather than tender loving care meant to alleviate hurt.

Situations such as these impromptu minor surgeries kept him away from the field of medicine altogether. Moreover, this is a perversion of intimacy, one where the only professional distance is political and not one of a physician interested in saving their patient's quality of life. Sasza lacks the experience but not the desire to quell his father's pain. Information is a form of protection, one that these mysterious comrades took great strides to obliterate. If momentary discomfort guarantees better strategy and furthers understanding of a true enemy, Sasza is willing to make that sacrifice.

The slender curve of his fingers manipulates the bolus enough to create a cavity for his father's breath. Władysław's bloody cough, however, dislodges it such that it smacks against the middle of Sasza's chest. He yelps and scatters, creating as much distance from his father on the loveseat as possible. The mound of indecipherable physiology plops onto the wooden floor.

"It has been tried, but the attempts have all failed."

"Why?"

Władysław wipes his damp forehead with his sleeve. "It comes down to blood types. Yours, specifically."

Sasza doesn't remember how it came up in his letters to his sister, but Sylwia warned Sasza never to reveal his antigens. Why, he never understood—being compatible with other types should be a boon, not a terrible truth to keep hidden. "If you need to borrow a significant amount of my blood, you could have just asked."

"Because it's not just *your* blood. Someone else needs to be drained for you to survive. And I found the perfect solution."

"Is that why you're blood drunk right now?" Unless Władysław goes out hunting bison in the dead of winter, there's no other explanation for the intoxication.

"I need someone on the verge of death, Sasza!"

Their raised voices and concerning noises will bring attention if they go on any longer. Sasza touches his middle finger to his thumb and pulls them across lips to cast a silencing ward around their residence, though there is no one around to hear them anyway. Pale blue dust splashes against the walls and windows, disappearing quickly.

Sasza shouts, "You could have called upon *Laurencja*, Father. She feeds off her terminal patients all the time!"

"Don't you for a second assume I didn't consider that. But she shouldn't know about the Flock. I've never told her, and you better not either." Władysław points at Sasza, his fingers tremble not of drunkenness but the hesitation to cast a spell.

"What are you going to do, Father? Curse me instead of trusting me?"

He exhales, rasping. "I would never, Aleksander." Władysław lowers his hands. "You're the only thing in this world that I do trust. Because of that, I must ask: will you give me your blood?"

Sasza already disagrees. "Who are you feeding off of that needs my blood?" He resents already knowing the answer.

"Empress Gita, of course! It brings her peace, spares her from the horrors plaguing her mind." He spits red onto the floor and looks at his son. "She's had enough of this world and Empire already, I see no fault in making her part of our experiment."

Sasza widens his eyes, and several swears smash into his mind all at once. Reasons cascade and pile upon each other in a neat stack rather than discord. The emperor and everyone else around him will notice the empress's health declining. If she needs to be placed in an infirmary, the only doctor they can trust is Laurencja. And that is *not* the doctor they will assign. The assigned doctor will be one who notices the blood missing from her body, and everyone else will catch onto the excess time they've spent together. The Czarnolaskis' days at the side of the Iwanowiczes will be numbered, and no amount of truth telling will erase the conspiracy of the Vampire States planting two of their own into the highest echelon of the Empire's government.

War will be guaranteed.

"Father, have you lost your *mind*? You realize you would have to drain both me and Lady Gita for this experiment to work?"

"I used to harvest blood from thralls, it's not quite so dramatic as you say." Władysław's face glows with a self-righteousness Sasza has seen before. The confidence in the correctness of his actions makes him sick. It's an expression he's witnessed when Władysław executed a deal or negotiated his way out of impossible-to-disprove accusations.

He eases himself off the love seat, slowly coming to standing. Władysław Czarnolaski, the man who made every choice to save himself and his son from those who want to reform the world in a torrent of blood, now wants his son a part of that flood. The problem isn't the nature of the experimentation itself—if Empress Gita wants to die, she's more than welcome to do so however she sees fit.

It's the irreversibility of the crime and that creating a vampire within the Imperial Court's highest echelon would stoke more mistrust of vampires.

"Father, Emperor Iwan already wants to declare war on the Vampire States. I'm doing all I can to stop it, and making a dhampir of *Empress Gita* would make it an inevitably. And if it doesn't work, I'm not sure if Emperor Iwan will forgive his wife's murder."

Władysław doesn't answer. He stands to meet Sasza and, for the first time, Sasza fears his father. Typically, he stood behind Władysław whenever someone approached Sasza with that same hateful gaze. But the predators and threats Sasza had been on the run from all these years stand before him, closer than ever before.

Sasza will not become a sacrifice. "Father, respectfully, I'm not letting you commit a crime against the crown to prove a theory that's already a fairy tale."

From an unseen pocket, Władysław produces a syringe. "That's not for you to decide."

"It will be a disaster if it doesn't work."

"But what if it *does*?"

"All right, Father, what if it *does* work, and Empress Gita is now a resurrected dhampir, likely the first of her kind? What then?"

At this his father pauses. Instead of making any kind of sound suggesting stalling for thinking, he simply stands there. Sasza swivels his head, searching his father's face for anything resembling an answer. None comes. Władysław, having climbed as high as anyone not of imperial aristocracy will go, has found a way to ruin it with no regard for his own survival or longevity. Cracks form in Sasza's heart—he both wants to give into the Flock to prove them wrong but has no plan for if they're right. Władysław just wants Sasza to go ahead with this directionless idea that puts both his son's life and that of his illicit lover's in jeopardy. It puts the stability of the Empire in jeopardy as well, but Sasza cannot bring himself to care about those millions of people in this moment.

His focus zeroes in on his own survival and, somehow, he is not the one being selfish in this townhouse on the outskirts of the Imperial Grounds.

Sasza slowly shakes his head and twists his foot back, preparing to flee the salon from his once protector. Like a snake, Władysław snatches Sasza's robe, trapping him in the fabric's folds. Sasza, despite lacking the enhanced strength of a freshly fed vampire, twists his way out of his father's vice grip. He cannot let that needle anywhere near his skin—that victory must be deprived at any cost. No blood for a vampire whose end goal is someone else's consumption.

"Aleksander, this is for both our sakes!" Władysław's eyes glow with frenzy.

"How is *war* for both our sakes? We'll be executed for treason."

"I assure you, we will not."

Sasza wriggles, slipping the robe off his shoulders. "You don't *know* that!"

Snarling, Władysław throws it aside, and it drapes over the loveseat's arm. Fueled by blood and a determined anger previously unseen, he bashes into Sasza. They crash into the wall adjacent to the roaring hearth.

Sasza's bare back slams into the soft, upholstered wall, knocking the wind out of his chest.

Władysław presses his arm against Sasza's shoulders, pinning him. "I will not let you die." He exposes Sasza's neck, perfect for piercing with the needle hovering in a shaking hand.

"And I'm not letting you take my blood, Father." The words come out strained, not by grief or misunderstanding, but effort. He's never gotten into a fight with a vampire, especially not one at the height of satiety. If he must defend himself, he will—university afforded him some training in the combat arts, but the salon's sanctuary is the last place he'd expect to use those skills. His knuckles brush against the fireplace's iron poker, its metal warm against his cold skin.

"So be it." Władysław sighs.

The needle pricks Sasza's skin like a kiss. Violent instinct awakens. Sasza grasps the poker, ramming the soft flesh between his father's ribs. Władysław coughs, staggering backwards. The syringe slips from his hands and onto the floor. The drunkenness robs the older Czarnolaski of the coordination required to retrieve it.

Sasza does not give him a chance. He wields the poker like a sword and pierces it into his father's chest, thrusting the iron through a plate of bone and muscle. Hesitation abandons him—Władysław would not give Sasza the same opportunity. If Sasza waited another second for his father's next move, his life would be over. In fact, two lives would end because Władysław lacked loyalty even to his own spawn.

With a shove, Sasza pushes Władysław back with his makeshift stake. Władysław's ankles hit the edge of the glass coffee table. His legs come up from under him, sending father and son crashing onto the delicate furniture. It shatters, spraying glass across the carpet. Blood's cupric smell fills Sasza's nostrils, making his mouth water, but his work isn't finished. Władysław breathes, chest muscles twitching around the rod. Sasza grasps it with both hands, raises it, and brings it back down. He mashes into the hole in his father's chest like it's a pestle on a mortar. Blood pumps out like a spring, painting over the carpet from Castle Wanda, spilling over the shards. The only sounds echoing in the salon are Sasza's grunts and the curious absence of Władysław's resistance.

When Władysław stills, Sasza, covered in his father's blood, weeps.

IT TAKES TWO CIGARETTES for Sasza to collect himself. He needed to drown out the scent of blood and settle his canines—he won't debase himself and feed on his father's corpse. But the corpse needs to be removed, and only one person came to mind who could handle such a problem.

"Sasza?" Laurencja shouts from the entryway. She arrived as soon as she could after Sasza made the call from the unused phone in the kitchen.

He doesn't go to greet her. Instead, he lets her find him in the salon.

"There you—" She covers her mouth to catch a scream. Her other hand grips the medical kit tightly, not wanting to drop the case against the already sordid ground.

With smoke billowing from his lips, Sasza says, "I didn't know who else to call. Apologies for the abrupt notice."

"No wonder you told me to come prepared. What...happened? Dare I even ask?"

Sasza spent the hour mulling over what to say. The truth feels a farce, while lying is unfair to Laurencja. Having memorized the placement of his father on the floor, he rises from the loveseat, carefully stepping around the carnage.

"I...didn't know what to do." His voice is so small, so child-like. Despite the severity and maturity of his crime, he wants someone to comfort him. The evidence lies motionless with a gaping wound where his heart should be.

He can't bear to look at Laurencja. Despite her crass demeanor towards her terminal patients, she's never been one to purposefully dole out harm. Despite Sasza's violence, he needs a doctor and a friend. Physically, there will be bruises on his chest and the dot on his neck might get inflamed, but no one else will see those minor injuries. Emotionally, however, he's shattered like the coffee table.

Władysław had put him in danger for his own single-minded ends.

"We have to clean this up." In Sasza's mind, Władysław's corpse is a chore to be tackled; to think of it as anything else will make Sasza weep again. Władysław doesn't deserve that, not for what he wanted to do to his own child. He played a moron and won a foolish prize.

Laurencja shakes her head, curls bouncing. "Not yet. We have to make this look like an accident."

"What?"

She looks at Sasza with glassy eyes. "I promised Zofia I'd keep you safe. I clearly fucked up somewhere if this is the problem we're dealing with. But I will not let you be condemned for finding a permanent solution to Władek's idiocy."

It's this admission that makes Sasza's want to spill tears again. This gentleness and offer of help are not something he expected from a woman who proved a trusted ally to both his parents.

"Sasza, I should have listened to you when you came to me. I'm so sorry for not...talking to him." She lays her kit on the loveseat whose serenity had been obliterated by familial strife. "I don't think you want me to touch you, so I won't. But what I need you to do is go upstairs and clean yourself. Take as much time as you require. I'll handle everything down here and make it look like an accident."

He bobs his head up and down, like a toddler promising not to play with delicate pieces of pottery rather than a grown adult who committed an act more irreversible. He doesn't care that he saved Empress Gita's life or protected himself from more dire consequences. Or took such a drastic step to keep the inevitably of a war between humans and vampires at bay.

Laurencja lowers her voice, speaking softly despite her trembling lips. "Can you do that for me, Sasza?"

Sasza's vocabulary vanished with the blood sinking into the carpet fibers. Any words to describe his father's failed experimentation got lost in the scuffle. Perhaps, for the better. They can die with Władysław.

Wordlessly, Sasza goes upstairs, leaving Laurencja behind in the salon, relinquishing trust and control to someone more experienced in cleaning up after Władysław Czarnolaski. Her magnum opus of covering up after his sins is removing evidence of his very own demise, with or without the help of the culprit.

Sasza elects to keep his hands clean of the matter, even as he washes the blood off his palms and wrists and watches it swirl down the sink's drain.

Echoing throughout the walls of the house, he hears Laurencja chanting spells. He recognizes the cadence—healing. His body moves before his mind has a chance to catch up.

Laurencja undulates her wrists with the same grace as a pianist over Władysław's chest. Sasza hears the faint splintering of bone.

"What are you doing?" It sounds loud in his head. He didn't mean to shout at Laurencja.

It does not interrupt her casting, but her singing stops. "Putting him back together."

"Won't that..." Sasza chews his lower lip. "That won't bring him back to life?"

She raises her eyebrows in that way she reserves for the truly ignorant. "No. But if you're going to be that worried about it, please go upstairs and into your room. Stay there. Scream. Cry. Do whatever you need to do. But I cannot be interrupted."

"What of his *clothes*?" Shredded and bloodstained, they still retain the evidence of a crime committed.

"Do you think I've never cleaned up blood before?" She clicks her tongue. "I'll be taking the clothes back to the clinic. No one else will need to see them."

"And the blood on the carpet?" There are so many uncertainties and opportunities for error.

Her hands stop moving, hovering over the hole. "I'm transferring the injury to his head. Your father got drunk and hit it. You came home. Here you found him."

It astounds Sasza how easily he accepts the lie. It is so much easier to believe that Sasza's (blood) drunk father stumbled and injured himself fiercely on his own furniture. The coffee table already has the requisite stains.

But Sasza doesn't move. His eyes remain fixated on the corpse in the salon and the unfolding deception.

"Sasza, I beg. Please go upstairs. It'll go faster if I'm alone. I don't need your company. Not this time."

"Why are you doing this?" He whispers, distraught, disbelieving.

She glares at him and flares her nostrils. "Because fuck Władek; Zofia deserves to see her child again."

Tears stream down Sasza's face again. He gives her a curt bow, and then goes to his room. He curls into himself like he's trying to find his way back into the womb, back to a time of no consciousness and no memory. In his hands, he clutches his largest pillow. He presses his face against it.

And he lets out low, bellowing scream after low, bellowing scream, muffled by fabric from the generosity of the Iwanowiczes, whom he had just protected from the whims of a man made mad by a Flock.

FIVE

I.

THE IWANOWICZES DECLARE A state funeral for their dearest friend, advisor, and Imperial Magician, Władysław Czarnolaski. The day of the affair is crisp winter, with the air cold and sharp as ice and the sun pale and beaming down from a cloudless sky. A frozen throng of dignitaries and citizens dressed in imperial red and funereal black occupy the slate gray grounds of Korona's largest plaza, the Pewter Square. Guards surround the periphery and line the promenade leading to the platform where Emperor Iwanowicz and his family overlook their citizenry, presiding over the somber affair with measured grace tinged with generations of tradition and decorum.

It starts with Emperor Iwan Iwanowicz standing at the amplifier. His silver, glittering crown presses down against his fluffy, chin-length black hair. His black robes shine like woven obsidian. The Iwanowicz family crest of a three-headed crimson eagle upon his chest blazes even from afar. The eulogy he delivers beautifully recounts a friendship that goes beyond the personal and is crafted in the most formal countenance to be worthy of an imperial address.

Iwona isn't sure Czarnolaski deserves the propriety. In her isolation in the Military Academy, Iwona had only heard rumors of him, each more colorful than the last. Since arriving in Korona, the stories of this man's antics proved a kaleidoscope of salon scandal and idle gossip. Some say he slept his way to his current position. Others say he cursed the imperial family, ensnaring them in the sort of trap that promises them his servitude and grants him protection. A tangled web of social relations not aided by, allegedly, a drinking habit which might have led to his demise.

Another story suggests that a betrayed partner had filled him with poison, but the killing blow had been a good bludgeoning to the head. She believes the version in which it truly was a drunken accident—it happened among the aristocracy with enough frequency that she memorized so many of the elaborate yarns spun to hide the perceived shame.

No such tales had been told in the Emperor's eulogy. In fact, she found it curious that at the end of his memorial, Emperor Iwan proclaimed Czarnolaski's mourning son, Aleksander, as his new Imperial Advisor. Passing on positions of expertise to offspring is nothing new to the aristocracy, especially if there are no siblings to compete with, as is the case with Czarnolaski the younger. That's the way of children with notable last names: they have positions handed to them.

But typically, the offspring are given some grace to mourn. A week is hardly enough time for such a stark transition. Her own family would at least entertain the pageantry of selecting other candidates for the vacant position. The Solstice Ball in just the next week, however, would explain the urgency of this succession.

It's likely the new Imperial Magician did not even want to follow in his father's shadow. She pities him.

This spectacle proves to be her first true task in the Emperor's Chosen. They lack the same visibility as the rest of the Military—their roster profiles match those of typical soldiers, and only the higher-ups and their families know the truth of their roles. While not glamorous or dangerous, Iwona's responsibility has been to stay in the back among the populace and to gauge their disposition towards the imperial family. Since the civil war, sentiment has not improved. It might have worsened after the tragedy known as the Jackiewicz Incident. Often whispered about and still unresolved, it seems omitted from all the Emperor's missives. Indulging in these public spectacles without referencing it whatsoever seems in ill-taste—funds wasted, rather than given back to the people. Iwona, however, isn't one to question the design. She has no connection to Daszek, and the Military Academy's mountain fortress is nowhere near the eastern part of the Empire. Even if she had been more aware of the Iwanowiczes' inaction in terms of sending aid in the last weeks of her schooling, she still would have joined the Emperor's Chosen, if only to boost her own pride.

"What the fuck does an Imperial Magician do anyway?" For a moment, she worries that it's her thoughts made loud for others to hear, but the originating voice is deep and gravelly in a way scratched by excess drink. A ruddy older man with thinning gray hair in a disheveled, oversized jacket too thin for the Odonic winter stumbles towards her.

"I cannot say I know, sir," she responds. Instead of making continued contact with his bloodshot eyes, she keeps her gaze on Emperor Iwan as he mournfully drones of the litany of accomplishments and biographical information of a man otherwise deemed a charlatan.

"No money for the people, but there's funds for this excess and to pay a twerp to fucking do nothing."

Iwona shrugs. She wonders if she should disclose her position. In her thick, black skirt, matching peacoat, and heavy crimson scarf, she resembles any other citizen. But she's not. It's a secret for her to keep unless otherwise stated.

"We keep seeing balls, galas, and holidays from those ruling over the districts, and to what fucking end? Their own depraved debauchery. That cretin up there?" He gestures, but at their distance and with his wobbling, it's unclear if the man means the emperor or Aleksander.

"Benefits without merit. You think someone as young as him has any interesting solutions? He'd only just been born." His voice is ragged, the cause of which is uncertain—drink or argument or lack of sleep or some other kind of ailment altogether. Maladies of the soul can have a physical presence, and she wonders if that rot within his psyche affects his senses as well.

Aleksander looks young, about her age. While she knows she has freedom to conduct her assignments in whatever way she sees fit, Iwona is not of any maturity or experience to be making decisions. As much as she wants to give him the benefit of the doubt in terms of perhaps earning his station, she knows what diligent work and a commitment to effort can yield. Age has little to do with a job well done, she's found.

Instead of contributing her own thoughts, she shrugs again. Her loyalty isn't to the people ruling the Empire, but to the Empire itself. It's why she wanted to be Chosen: to have nothing to do with the aristocrats who create problems that make her position a necessity. She doesn't know what their first true assignment will entail, but she has a feeling it will be used to excise something nasty ruining the heart of Odonic rule.

"You know that cockroach scuttled in from the outer Empire? Do you know anything about the outer Empire?"

Iwona tilts her head to the side. "I did hear about the Jackiewicz Incident. But that family has been working on recovery for several months now." At least, that's what she last heard—a Jackiewicz further down the family tree attended the Academy at the same time as Iwona. He wept furiously to learn that his cousin and uncles had survived. Many details of the tragedy have been redacted.

"Are you some kind of sympathizer?" He glares at her. "Aristocratic survival doesn't mean shit for safety. I thought someone else all the way back here with the rest of us would know better."

"Is he causing you trouble?" A mellow, but stern voice like strongest coffee interrupts the interaction.

"Oh, Mr. Górniak!" The man bobs his head forward. "I did not think you were going to be here with the rest of us rabble."

Iwona recognizes him as Ilya Górniak, Finance Minister to Emperor Iwan. He's a shorter man than she's used to seeing around the Academy. In her heeled, winter boots, she can almost see the top of his military-style capped hat. He dresses elegantly, in a tailored double-breasted black coat, hands hidden within its large pockets.

"Among the rabble is where I prefer to be," he replies. "You'll have to forgive my comrade. He forgets that we're attending a solemnity."

She glances at the dais and notices that only Empress Gita Iwanowicz and Aleksander from the supposed inner circle are there. "He's not causing any trouble, sir."

Iwona probably should not disclose her identity. And she shouldn't feel safer now that someone from the Emperor's Imperial Council stands beside her. When the Chosen are to protect the Empire, these are the figures they should keep an eye on. With Mr. Górniak so immediately in her vicinity, she feels a personal responsibility for him. The intoxicated man has no softness for anyone in higher social classes, he's made that abundantly clear; she has no way of knowing that he isn't a real threat.

"This event is far too peaceful, Mr. Górniak. Apologies if I seem a little disgruntled."

Mr. Górniak performs a warm smile well, but none of it reaches his eyes or his wrinkles. "There is a time and a place for everything, and this is neither."

Questions flood Iwona's mind. One of the tricks she learned from Ute when it comes to navigating other aristocracy and getting the information she wants, however, is to stay as mute and demure as she can muster. It had nothing to do with femininity. It has everything to do with charming, aristocratic learned helplessness. There are the manipulators and those who absorb the manipulation, an exchange of toxic energy which proves the real fuel in decision making and strategy.

"I don't think peaceful is the right word," Iwona offers. She tugs a strand of her hair. "It is somber, but that's to be expected."

There wasn't even a fanfare or applause upon Aleksander Czarnolaski's appointment. Granted, the emperor asked there not to be, but time and again she had witnessed clear defiance of those rules. She was among the throng cheering during the Academy's full class graduation, even though solemnity was also requested then.

"See, comrade? Some of us can have a neutral disposition."

The man scratches his mustache as he laughs, a languid awful noise that scrapes over his throat. "Peasantry get slaughtered, people are starving, and here we're supposed to celebrate the offspring of a man who did fuck all."

"Aleksander Czarnolaski is nothing like his father, I can tell you that much."

"A sprout so fresh should not be raised on such a pedestal."

"Perhaps, but everyone needs to start somewhere, comrade."

"You keep using that word," Iwona says. "I can't say I've heard anyone use it so casually for others." The words are clumsy; she cannot let either man know that she recognizes him as the Finance Minister, even though men of his shape and his name combination are frighteningly common regardless their status.

"Well, if you feel it's uncommon, that's because it is." Mr. Górniak produces a pipe and presses it to lips hidden beneath the shadow of his mustache. He lights the packed tobacco with a snap. "Some of us have a disposition towards believing in equality. And what better way than to start addressing each other with fellowship. If you'd like to hear more, there will be salons throughout Korona in the New Year."

Mr. Górniak places his hand on the shoulder of the man who initially approached Iwona. His shoulders slump, and he says, "We could always use more people interested in learning more."

If a spell had been cast, Iwona cannot detect it. But the change in the man's demeanor frightens her. The fight should not leave a person so quickly. It seems the wrinkles on his face might have smoothened, but that might be a trick of winter's colorless sunlight. Spell-casting had never been Iwona's strongest suit except for combat, but even she knows it needs a gesture and an incantation; Mr. Górniak performed neither.

"I'll consider it." Iwona doesn't know if she's telling the truth or lying. What she does know is that she needs to tell Captain Łukasiewicz later of this strange encounter with someone the emperor has selected for his own closest advisors.

II.

The metal prosthetic creaks and cracks in the cold, wintry air as Ute arrives at the Imperial Palace by autocarriage. It vibrates with the vehicle's consumption of magic, and it's a discomfort she had been given pills for. In fact, she has an entire regimen of various medications and potions to deal with the trauma. So far, the most disorienting thing is that, when she removes the large hunk of metal for sleeping, she sometimes feels the phantom of bone and muscle. Fingers reach and grasp where fingers no longer exist. The doctor said it will go away with time, but not quickly and never thoroughly. It's a relief she's willing to chase with chemistry, and perhaps the minutiae and responsibilities of her position will provide ample distraction.

The Iwanowicz Palace looms over the roundabout as the autocarriage makes its turn. A pristine, marble exterior carries several dozen flags of each of the aristocratic families, their woven fabric wafting in the cool, winter wind. Snow lays along the ramparts, terraces, and gilded tiling. During this time of winter, the sun never quite reaches its apex, leaving long shadows along the Palace's exterior and robbing it of any sense of warmth or hospitality. She had only seen its silhouette as part of the logo for the Imperial Gazette. She cannot recall ever seeing the building in person; it is as gorgeous as it is impressive.

As the autocarriage rolls to a stop, Ute pops a pill to dull the inevitable ache at the seam between flesh and the metal as it reacts to switching from cold to hot. It also has the added benefit of slowing her heart rate, which has been sprinting since she realized just how close she would be to Her Highness Świetlana. Ute wonders how she's changed in the years since their shared schooling, hoping that she will be remembered.

After all, she had thrown away the most lucrative position with the Empire's military for the Emperor's heir.

Before getting out of the autocar, she checks her hair in the mirror. Wave-like layers are the style in Korona, and she thinks it works with her short, lavender-gray tresses. They soften the Military-worn planes of her otherwise young face.

The gravel driveway and the low steps leading up to the double-doored entrance are all cleared of snow, piled neatly against once-verdant bushes. A butler in a thick, red-and-gray uniform emblazoned with the Iwanowicz sigil greets her and offers her a hand. Ute had forgotten the politeness theater shared among the upper ranks. She almost ignores him, but thinks better of it, giving the butler her gloved, left hand. He guides her towards the entrance beneath the portico held up by four titanic, striated columns. Another servant opens the dour ash-gray doors for them.

Ute walks inside and witnesses an opulence long forgotten. Where the military prided itself on its lack of identity, its clean lines, pristine halls where nothing lived except for the killers-in-training within, the palace added vibrancy and vivacity to a space half as occupied. Either by magic or the perceived sorcery of horticulture, flowers bloom and large trees unfit for the wilds rise from enormous pots. Several staff members carry vases and fabrics, hustling to prepare for some kind of event.

"It's quite busy, it seems," Ute says to the butler.

"Oh yes, the Emperor's Solstice Ball is happening in just a few days. Her Highness has had most of us diligently preparing."

More like frantically, but Ute keeps her mouth shut. There's an energy bouncing between these walls that she cannot capture. It's frenetic, it's nervous. She hopes it will not be her problem—Ute did not join the military to manage other people's hysteria. Even though it is no longer her post, she hopes to remain as a servant to the crown and not one who needs to manage service.

There are features within the palace she hadn't even considered could be placed indoors. Crystal chandeliers sparkle against the spotless, tiled floor. Due to the winter season, a thick, cerulean carpet rests upon the long steps guarded by statues of Iwanowiczes past, collecting moisture so that no one trips walking up or down. The butler doesn't take her that way. Instead, he leads her past the enormous fountain decorated with the three-headed eagle that is the Iwanowicz crest. Water spills from its beaks in a pleasing trickle into a pool large enough to lazily lounge in. The water also shimmers beneath the opulent lights, illuminating the florid vines and patterns in the mosaics beneath its surface.

"Ah, first time in the Imperial Palace, miss?" The butler leads her down a connecting hallway lined with more statues and doors. This space also indicates preparations for a festivity with its ribbons tangled with flowers.

Ute purses her lips. "I believe so, yes."

"Oh, how wonderful. I hope you find yourself welcomed."

If being escorted is welcoming, then she feels that acutely. They make it down several such hallways, but the lack of turns suggests to Ute that they remain in the palace's central structure, rather than its residential wings. One wing is for visiting aristocrats, while the other is reserved for the imperial family.

Two enormous sets of wooden doors open to reveal the palace's main ballroom. Black columns veined with red reinforce the paneled walls framed with gilded leaves and flowers. Benches upholstered in gold and crimson line the walls. In between each one sits several seasonally impossible bouquets and arrangements. Golden ribbon flows from one bouquet to the next. The fabric glitters in the scant winter sunlight visiting through the floor-to-ceiling windows leading to the snow-covered back garden. Along the frames, darkened spheres connected with wires hang almost like more decoration rather than sufficient lights.

At the far end of the left side of the space are two curving sets of stairs leading to a balcony with a tangle of iron banisters. Draped over it is a tapestry with an embroidered Iwanowicz crest. Did her family emblazon so much of their living space with their sigil of a boar pierced through its heart with an arrow? She hopes not, but it has also been many years since she last saw the Myśliwski estate. Many more will pass before she returns.

In the middle of the ballroom stand Her Highness Świetlana and a tall white-haired man Ute can only assume is Aleksander Czarnolaski.

"Your Highness," the butler calls, his voice echoing across the room. "I present to you, Ute Myśliwska." He nods to her, granting permission to get within the imperial daughter's personal space.

Ute is careful to maintain a professional countenance while crossing the shiny, wooden floor. Her heart quickens. Relieving her buried desire for Her Highness before leaving did not calm her, in fact it made her more nervous about this appointment. Does Świetlana remember Ute? Has she somehow found out that Ute purposefully failed her final in order to be immediately at her side? Does she even need a Magical Advisor? Ute has assumed that the position is completely ceremonial, but what if that's further from the truth?

This could be a kind of job interview, one that Ute has no interest in failing.

As she approaches, Świetlana hops off her stool and sprints. Her Highness sweeps Ute in an embrace too warm to be shared between an aristocrat and her servant. Ute wraps her arms around Świetlana's back, enjoying the calming effect of their bodies pressing together. Her Highness's soft, black hair swept in its ponytail softly brushes against her arms. Ute forgot how short Świetlana is—they're the same height, even though Her Highness seems much loftier in Ute's dreams and memories. She blushes upon realizing how Her Highness's ample bosom squishes against Ute's flat, battle-hardened chest. It's crass to notice, but Ute cannot help herself, even if Świetlana is technically her employer.

Her Highness pulls away first. "It's been so long, Ute." Her deep purple eyes glint like amethysts and painted pink lips offer a smile. "When I got the news that you would be my advisor, I couldn't help but wonder if it was the Ute from my lyceum years. I'm not sure I can be happier that indeed it is! We have so much to catch up on."

She catches Ute's left wrist and gently pulls her towards Aleksander, who has not moved. It doesn't seem that Świetlana has noticed the prosthetic. It hasn't bothered Ute since she went inside, and plenty of military personnel endure injuries which warrant such equipment, so she's unsure if she should call attention to it. She decides not to, unless asked. With how early she is into her rehabilitation, it is more cosmetic than functional.

"Allow me to introduce you to Aleksander Czarnolaski. Call him Sasza." Świetlana returns to her seat at the elevated table smothered in a white tablecloth threaded with gold. She has a tall stein of strong coffee, matching the one Sasza nurses.

Ute nods politely, noticing that Sasza isn't sitting on anything—he's just two meters tall, towering over Ute. A lack of sleep scars his deep-set amber eyes and his high cheekbones age him far beyond his twenty-three years of age, if she assumes he's the same age as Świetlana. His short hair is shaggy and white, falling over his eyes in a uniquely adolescent style.

His lankiness suggests he's an academic, not someone raised among the aristocracy or trained in the military. The primary rumor floating around the courts is that no one is quite sure from where the Czarnolaskis originated. Some speculate that they are the rare exception to the nepotism which rules over all appointments related to the ruling class. Others propose that they are ambitious lesser aristocrats who still had access to the hierarchy but never tried to climb it themselves. Ute isn't sure what she believes, yet. From his demeanor, however, it wouldn't surprise her if he politically threatened his way into his position.

He places his hand on his chest and nods his head. "It is a pleasure to meet you, Miss Myśliwska." His voice is thick and smooth like red wine, only slightly gritted with exhaustion.

"The pleasure is mutual." It's all pleasantries. She knows it's likely that Sasza had gotten to his position through necrotic nepotism. At the same time, Ute wouldn't be here if not for her own pursuit of advantage by any means possible. It was Iwona who had always believed in the virtue of hard work. It was Ute who always needed to take whatever leg up she could get.

A servant arrives with a third stein of hot coffee. Ute isn't sure how to use her arm in polite company, so she takes it gingerly with her flesh hand. The coordination leaves much to be desired, but neither Sasza nor Świetlana take note. She gently sips, careful not to burn her tongue.

"Unfortunately," Sasza says, drinking his own mug. "We are both on our own—my father, may he rest, previously held my position, but he's no longer with us to offer instruction or guidance."

"My condolences." Ute had heard of the state funeral for the late Czarnolaski.

Świetlana turns to Ute. "I hope it's not too much a disappointment that your position is technically Magical Advisor rather than Imperial Magician—I'm not emperor, but I asked my father if I could have one such companion." She frowns. "I wanted it to be Sasza, but my own father beat me to the appointment."

Sasza shrugs. "If it's any consolation, I've been at the role officially for a week and not much has changed. I'm still playing telephone between you and your father, but perhaps now Ute can get involved in the fun."

Świetlana elbows him. "Don't demean your work like that. It's not a game of telephone because you're actually competent."

They laugh like old friends sharing an inside joke. Jealousy stings; the way Ute's shoulders rise to her ears suggest that the nervousness is affecting her physically. She's been away for too long, and another has taken her place at Świetlana's side. The rumors of the ceremonial nature of the role might be false. Moreover, Ute had never had a personality as serious as Sasza's already seems. Świetlana might prefer that.

"I have to ask, my apologies: is there anything going on between you two? Some political arrangement I should otherwise be appraised of?"

"Absolutely not." Sasza answers first and a little too quickly. "The relationship we have is strictly professional. Ow!"

Świetlana poked him in a rib buried under several wool sweaters. "There is friendship here, no romantic or political promises of marriage. We'd both rather keep it that way, and I'm sorry if gossip made you think otherwise."

At the Military Academy, all the students shared the same status of soldier. Entanglements are discouraged but not strictly forbidden due to the mutable nature of post-adolescent feelings. It was rare for the other soldiers in training to have arranged marriages or partners waiting on the other side of five years of schooling. But since it's impossible to be higher in status than offspring of the Emperor, Ute understands that for Świetlana, flings and relationships must be a calculated endeavor.

It doesn't help that the rumors surrounding the older Czarnolaski suggest that he slept his way into his position, but it's never been made clear if his affections flowed towards the emperor or the empress. Ute would not be surprised if Sasza's an apple which fell within the shadow of Władysław Czarnolaski's perverted tree; he's an aristocrat just like the rest of them. She understands pulling upon the threads of loosely wound familial relationships for personal gain.

Her judgment is projection. She too schemed her way into being Świetlana's Magical Advisor at the cost of her own arm and a role in the Emperor's Chosen. No one knows this but her. Unless she muttered in her sleep to whoever her watchers were, there's no reason to suspect any ulterior motive of her presence and unexpected ascension.

"Anyway," Sasza says. "How are preparations for the Solstice Ball proceeding, Your Highness? They seem almost complete."

"They're going, I suppose. The theme is glory and gold, hence all the gold and Iwanowicz colors. I suggested to Sasza that perhaps we should postpone it, given his father's passing."

Ute nods, understanding the notion of offering even the most vestigial respect.

"My father, may he rest, enjoyed these affairs, alas." He sips his coffee. "It'd be an affront to his memory to have it omitted. I believe Emperor Iwan intends to toast in his memory. Father would have loved that."

"Lord Czarnolaski would have enjoyed the acknowledgment, yes." Świetlana takes a long drink, shuddering from the heat.

Ute says nothing and observes them. She cannot shake the feeling that Her Highness mourns Lord Czarnolaski more than his son seems to. Her face sinks appropriately with brows furrowed while nothing of his visage has changed. Everyone grieves differently, and Ute admits that she knows nothing about Sasza, so perhaps his skill lies primarily in not betraying his feelings.

But if she's going to be Her Highness's Magical Advisor, she needs to know who stalks around Świetlana, regardless of how cordial their interactions seem to be from the onset. Sasza bothers Ute, but there is nothing to justify the feeling. They're all humans in this space, and if he were infiltrating in a plot to overthrow the Iwanowiczes, he'd have been ousted much sooner than staying long enough to take his father's place by the Emperor's side.

Sasza glances around the hustle and bustle of the Ball's set-up but sees something and ducks his head away from Świetlana and Ute. She follows his glance and spots an incredibly well-dressed man in his late forties or early fifties waving at them. From their distance, Ute does not recognize him, nor can she accurately tell his age. The wavy dark gray hair on his head suggests an almost parental maturity, as does the well-kept facial hair obscuring most wrinkles. Most young men also don't wear kerchiefs to obscure the shape of their soft chins.

Her Highness returns the gesture, but not after swatting Sasza on the arm again. "That's not typically how you react to Minister Górniak."

"We…had a bit of an argument. My apologies, that was unprofessional." Sasza straightens and jerks his chin at Minister Górniak in greeting.

She cannot say she's heard of a Minister Górniak. "May I ask who that is?"

"Financial Minister Ilya Górniak."

Her brows raise high. "Oh?" It's a name common for the working class. It's not an aristocratic lineage, that much she knows for sure. It wouldn't be the first time she had heard of an aristocrat abandoning their pedigree; Iwona had been her main example of someone who took on a different name in pursuit of honor, rather than hiding in shame. Most who forsake their family names do not ascend to a position so close to the emperor himself. Ute wonders about the minister's methods.

Sasza clears his throat with a sip of coffee. "I should give you more context: we had worked together on the recent mandate allowing the proletariat into aristocratic education, should they qualify."

Ute tries to not widen her eyes like an owl either. In the Military, it was common enough that the aristocracy and the proletariat trained and mingled together; their training facilities are the few places where delineation of status had been explicitly discouraged. There is another—the Institute of Manners in the Empire's Central Steppe—but that results from the fact that it occasionally allows students from countries beyond the Empire as well. Different titles mean different things between languages, and no one wants to accidentally incite an international incident out of ignorance.

She knows of her own interactions that the working class and the aristocratic students regarded each other with distance and disdain for their own self-preservation. For an aristocrat to willingly work for the advancement of the proletariat is simply unheard of.

Ute sips her tea. "Things sure have changed since I went to the Academy."

"The *Academy*." Sasza drags out the word with an impressed inflection. She sees the ghost of a grin on his face, and she doesn't know if he means to compliment her. "You really did well with this advisor. Your Highness."

Świetlana shrugs with a laugh. "Yes, well, I also attended lyceum with Ute. I recognized her name immediately when they presented me with my options, and the other candidates simply weren't viable."

Ute is grateful for the table's sturdiness. Świetlana had *chosen* her from several other possible advisors. It makes her heart beat in an uneven rhythm to know that her wager paid off. Her arm stings as if to remind her of the cost. Worth it. Though they are not equals, their statuses are not so far removed. Instead of working for Świetlana in secret without even getting to see her, Ute can be in her presence so long as she continues her work as Her Highness's Magical Advisor.

"So yes, between the training and the familiarity, I really did do well for myself in selecting this appointment."

"Thank you." The phrase comes out mouse-like, as Ute etches the image of a proud and smitten Świetlana Iwanowicz deep into the recesses of her yearning mind.

SIX

I.

CIVILIAN LIFE IS A series of rituals that had eluded Iwona during her entire training at the Military Academy. Every piece of recreational activity had its ties to the Military, be it the Military Theater, the Military Gallery—Iwona was surprised the town that serviced the Academy wasn't also named Military Town. It might as well have been, as students were not privy to its true name.

So, when Iwona enters the loud tavern in the Centrum of Korona's Worker's District, it has the exact opposite air. Iwona can barely hear her own thoughts over the drunken din and the poor attempts at musicianship. Everything about this tawdry establishment is the opposite of the professionalism branded onto her countenance. No hardened soldiers, unable to handle their woes, seek solutions at the bottoms of bottles. The cushions on the seating contain stains from a bygone age and there are nicks in the wooden booths and exposed beams keeping the barn-like ceiling aloft. Some have been filled with different shiny, black liquids, others left to splinter. Drunks yell at each other mostly in jest as Iwona swims through the crowd. Though Iwona had never considered herself the most aristocratic of aristocrats, this establishment feels far beneath her.

Suddenly, she understands her mother's almost pathological distaste for the proletariat. Agreement with the sentiment, however, is nowhere to be found.

"There she is!" Captain Łukasiewicz's voice pierces through the clamor.

Iwona gives her a pleasant wave, then pushes through the swaying bodies, trying not to get any liquid or worse on her clothes already dampened by winter.

The unoccupied side of the booth has a giant hole in its cushion. Iwona takes her coat off and folds it into a pillow. Winter's damp will seep through her trousers, anyway, and the tavern's close warmth will offer it a chance to dry, assuming the boisterous, sweaty humidity doesn't get to it first.

"Thank you for the invitation, Captain."

Captain Łukasiewicz slides a large mug Iwona's way. The crimson liquid inside smells of a hearth and festive spices. "It's my pleasure. I do a dinner like this with each member of the new cohort. How are you finding the work?"

"Easy enough, I suppose. I can't say standing towards the back of the congregation at the state funeral is the most difficult of jobs."

"No, and it's a good way to get acclimated to the discipline. I haven't heard any rumors of us even being there, so I can applaud you for that." Her face lights up as the barkeep brings over a przekąska of steaming bread and glistening smalec. Captain Łukasiewicz takes a piece and dips it into the lard dotted with crispy pork.

As Iwona takes her own piece, she says, "I did meet the Finance Minister. So, it wasn't entirely an uneventful shift."

"That far in the back?" Captain Łukasiewicz tips her drink back. "Interesting, I'd thought he'd be closer to the front. I've only ever heard rumors about the man, so, you'll need to tell me what he's like."

Iwona shrugs. "He calls everyone he interacts with, 'comrade.' I found that interesting."

"That is interesting." With a full mouth, Captain Łukasiewicz continues, "You know he actually worked his way into his position? Górniak isn't just an assumed name. Truly, the man has no affiliation with aristocracy."

"Is this one of those rumors you mentioned?"

"No, there's really only one rumor: he made a bedmate of the former Imperial Magician's son."

"The young man who just got elected to the position?"

"The very one."

With the way Iwona admires Captain Łukasiewicz, she cannot fault someone who looks about her age to be lusting after someone several decades older. But to be acting on it? That's an entire other set of complications she never had room for in either her heart or her mind.

"Do you think that rumor has anything to do with him being the Emperor's aide so young?"

"No, aside from that one relationship, the lad has a clean record. Hard working, graduated top of his class in university. Honestly, Aleksander Czarnolaski is one of the most boring people to ever come under the Emperor's employ. From what I can tell, he just believes in the virtue of work and expresses that accordingly." She cups the top of her drink with her hand curled like a claw. "We should perhaps toast to the virtue of work. Zdrowie?"

A proud smile cuts through Iwona's shyness. "Zdrowie."

"Zdrowie!" The mugs clank against each other, spilling a bit of the wine on the already filthy wooden table. "That probably should have also been dedicated to the late Czarnolaski, but we can toast to that later. The night is young."

Because of winter's penchant for the nocturnal, night started at sixteen hundred and hasn't relented. The lamps on the streets of Korona serve as the only source of light during what should otherwise be day. In the Empire's northernmost reaches, some towns and cities don't see the sun for several days at a time. Though Korona's daytime isn't in short supply, to say that the night has barely started is an understatement.

"If you say so." She takes another drink, the acidic warmth collapsing deep into her belly. Unlike her peers, she eschewed recreational alcoholism during her training years. But now that she has achieved her goal, she can perhaps let go of such discipline, at least for an evening.

"I'm sure you're wondering why I had you join me for dinner here rather than somewhere quieter and classier." Captain Łukasiewicz softly burps. "I've been away from the aristocratic pansies for long enough that I can wander among the people they'd consider 'rabble.' Their food is pretty good and the conversations even more interesting than idle gossip about who's fucking who. It can be fun, but if that's all you're hearing? Boring. The conversations around these parts are so much livelier and more relevant to our calling."

"Is this a lot of what the work is? Gathering information?" Iwona smears some more smalec and takes a bite of the bread. Food like this had been hard to come by at the Academy, given their mindset of food being fuel and preparing soldiers for the scarcity that comes with the battlefield.

"Indeed. The aristocrats play this game with each other all the time, strategically inserting themselves among relevant positions and into certain social situations. If they did it more among the proletariat, there'd be actual solutions to the Empire's ills, but you're going to pretend you didn't hear that."

"I have to agree though." Iwona rinses her mouth with her drink. "I denounced my family name, so I think I have more in common with the people here than those living in their townhouses and grand estates." But even she wouldn't consider the Ogrodniks on the same social strata as this tavern's patrons. The people here have exhaustion wrinkling their faces several years too soon and an affinity for twitching and fiddling that can only be explained by drinking and failed attempts at easing pains medicines and magic cannot reach. They yell at each other because they cannot yell at the ones in power causing them the stress they cannot relieve.

Iwona used to eavesdrop on her former family members all the time. The food and drink provided by Captain Łukasiewicz gives enough fiddling to occupy herself to hide her infiltration. The first chat goes like this:

"My daughter brought her girlfriend to our home to live with us."

"Oh, that's lovely. How long have they been together?"

"Lovely? Not at *all*. They're too young to be cohabitating—they should be youthful and apart. The relationship's only a year old. They need at least another year—no, two! Two more years before they even consider signing a lease together."

"If you're so opposed to it, why let it happen at all?"

The other person groans. "I'd be a shit parent if I didn't. I already had to bail her out for stealing bread."

"Shit."

"It is what it is. I've tried getting her a job in the city. There are none, not without the right certifications or other testing. I don't think I'd qualify for my job now."

"How long have you been there?"

"Long enough to know that there are some things that can't be taught, only learned."

Iwona had never in her life considered how she would afford food and housing. It's been provided by employment or relations that are family in all ways but legal. These struggles are news to her—no one in the Military Academy wanted for necessities, though luxuries proved few and far between. No one starved, and the only thing to complain about was the necessity of free health care.

Because she had her path set for her through such specialized schooling, Iwona had never once worried about her job prospects. Even if she were to ultimately decide against a Military track, she never thought about how much power that simple diploma affords her. She can work whatever job she wants, without really considering if her training makes up for her lack of field experience.

This irks her, because she had heard of the motion to allow proletarian students into the aristocratic schools in order to bridge the gap of opportunity. She cannot tell if it is too little too late or too optimistic in its execution. It's still aristocrats making employment decisions at the end of the day; this was true for the Ogrodniks serving her former family as well.

Captain Łukasiewicz had ordered a steaming plate of pierogi filled with potatoes and cottage cheese, smothered in apple sauce, with sour cream nowhere to be found. The meal swims in fat, but Iwona's hunger overrides her aesthetic senses. She takes a bite and finds that even the fanciest of food parcels seem comparable. Perhaps the sour cream serves as the only difference between proletarian and aristocratic food. She doesn't look too closely at this dish, complements of the Emperor's Chosen.

Eating leaves her with enough focus to zero in on another conversation:

"I haven't been home in a few weeks."

"I was beginning to wonder—you usually don't spend this much time in Korona."

"Well, see, a bridge collapsed, and the Minister of the Interior has done fuck all to fix it. What the fuck's the point of an infrastructure budget if none of it is going to be spent on, well, fucking that." The speaker sputters as they drink too quickly, and Iwona catches a glimpse of them shuffling off to the latrine with all the elegance of a soggy cat.

The thing that sticks with Iwona is the fact that none of these problems are new. Aristocrats have always dragged their feet as far as execution of the things promised to their subordinates—the closer to the Emperor, the truer this seems to be. There were talks at the Academy of a new necessity for a position called district police, but nothing had come of that, as far as she could tell. All these opportunities for non-aristocrats, but none of them seem to be manifesting in anything good. Sounds about right, in her experience.

Captain Łukasiewicz says nothing except for ordering yet another drink—Iwona can hardly keep up. To stop her head from pounding, she eats more than she's accustomed to, hoping the carbohydrates soak it up and prevent her from getting sick. It's in this daze she catches onto one more exchanging of words:

"Troops have started demanding tithes in our market for…oh, what did they say? Pre-payment for our protection."

"Protection from what?"

"Ourselves, most likely. We need people to work, but no one wants to work, and those who do work call a strike every day. It's nothing we need police presence for."

"Are you sure no one wants to work?"

"I phrased that wrong. I've seen the wages. I've seen the promises of care beyond the wages. They're pathetic. The people ruining themselves on someone else's time are not much better off than those wasting away trying to find labor."

"Can't you petition the business owners to pay more? Isn't that the whole point of having those fancy degrees? At least, that's what my parents said worked for their friends."

"Those certificates mean nothing except now things that once cost fifty grosze now cost one hundred, but no one's getting paid for the labor. The emperor sends no support to the jobless, even though the solution is a sack of cash. No, instead, they're sending troops to prevent riots. They watch over us lowlives, wondering why they get paid to do nothing, and we get paid nothing to do everything."

"Sh, someone might overhear." (Both Iwona and Captain Łukasiewicz purse their lips at each other.)

"Speaking isn't treasonous, yet. But that doesn't mean they trust us to stay calm."

"Perhaps they do, since, as you said, they're not throwing money at the problem."

"Oi, you're a clever one, comrade. I'll give you that." The speaker pauses to take a drink. "If they don't want to throw money, give us grain and potatoes, not fit youth equipped with weaponry."

Iwona shudders at the use of that word. *Comrade.* It's a call for unity, but against the aristocracy, those with wealth and resources who created these divides in the first place.

Captain Łukasiewicz, judging by her raised eyebrows and fluttering blinks, also heard the term.

Someone calls for a rowdy round of patriotic ballads that avoid any reference to the Empire or its rulers. Everything about nationality, nothing about the negligent fools at its helm. Iwona keeps drinking and snacking. Her head throbs as if keeping the rhythm like a drummer boy. She cannot tell if she should consume alcohol more often or less often; the next day will be a nightmare of aches only time and lying prone in her bed will soothe.

"Just as I suspected," Captain Łukasiewicz says once the adulterated singing abates. "The people have noticed the military mobilizing, despite the lack of threat and the lack of immediate danger."

"What about the Jackiewicz Incident?" Iwona asks, slurring. "That's a threat."

"You're right. Because they know whatever happened there has nothing to do with whatever the emperor plans. It's all *a perceived* threat, but that threat is what we're following up on in a few weeks."

"Oh?" Iwona leans forward, only to have her elbows catch on the sticky table.

"Obviously, I will not be divulging the details, as much as this mulled wine bordering on samogon wants me to." She throws back another gulp. "But the true responsibility of the Emperor's Chosen is to prevent war. Eradicating threats. Beyond anyone's notice."

Iwona shudders at the unabashed mention of their station. "How do we know war is coming though? I admit, I wasn't old enough to know anything of the civil war, but I feel like there's some kind of storm coming."

Captain Łukasiewicz bring her face towards Iwona, with her alcohol-stained breath filling the close space between them. "They say it's the vampires. But I don't think it's true. Not with the non-aggression pact and their general disinterest in the lands beyond their borders."

"What do *you* want me to believe?"

"Whatever will make you good at your job, Miss Ogrodnik." Captain Łukasiewicz drains her drink and calls for another. She sways, waiting for her beverage to arrive. In a low voice rocky like the battlements of a misbegotten fort, she says, "Being Captain of a Regiment means that the only thing I am responsible for is your safety and your ability to go on another mission. What's also my responsibility is your ability to execute your tasks, and I don't mean physically. Which is all a roundabout way to say: war is not your concern until I tell you it's your concern. Do you understand?"

Iwona understands the individual words spoken to her, but not the collective implication. "Then why have dinner with me here?"

"Because I needed someone else to hear everyone's ravings to prove that I'm not going mad." She tuts and finishes off her beverage. "*Comrade*."

II.

On the Imperial Palace's grounds, there are acres and acres of recreational facilities, some up above but others carved out of the stone down below. Such underground constructions are deeply familiar to Ute. At the Military Academy, for all its advancement and supposed care of its students, kept the facilities candlelit and subject to the elements.

Unlike the Palace's subterranean courts. Autobatteries and autocells power large trough-like vents that snake across the high-ceiling catching and releasing echoes of balls pinging and ponging. The metal in Ute's right arm creaks at the sudden change in temperature. A vast plain of green asphalt painted with straight white lines spreads out as far as she can see. Aristocrats run around, smacking the balls with their racquets, dressed in revealing clothing appropriate for summer but completely out of place as snow once again blankets Korona. Their servants have shed their stiff uniforms, running around in leisure wear to collect stray balls and make sure their lieges stay hydrated. If there wasn't a steel and stone sky, Ute might have thought these courts to be outdoors in a warmer season.

It reminds Ute of her own family's home—an estate not too far from Korona. The botanical garden stayed lit and warmer through the winter, while people in town froze to death in the streets due to fuel shortages and the wait times for their buildings to upgrade to autobatteries. This had bothered her growing up. Though she didn't recognize it, she didn't want to be complicit in the indulgent resource mismanagement that came at the expense of the citizens' lives.

But her recovery requires her to partake in this comfort far from elemental barbarity. Mandated physical therapy would build the strength and dexterity required for her position. Tennis and its other racquet sport siblings might feel the most familiar, despite the distance from danger. She has her own instructor alongside another young person whose sole responsibility is to chase after balls that go off onto other courts. Ute isn't sure if they're old enough to be legally employed.

She doesn't think about it.

Not as she swings with movements foreign to her less dominant arm. Not as she trips and catches herself on the brand-new bit of engineering welded to her skin. Not as she chases pain medication with cloudy water full of nutrients even though easing pain now means a shorter long-term recovery.

This first session feels much longer than its two hours. Perhaps she had gotten back into rigorous physical activity too quickly. Ute starts off in a bit of a fog—light-headed from the heat and magical residue wafting in the air—and ends it tired. Her skirt sticks to her skin, the soft bulges between her thighs aching with the regret of not wearing longer underpants. Untidy strands of lavender-gray hair flop against her face. She begs for another drink before the burning where her right arm used to be flares into an inferno.

"Ute!" Her Highness calls to her from the next court over. Sweat beads like dew on Świetlana's skin, and her black hair swings from side to side as she jogs over. Her white dress is short for the season, just skimming her knees while her socks rise not much higher than her white flats. She looks almost girlish, free from the confines of regalia.

"Interesting seeing you here, Your Highness." Ute didn't imagine that Świetlana had time for recreation, not with the ball coming up and the aftermath of a national funeral.

Świetlana wipes her forehead with the ragged cotton band on her wrist. "I could say the same. I thought you had rehabilitation."

"This is my physical therapy." Exertion takes Ute's breath between statements. "Rebuilding my kinesthesia."

"Oh." Świetlana taps a finger to her bottom lip. "That makes sense to me. Would you like to play a set or two?" She gives Ute a wide smile.

Despite her own tiredness, Ute isn't sure she can refuse Her Highness. She looks at her therapist, who has already stepped aside, giving them space. "I would enjoy that greatly."

It's not the first time it's seemed like Świetlana's staff can read her mind. Unlike other aristocracy, Her Highness doesn't ask for things, she's just given them. Most aristocratic last names have inherent value, but none more so than Iwanowicz and it shows.

Ute picks her wooden racquet off the ground with her still clumsy hand. It hurts. The new muscles twinge with soreness that she's going to need more pills and poultices for. She wiggles her right shoulder. Each movement causes flickering pain, and she's not looking forward to seeing what the abrasions in her skin might look like from the belts. But she wants to indulge Świetlana, especially when she's so carefree. A little disheveled, a little sweaty—it makes Ute ache for her scent and wanting to know just how sticky Świetlana's skin feels against hers.

They take positions on their opposing sides. Świetlana bends forward, her short legs stretching as she prepares her serve. Strong fingers curl around the ball. Her body snaps, throwing it into the air, and in a perfect, bending arch serves it to Ute. The ball flies her way, much slower than what she had just endured in therapy. Casual, and, if Ute allows herself the word, fun.

She hits the ball, returning it easily. An almost lethargic hit, that Her Highness returns with the same leisure. Ute's poor knees and calf muscles beg for respite. But she cannot quit, not when approval is so easy to build, and especially not during this casual approximation of a game.

Świetlana hits again, and Ute returns. The only sounds coming from both players are breathy grunts. They exchange the ball at such a steady cadence, Ute's eyes wander to Świetlana's form. The way her hips and shoulders sway with each swing. The fact that she plays tennis at all suggests to Ute she has some proficiency with a blade—most aristocratic firstborns undergo weapons training, given that they need to be both general and diplomat. She wouldn't be here if she were an archer instead, Ute thinks. She doesn't think Świetlana is a brawler; non-military civilians have their own sport to partake in and Świetlana's hands don't seem to have the requisite blisters and callouses. If Her Highness were a mounted fighter, she wouldn't be in the courts and instead would be off riding a horse or some other steed in a different indoor facility on the other side of the Palace grounds.

Ute misses a shot. It wasn't her distraction, but Świetlana interrupting the rhythm. She doesn't know if she should shout an apology or point out Her Highness's error.

"Want to go again?" Świetlana calls to her. She folds forward, catching her breath.

"Only if you want to, Your Highness," Ute replies. Her own shallow breaths suggest she stop. Too much exercise with not enough healing. She doesn't need to prove herself—Świetlana chose her specifically. This abrupt play is for diversion, not performance. "Actually, I'm not sure I can."

At that moment, pain tears through her right shoulder. Though the metal arm remains connected, it strains as if the ground pulls on it. Ute yelps through a clenched jaw as she sinks to her knees. Her therapist rushes over with a small pill and water. Ute chokes it down, and the relief takes a few breaths to kick in. The pain melts as if it never happened in the first place.

"What's wrong?" Świetlana says, crouching next to Ute. Unpolished brows knit in concern.

"New arm, new pains," Ute replies. She tries not to curse in front of Her Highness, the opening K of a swear sticking in the back of her mouth. The pain reappears, gasping, but steady breaths suppress it.

"Well, I can't let you go home like this, not in this condition. Would you like to eat at the palace? It's almost dinner time."

Ute had originally planned to go back to her own studio in Korona. She also looks down at her sweat-spoiled tennis uniform. The leggings and sweater she had worn to keep the cold away during her commute are not appropriate. "I...I don't have anything to wear."

"Oh, please, let my staff figure that out for you." Nothing in Świetlana's amethyst gaze or concerned face suggests refusal as an option.

Then Ute's stomach grumbles. "I will stay for dinner, yes."

"Wonderful!" Świetlana reaches to grab Ute's hand, but refrains. She clears her throat as she stands. The attendant who had been her opponent earlier runs over. "Please arrange a shower for Miss Myśliwska and some fresh clothes, and then show her to the smaller salon. Make sure it's reserved for me."

The attendant bows, waiting for Ute to finally stand. She rests her left hand under the metal arm to support it. She will likely have to remove it for dinner or wear a sling. She doesn't know which is worse. But her comfort needs to come over politeness.

"Are you feeling better?" Świetlana asks.

"Yes, I think so." Her therapist is already arriving with the sling, giving Ute no say in the matter for the time being.

"That makes me glad. I will see you in about an hour. I have to clean up myself."

Ute perversely wishes Świetlana didn't. Feminine musk gently wafts behind Świetlana as she leaves the tennis courts. It takes Ute a moment to compose herself before following her assigned attendant to the Palace's main building.

UTE HAD NOT BEEN cleaned by someone else in a non-medical setting in five years. The efficiency she had become so accustomed to leaves her entire body when a maid old enough to be her mother peels her clothing off with much care taken not to aggravate her stump. The flesh around it is red and puckered, splotched like Ute's chest would get from too heavy a workout. The therapist left instructions for how to take care of the skin once separated from the metal. Despite the ease with which Ute can dress herself one-handed, she appreciates having someone else to help. Having an extra set of hands makes applying the lotions much easier as well.

Her heart races as she approaches the salon. She had not yet been alone with Her Highness. Their work together had all been meetings and other orientations—meeting the staff, introductions to her father's various secretaries, but not Emperor Iwanowicz himself. It should strike her as strange.

The feeling disappears when she sees Świetlana with her hair gathered on top of her head and wearing a mismatched combination of dark sweaters and light slacks. The homey couture matches the house clothes Ute put on and the way her own damp hair presses against her scalp like a slate cap without any sort of style. The fabrics and colors don't quite match, but the fashion and decorum are clear: dinner will be casual as well.

The small salon has a plain, wooden floor assembled from tessellating triangles in different tints. Flowers in shades ranging from deep blues to soft pinks decorate the wallpaper. A large chandelier hangs from the ceiling with small glowing orange autocells filling the bulbs, releasing heat as well as light. The square table in the center has been set up with tea and a rich stew accompanied by crusty bread.

Świetlana focuses on Ute's face as she approaches. "I'm so glad you could join me. Are you feeling better?"

"I am." Ute looks to the fabric hanging from her right arm, bunched in a knot where she had removed the stump. "I apologize for not asking earlier, but I simply couldn't keep—"

Her Highness raises her hand softly. "I will accept no apology. You should do whatever makes *you* the most comfortable. I will deal with anyone who says otherwise." She then takes her teacup full of coffee and sips.

Ute lowers herself in the seat, breathless at Świetlana's compassion. "Thank you, Your High—"

"Only call me Your Highness in front of my father."

"Thank you, Świetlana." She doesn't remember if that's how Her Highness had conducted herself while they were in lyceum. Ute should recall if she used the full name or something else, but the specific memory escapes her.

"Of course. If I can take away one more worry and make you better at your work, then I will."

Is she so assertive with all who serve her directly? Is she like this with Sasza? Ute pushes these thoughts aside as she puts her focus towards scooping the stew with a spoon in her clumsy hand. "I also appreciate the meal."

They exchange a smacznego and dig in. Świetlana, however, has more to say. "Thank you for being flexible and eating with me. I know I didn't give you much of an option, but it seemed rude to let you go home exhausted and on an empty stomach."

"I suppose, Your—Świetlana, but I can handle myself well enough."

"It's not that I don't doubt you, but you've seen the weather outside. Oh, that reminds me!" She pulls out a small notepad and a pen, jotting down a note in the margin of a sheet blackened with other crossed-out phrases. "Let me arrange a valet to take you home."

Ute doesn't even let herself protest. "Thank you." Such graces seem like a silly reason to expend her allowance of disagreements with Her Highness.

"I do want to let you know that I think a weekly dinner like this would be wonderful. If there's anything I can do to aid your physical therapy, please let me know. I love playing tennis and to have someone I'm familiar with as a partner would make it that much more exciting to me."

"I'll gladly be that partner for you." Neither of them mentions Sasza; if he had played, he would have been there. But she also doesn't take him to be terribly physically active, either for combat training or his own recreation. If the rumors of his humbler origins are true, then it's likely he never had to learn swordplay or any other weapon. Nothing in his resume suggests studying offensive magic either, which makes her wonder why he's the Imperial Magician and not anyone else.

"It would also be good to have one place where we can simply be, without political theater." Świetlana dabs a stray dribble of tomato broth with a torn-off piece of bread. "I know you serve me and you're technically part of my staff, but my father has asked to hold off until the New Year for you to join the meetings of his Imperial Council."

Ute simply shrugs. Those words largely don't mean much to her, especially since no one has truly outlined her tasks as Magical Advisor, aside from keeping Her Highness company. She knows Świetlana has other secretaries, so it wouldn't be required of Ute to take on those roles as well.

"I'm sure it would be good for you, Ute, to meet the others that advise His Majesty, but that upcoming meeting is far too special, it seems. I hope that agrees with you."

"I don't see why it wouldn't. He can run his staff however he wants."

"I am glad you agree, Ute." Świetlana gives a small grin and continues eating.

They eat in silence for a long time, until Świetlana starts talking about her favorite tennis players from across the Empire, how she wants to host an annual tournament to boost regional pride and to open up such sport to the working class. How she wants it to be an entire celebration of Odonic pride, kind of like the Inventors' Fair for academics, but for those who enjoy sports. Ute amicably agrees with these measures, enjoying how Her Highness shares ideas rooted in genuine interest regardless of the opinions of others.

A minute disturbance nags at the back of Ute's mind. How any of these entertaining plans are relevant to His Majesty's meetings can be anyone's guess. Perhaps it's something she wants Ute to research and present once the sessions start in the new year. But Świetlana doesn't leave much room for such logistics. She's not talking to Ute like Her Highness should speak to a servant.

Ute wants to be that space for Świetlana; Her Highness deserves someone who can converse with her, not just take orders. A friend, a confidant.

Whatever Świetlana needs her Magical Advisor to be, Ute will gladly take on that role.

SEVEN

Much like the previous year, the final gathering of Emperor Iwan Iwanowicz's Imperial Council includes several members who only attend biannually. The one that keeps Sasza completely on edge is Lady Bianka Lewońska, the Minister of the Interior.

She might have been beautiful once. Some humans inject vampire blood into their faces in the hopes of reversing aging, but all it does is draw more attention to weathered skin. Tall and lithe in a way that suggests she doesn't need the frivolity of excess feasting, her face carries a severity etched from hatred.

She is a woman whose grief has warped into cruelty. It follows her like a shadow, hanging over her like a fragrance, as she approaches her seat around the long council table. For the second time this year, her seat is filled, as are many others. Ilya takes his spot on the opposite side of the table, engaged in a conversation designed to avoid making eye contact with Sasza.

Some chairs remain empty, however. Świetlana had told Sasza that the Jackiewiczes declined attendance. They wanted to ring in the New Year with their own, and Sasza understands the decision.

He notices another absence. Her Highness arrives alone, without Ute, and takes her seat across from Sasza. They flank the emperor, whose wife sits at the other head, still wearing a black mourning veil for Władysław. Sasza and Her Highness nod at each other from across the runner embroidered with three-headed eagles, crowns, and swords, the gold threaded throughout glinting in the autocell-powered light from the chandelier. A stage set; the players prepared.

This meeting is the one they rehearsed for. They practiced their statistics, quizzed each other on percentages and volumes, peppered each other with questions, role-played as different members of the Imperial Council. It's the closest to fun Sasza has experienced in quite some time. Given the weight, the feeling of diversion feels entirely inappropriate.

The emperor, however, does not give Sasza a chance to deliver his opening argument against a war. He rises, shoulders pulled back to hold the crown resting heavily on his head. He takes his time scanning the attendants, relaxing his thick brows from their furrow. From within the folds of crimson robes he reserves for ceremonies, he produces an inky black, thick envelope the size of a parcel. The three-headed eagle wielding a sword and shield—the Military's crest—embossed on its surface has never looked so menacing.

"After many months of investigation, I have finally received the definitive report on the Jackiewicz Incident."

Whispers break out among the attending aristocrats. Sasza, however, keeps his mouth shut and stares hard into the hands clasped in his lap. Despite his individual meetings with the Emperor, such work had never once been mentioned. Anger and the hurt of betrayal manifest as an ache at the nape of Sasza's neck. Not once had it come up—Sasza perhaps should have hinted at his own findings and inquiries. But his work had neither yielded anything concrete nor did its open doors lead to further curiosity. The emperor kept his own exploration close to his chest. Perhaps the reason Władysław never pursued answers to any of the questions remaining in the aftermath had been because he didn't think the emperor would be investigating the incident himself.

Unless it was for his own benefit, Władysław was not the kind to initiate his own projects. If the emperor didn't ask him to investigate, he wasn't going to. With the Flock an imminent threat on his tail, there never had been a reason to delve deeper.

Meanwhile, the emperor did not employ any of the two-dozen people selected to manage the Empire in the pursuit of the truth behind the attack. The papers collected in his bejeweled hands tell Sasza that Emperor Iwan has done the opposite of ignoring the tumult in the Empire's easternmost reach.

"Our great Odonic Empire still weeps for the lives lost in Daszek, the city ruined, still in the arduous process of rebuilding. But we excavated much from the rubble. The casualties are far greater than we can have ever imagined. It saddens me that the Jackiewiczes could not be with us in this week of the solstice but nevertheless. Our hearts and our prayers go back to them, that the new year brings them less tragedy.

"From within the rubble, however, several interesting things have been found, starting with this." He puts down his papers and hails a servant to bring over a plain, wooden chest and place it on the table. He opens its hatches and the lid clicks. Emperor Iwan reaches inside and pulls out charred, leather armor, unmistakably the regalia of the Vermilion Envoy. The headless eagle of their insignia rises from the once moonlight-white fabric now stained gray with smoke. That any material survived the blaze the Jackiewiczes inflicted to save their city seems suspicious.

"We do not have them here, but the remnants of vampiric weaponry have also been recovered. There are no reports of vampiric military brigades entering the city. They likely had lain in wait for the opportune moment to strike and take our intellectuals from us. The Emperor's Chosen were not there to report for us; I do not blame them for having missed signs they cannot have seen." He leans forward onto his knuckles. "After we had worked so hard to create a new aristocracy, the Vermilion Envoy tried to take it from us. This attack was not just an attack on Daszek, but on the Empire itself."

Sasza's stomach curdles. That's how the Military got permission to requisition mass production of undead blades. The scant evidence points to the Jackiewicz Incident being an attack from the Vermilion Envoy, but deep in the recesses of Sasza's logic, he knows it's not true. Sylwia or Władysław would have mentioned aggression from the Vermilion Envoy more often than never at all. If the vampires were preparing to go to war with the Odonic Empire, someone else had to have known, someone other than the emperor and his Chosen.

The emperor lowers the ruined leather and makes sure to look across his closest allies as he speaks. "For this reason, in the year 1918, the Empire will become whole again. No more Vampire States. No more land that doesn't fall under our rule. They have prospered for too long and given us nothing. We shall be a reunited Odonic Empire, like the one from centuries ago. One land. One empire. One people."

The emperor pauses to sip water from his tall, crystal glass. No one says anything. No one makes any sound suggesting support or concern. The council chamber sits as still and quiet as it does beyond the council's meetings.

Sasza, however, stands, almost knocking his seat over, jerking his head at Emperor Iwan. With all the strength and conviction nestled within his chest, he says, "No."

Emperor Iwan tilts his head at Sasza. "No?"

Heat burns his ears as he hears each of his own individual heartbeats. He and Świetlana rehearsed the evidence against a unification war. It's all grounded in truth, in numbers. Esoterica people trust. Sasza glances at the empty seat beside him—the one reserved for Władysław as a memorial. His father had never spoken out of turn. He would likely start talking his way out of Sasza's outburst with the only objective being to protect his offspring.

Though Sasza values his own life, there is more at stake than the life of one aristocrat no one suspects belongs to their hematophagic new enemy.

"The Empire still hasn't recovered fully from the last civil war. There aren't enough people to work in the factories, let alone join the army, and especially not if they're starving. Our veterans have still not returned to the service, and I think a draft will cause a greater crisis of faith than the war itself." His voice wavers as he speaks faster. "Moreover, there's not enough food to feed everyone. It's not just the blight—people have to choose between freezing to death and starvation, and I'm not sure there's anything to be done about it now. As a political entity, we sit at the nadir of a chasm of debt, and we literally cannot afford to sink any lower."

The specifics slip away from him in the deluge of fear. No one else seems as afraid, but perhaps they have a handle on their composure. The other aristocrats also don't share the same secret Sasza does. He's a vampire—the people in this room must have figured that out by now. It's in his smell; it's in his countenance. They've seen the way he doesn't seem to express any emotion or response while eating or drinking, be it delighted or disgusted. He will be executed for treason by affinity. And if he isn't eliminated, there be no opportunity to warn Sylwia of impending war.

Sasza darts his eyes to Ilya, who had given him most of the records to back up his argument against any conflict. The Finance Minister does not meet his gaze. Sasza looks at Świetlana. She also cannot meet him. Much like his sister warned, Sasza has finally found himself in that very political den of wolves, alone.

"Please, Your Majesty, reconsider this plan. There must be a better way." Sasza struggles to contain the panic electrifying every fiber of his being. No one on the Imperial Council has ever spoken back to Emperor Iwanowicz before, especially not anyone with the last name Czarnolaski.

Lady Bianka sniffs. "Respectfully, Czarnolaski the younger, you were a child at the time of the first war. There is no way for you to have the life experience to know how good another war would be for the Empire. Without that conflict, we might not have clawed our way out from ruin's maw. Yes, it cost lives—I lost three of my own boys in that conflict. But it created jobs. Opportunities. It reopened trade, and we are going to need to make exchanges to not fall, as you said, further down a chasm of debt."

He squares his jaw and says nothing. He cannot admit how correct she is; he is too young to have witnessed the previous civil war himself. But he's been among the people, more so than any of the aristocrats in this room save for Ilya. Sasza himself started off as a provincial vampire, feeling more kinship with the proletariat than the generous aristocrats who allowed Sasza and his father to partake in their luxuries. It's a generosity that only extends as far as their insular networks go.

Meanwhile people from across the Empire abandon their farms and move to towns where industry is now moving towards the sort of automation invented by the proletariat to make their lives easier, not replace them entirely. The new aristocrats only see the efficiency, not the loss of labor and expertise. They don't understand this crucial distinction for a thriving citizenship.

A senseless war will only enhance the social and economic discrepancies and completely undo the initiatives Ilya and Sasza had conducted together in the year prior. Ilya does not seem to care about his own life's work or self-esteem; the man still says nothing.

Lady Bianka adds, "Unless you think that charred regalia is a fake?"

Sasza arrives at a loss. He hasn't read the reports himself nor seen what had been pulled out of the debris before this meeting. The ruined fabric beside him seems real enough, but why had this evidence of aggression taken so long to appear? There's no reason for any of the Jackiewiczes to keep such a secret from anyone. Sasza had taken classes with the youngest, Lucjan, and regrets not thinking to reach out to him except at this very moment.

Emperor Iwanowicz gives Sasza a soft look, the kind a parent would give toward an upset child. "This will be difficult for you and Świetlana to bear. But the country must unite, truly. The Vampire States have not taken responsibility for the violence, we have to claim it for ourselves."

"I apologize for my naiveté," Sasza finally says, keeping his voice level and his gaze fixed on the Emperor. "I apologize for second-guessing the crown's stability and authority. If you, Your Majesty, think this is best for the Odonic Empire, then it is best for the Odonic Empire." He bows his head forward mechanically, wishing it could fall off and have it all be over. He pulls the seat beneath him and tries not to slump.

"You are forgiven, but of what, I'm unsure. You are a man grieving a father who was dear to us all. It is all right for your emotions to be taking over your thoughts."

Sasza blinks slowly, feeling his lids slide over his aching eyeballs. This isn't about grief or his father's departure. This is about maintaining the stability of an already suffering land.

For the rest of the meeting, he decides to keep his mouth shut. He worries that saying anything or protesting more would raise suspicion both about his father's passing and the fact that neither Czarnolaski had ever been human. He sits quietly, absorbing the logistics of going to war with the Vampire States. The declaration will be put forth at the Solstice Ball, in only a few days' time. His throat grows sticky at the thought of warning Sylwia. If he sends a missive out *now*, it might arrive at the same time as the formal declaration of war. If he doesn't tell her anything, she'll think he betrayed her and the rest of their kind, regardless of his lack of political kinship.

There's only one option: prevent the entire conflict from erupting in the first place.

If Sasza must do it alone, so be it.

THE EMPEROR DISMISSES THE council. Świetlana stays behind but gives Sasza a stiff nod which promises a conversation later. As Sasza attempts to rush past the decadent displays and disappear into his autocar and return to the isolation of his lonely townhouse, Ilya calls his name.

"A word? In my office," he says. His hands hang down his sides, shoulders relaxed.

Sasza halts and tilts his head back to look at him. Ilya didn't once speak up. He offered no guidance as Finance Minister against this ill-advised act of violence, leaving Sasza to speak out-of-turn against the most powerful man in the Odonic Empire.

Because only a Czarnolaski can speak back to an Iwanowicz, it seems.

"Please?"

The word's soft delivery has Sasza turning to Ilya. Perhaps in private, Sasza can ask for assistance. Obedient like a kicked pet, he follows Ilya down several halls to the Finance Minister's private office.

The recent aftermath of frantically pulling records for Sasza to eventually never use in an argument with the emperor remains strewn about the room. Papers, open books, and other detritus of excess study. All for naught. Why did he put so much work in if Ilya wasn't going to help present contrary evidence?

The once welcoming light warming the plain walls and their cabinets feels distant and cold. Sasza marches inside the rectangular room towards the heavy, dark desk flanked on both sides by narrow tapestries decorated with the emblem of an Empire Ilya barely swears allegiance to. Sasza braces his hands on its smooth surface, seeing the faint reflection of his face in the wax. He takes several deep breaths and waits for the door to shut before turning to Ilya.

Sasza's cheeks puff up with words ready to burst from his mouth. Usually not the one to cast the ward, the Finance Minister envelopes the office in silence so Sasza can unleash what festers in his heart.

"You cannot let him go through with it," Sasza says, throat thick with rage. "It's the one time I asked anything of you, and you *abandoned* me."

Ilya says nothing but looks at Sasza with those aquatic blue eyes of his.

Despite Sasza's quivering lips, he is not going to stop. There is nothing to grieve, there will be nothing to mourn. Not if he has anything to do with it. "You had told me yourself; the Empire is in decline—you saw the records, there's absolutely no logic behind the emperor's—"

"I know, Sasza." He holds Sasza's upper arms tightly, like a father attempting comfort. "But nothing in my records can refute the evidence His Majesty presented. It was news to me as well, Sasza, I swear."

"This vengeance will destroy the Empire as we all know it. You know that will be the outcome." Sasza places his hands against Ilya's chest, kneading the edges of his waist coat like a kitten searching for milk, seeking comfort. He bows to whisper into Ilya's ear, "I'm a vampire."

Someone else who isn't Świetlana has to know. Once the truth leaves Sasza's lips, however, he's unsure if he can trust the Finance Minister. His affinity will not protect him; the realization hits too late for Sasza to take back his truth.

Ilya pulls away from Sasza, gazing deeply at him and replies, "I know. Władysław, may he rest, and I go back very far. I made the introduction between him and the empress all those years ago, keeping the vampirism a secret. I assumed you must have been one as well."

"And yet you still wouldn't speak." Though Sasza attempts to take a step back, Ilya grips Sasza with more strength than Sasza ever expected out of the older man. It roots the vampire in place.

"There is no stopping it, Sasza. And it's not because of your youth that I'm telling you this—far from it, in fact. You're mature enough to know that the people aren't unobservant rabble. In fact, I'm helping the people mobilize."

"What, with your salons and aristocratic ass-sniffing parties?"

Ilya snorts a laugh. "No, not like that. With equipment, and organization."

"It's that very organization—the Flock—that came up in my own research. Unless there's a vampire branch of it, I think you might have some crimes to answer for, Ilya."

"I will not take blame for an atrocity I had no hand in."

"But one of the others—you said yourself that it's decentralized, but you must communicate somehow. I refuse to believe violence enough to catch the emperor's eye would—"

"I *will not* take blame for an atrocity I had no hand in. I assure you, the proletariat I'm looking to elevate would not have attacked their betters, not in a way that would warrant a defensive fire-bombing. If there are vampires among the Flock, they are not loyal to the Envoy. Their States already have equality."

Ilya has no idea the truth of the Vampire States. They have nobles. They have thralls. They have dozens of social and economic strata between humans and blood-drinkers. Equality is an illusion. There is less difference, therefore less strife. The poorest of the vampires are faring much better than the poorest of the humans, but attacking the strongholds of vampire culture and survival will not make either richer.

Sasza will have to appeal in another way. "Please, Ilya. I know my father would have stayed back and let atrocities unfold if it meant preserving our status, but...but, I'm not like that."

"I know."

Desperation cloaks Sasza's tone. "There's not a whole lot I wouldn't do to keep myself safe. And if keeping myself safe preserves the lives of thousands if not hundreds of thousands of others, then I'll do anything."

The man takes Sasza's chin and holds it in his right hand rough from paperwork and intensive study. "I know."

Sasza scoffs. "So much for faith and power."

Ilya's brow twitches in a furrow which can only be described as offense. "You have not considered it."

"And why should I?" He leans his face closer. Their noses touch. "Will admission into your cult guarantee me protection from the violence His Majesty will wreak across these lands? Will it keep me safe despite any loss of status? Despite the fact that I'm literally one of the people Emperor Iwan has condemned to war?"

"The Flock cannot promise anything, not for the individual." His thumb brushes some wetness off Sasza's cheek. "Between us, however, I will not lose you to the whims of Emperor Iwan Iwanowicz or any of his ilk. In fact, I would like to see you on the opposite side of the Iwanowiczes, as a challenge to their rule."

Sasza's head spins. The new messages Ilya sends him conflict with every next word. How can he have a plan to protect Sasza and the people of the Odonic Empire if he won't even stand up to the emperor in the privacy of court? What is this ascension that he sees for Sasza, especially if the vampire won't join his Flock? Has he not considered that advancement will not save him—it didn't save Władysław; it will not preserve his son.

These grown men have all been fools, with the full extent of their idiocy remaining to be seen.

"But that's all for the future." Ilya kisses each of Sasza's damp cheeks. "Tell me, Aleksander, what do you need right now?"

"I need—" There's only one thing Ilya is good for in this moment. All forms of polite language fail Sasza when he murmurs, "I need you to fuck my face."

"Are you sure?"

"Expel the thoughts; I've had enough of them."

Ilya kisses Sasza on the lips as he grasps Sasza's wrist. He twists, pulling them both down against the office's carpeted floor. Sasza's back hits the surface hard. Pipes beneath the floorboards exude warmth, soothing whatever aches the impact may leave behind. He undoes his cravat and the top buttons of his dress shirt as Ilya straddles Sasza's neck.

With fast work of his trousers' buttons, Ilya frees his thick cock, more girth than length, but perfect for filling Sasza's mouth. The uncut head parts Sasza's lips and enters without ceremony. Its wrinkled, veined skin kisses the roof of Sasza's mouth, his nose nestling in the musky fur at its root. Ilya doesn't let Sasza get accustomed to the swelling of his cheeks before he starts bucking his hips.

As Ilya's groin slaps against Sasza's face, secretarial fingers tangle in Sasza's white hair. He does his best to protect Ilya's shaft from his teeth, but as the muscle glides in and out of his mouth, Sasza grimly wonders what the Flock would do if he closed his fangs, slicing through Ilya's prick like a knife. Would they come for revenge? Would they also lead a campaign against the vampires because one of their own had been taken out by one?

Ilya lurches forward, pounding Sasza's face. Saliva dribbles down Sasza's chin. His mouth stretches like a cunt, and instead of that pressure, all Sasza thinks about is how likely it is that Ilya is willing to sacrifice the vampires if it means eliminating several aristocrats in the fallout. After all, that seemed to have been the objective of attacking Daszek, putting the heartache on the Jackiewiczes by destroying the intellectual center they had spent so many years building.

The Finance Minister hides his involvement, that much Sasza is sure about. The temptation to bite grows, though he knows that eliminating one of the Flock's leaders will not bring the others out of their shadows. One death will not be enough—even eliminating Władysław had yielded nothing. No one came to retaliate. It did not make Sasza's situation better; it did not make it worse. The emperor is going through with his war, with or without acknowledgment of his Magician's concerns and with zero protest from people like the Finance Minister who has the most insight into why reunification is a fruitless endeavor.

As punishment, Sasza should take a bite and remind Ilya that he's exactly the kind of monster Iwanowicz fears. Instead of blood, however, cum spurts deep into the back of Sasza's mouth as Ilya bottoms out. Sasza swallows like the perfect servant. He sucks on the tip, rinsing the soft foreskin, relishing that sweet, salted cream. His mind still races as Ilya pulls out, panting as he falls forward onto his elbows. The hem of his untucked shirt brushes against Sasza's face. He smells like work in winter: sharp, bitter, and musky. Perhaps a little bit of strong pepper.

How Sasza wishes he could nibble on that soft skin while blood pools in his groin. It would spray and drench Sasza's face, more going to waste than to sustenance. After all, his restraint and propriety hadn't made his survival any less precarious.

Ilya lifts himself and rests on his ankles, looming over Sasza. "That wasn't all you wanted, was it, Sasza?"

He shuffles back and rests atop his partner, pushing his tongue into Sasza's sore mouth. Sasza responds in kind, scraping the remaining semen from his slick, tender cheeks. Their curling tongues mix their shared spit. Ilya pulls back with a loud smack, a thin thread of bodily fluid connecting them.

"How could you tell?"

Pushing his hair from his flushed face, Ilya says, "You're still thinking."

Sasza's vision remains crystal clear as he strokes a hand up Ilya's soft stomach. "Get on your belly, then, and we can fix that."

Ilya gets off Sasza and gestures to the desk. He presses himself against the short carpet lining his office. Sasza undresses, throwing off the layers in the full knowledge that Ilya cannot see his naked frame—Sasza denies him this pleasure. It's the smallest penance; the only way Ilya can truly atone for his spinelessness is to march into the emperor's private quarters and protest. He won't.

Instead, Ilya presses his head against the floor with his round ass raised to the ceiling. Rutting is the only ruin Sasza can act upon, paling in comparison to any more permanent alternative. It will satisfy Sasza for the duration of the session, but the rage will linger long after.

Sasza opens the secret drawer where Ilya keeps the oil and pops its cork. They've fucked in his office before—several times—but none of their encounters have had Sasza so engulfed in his own frustration and disappointment that it looks exactly like desperation.

He straddles the Finance Minister's half-dressed legs. Oil drips into the meaty crevasse. Sasza, impatient, does not tease his hole with an index finger or thumb, but plunges his long, lithe middle and ring fingers deep inside. Ilya howls in pleasured pain, and Sasza does not think to check on him. He chases the numbness that comes with lust at any cost.

He saws his middle fingers in and out, relaxing the taut ring of muscle enough to swallow Sasza's lean dick. This singular focus ensures he cannot capture any of his racing thoughts, especially as Ilya loosens. He removes his oil-slicked fingers and replaces them with his pointer and his thumb. The hole gapes, puckered like lips. Sasza mashes his tongue inside his own mouth, gathering saliva and remaining semen into a thick glob. He spits into the eager opening.

Ilya whines his name. As a treat, Sasza doesn't remove his fingers and runs his tongue across the rim. He doesn't want to hurt Ilya much, just enough as an ultimately gentle punishment for his lack of transgression against the emperor. Enough to know that this youth is not pleased at all with the older man whose counsel and solace he sought several times before.

Pretty words are nothing without action, and Ilya is as absent as Sasza's deceased father.

Without awaiting permission or confirmation, Sasza lines his cock head up with the abused entrance. He plunges in; Ilya wheezes. Sasza starts off slow, allowing Ilya to squeeze every centimeter of his length. But once the squishy flesh sheaths Sasza's prick, instinct takes over. He pounds into Ilya. The older man squirms beneath his lean, academic frame.

Sasza's hips bounce like the boughs of a birch tree in a summer storm. Sweat drips down his neck from the effort. Frantic and rigid, he pulls his cock out and grunts with each re-entry, plowing into this person he thought of as a colleague, a man who wanted Sasza as a comrade. This man could have kept being a lover, but instead he will serve as a receptacle for Sasza's frustration.

He breaks like a wave crashing against a shore as he spills deep into Ilya's guts. Stars flicker in Sasza's vision as he falls against the flesh still wrapped in his Imperial Council best. The fine fabric acts as a towel. Sasza struggles to breathe.

"You're crushing me, Sasza," Ilya groans, unable to expand his lungs.

For a flash, Sasza contemplates staying like that, suffocating Ilya with his own office decor. The effort of this betrayal is not worth it. Sasza's head spins as he raises himself on trembling arms. The feeling in his toes is gone as he sits back. His dick pops out of Ilya's asshole, all flaccid and spent, slick with his own cum and the oil. White drips from the tip.

Sasza's head feels empty like a burlap sack as he drags himself onto the silvery suede cushioning of the bench next to the desk. His damp thighs will leave a stain. He wipes his hand against his face, cheeks wet with a few escaped tears and exertion's wetness. That seating has seen worse messes from both of them.

He stares as Ilya rolls over. His exposed stomach and cock are flushed red, rubbed raw with a slight burn. The man struggles to get himself marginally decent—Sasza allows him the vulnerability of witnessing his sexual come down while the inflamed particulate in his mind settles like ash.

Ilya goes to his attaché case and produces a box of cigarettes. The branding makes Sasza eyes widen; it's the turquoise Peony brand popular in the Vampire States, made of a much different and more potent plant. "Blood tobacco?"

"I save it for dire needs of comfort." He pulls one out and snaps to ignite its tip. "For you."

Sasza holds the elegant, black paper cigarette between his fingers. His father had forbidden him from even trying it, for fear that such shipments would clue others into their truth sooner. Father is dead, however, and can no longer stop Sasza from giving into more reckless vices.

He takes it into his lips and, much like when blood touches Sasza's tongue, he can taste the complexities found within the crushed plant fibers. Warm spices and a hint of sweetness fills his mouth as he takes a much longer drag than he does with the human-grade tobacco. The oblivion hits harder and hits immediately. It settles into Sasza's mind like a fog, bringing peace. His head hits the top of the couch as he passes the cigarette back to Ilya.

Ilya takes an equally long pull and exhales, smoke billowing from beneath his facial hair and thick lips. Sasza worries—the compounds are in too powerful a dose for humans. Instead of fainting or falling victim to violent emesis, Ilya takes another small puff and hands it back to Sasza. His disposition changes as much as Sasza's, both of them relaxed in a smoky haze. Ilya should be feral and sick, not relaxed and self-satisfied.

Sasza doesn't understand how Ilya could have possibly developed the tolerance for blood tobacco. There's nowhere for humans to procure it, not in Korona—most vampires wouldn't make the sale for fear of liability and consequence. He must have an alternate source. And he must have trained his body into an immunity.

It is with this subtle deviation in human biology that Sasza realizes that there is more to Ilya than meets the eye. He's not the only one with some kind of magical or supernatural secret.

Sasza leans his head against Ilya's shoulder, leaving his thoughts behind in a post-coital fugue, buffered by sweet smoke. Their fingers entwine as they pass the cigarette between each other.

They stay like that for a very long time.

ONCE THEY FINISH THEIR cigarette and Ilya eventually passes out like people are wont to do after too much blood tobacco, Sasza covers him with his own jacket and leaves. He's spent too long in the Palace and seeks his own home. As he rounds the corner to go to the main staircase, an arm hooks around his and pulls him in the opposite direction. The tiny trap is none other but Świetlana, fuming and in need of the counsel of her father's Imperial Magician.

"Your Highness, I—"

"Don't speak, you're coming with me." Though she walks as quickly as her short legs will carry her, Sasza catches the irritation along her waterline and in her eyes, red as dawn's first light. Makeup stains mark where tears ran down her cheeks.

A robe hangs loosely from her shoulders, her sleeping gown struggles under the weight of her relaxed bosom, and her hair mostly tumbles down her shoulders. Sasza had completely lost track of time in seeking solace from Ilya. It reminds him of his more reckless years and with that comes slight embarrassment. It fades quickly when he realizes the rage Świetlana feels has nothing to do with that diversion.

She leads him to the third floor where the Palace's permanent residents make their living. The guard outside her bedroom unlocks the door. In thanks, Świetlana says, "Leave us."

Before they depart, the guard winks at Sasza. His stress outweighs his annoyance at another impending set of rumors that he and the emperor's daughter are involved somehow. Let them talk; worse is yet to come.

Świetlana closes the door, locks it, and snaps the ward into place. He doesn't bother taking a seat, instead standing awkwardly in the center of her plush, lavender carpet. The room is in the same pristine state as it would have been after the staff had their way with it. In his post-orgasmic haze, he doesn't want to put any part of his body on the even sheets.

"I apologize—"

"For what?" She walks past him. "You smell a bit more like an ashtray than usual, tinged with another substance I'd rather not think about, but that's the least of our problems."

Sasza blushes. "How did you know I was still at the Palace?"

"I asked the valets, and they told me your autocar was still in the lot. So, I went to the only other place I assumed you'd be. That's when we ran into each other."

As he nods, she crosses her room and sits down hard on her bed. Despite the plush blankets and the myriad stuffed animals artfully displayed, it exudes more modesty than the monstrosity Ilya sleeps in. None of the papers from the previous evenings spent cramming for an argument neither of them made remain on her desk. In fact, all that laid there was Świetlana's scribbled notepad and planner. No evidence of excess research.

"What did Ilya have to say for himself?" She asks, words coming out like bites.

"That's what I stayed behind to figure out."

"Oh, is that it?"

Sasza must have done a terrible job putting himself back together. He knows his hair is a mess, and he didn't bother redoing his cravat. "Mostly. I too do not understand why he essentially sided with His Majesty through his silence. He said the biggest problem is that there's no doubt that it's vampires that attacked Daszek."

Lady Świetlana rubs her tear ducts. "Please tell me you do not believe him."

"Of course not. I feel like my father would have known if that were the case."

"Do you think Ilya set us up to look like fools?"

"No, that I don't believe either." Sasza tucks one arm under the other and rests his chin in his knuckles.

"You know him better than anyone else in the circle."

"Unfortunately. But given Ilya's objectives and politics, the idea of a war is advantageous to him." When Lady Świetlana's mouth forms a question, Sasza answers with, "Yes, a war would cause many more problems for the proletariat, but it might be what erodes any goodwill they had towards the aristocracy. If slaughtering thousands ensures that some of the dozens at the top perish, I think he's willing to make that sacrifice."

Lady Świetlana groans. "Why are they all so fucking stupid? Because here's my view on the situation: I think that evidence had been planted. After centuries of peace, I refuse to believe that the Vampire States would have any reason to turn their weapons towards the Empire."

There are not enough words to help her understand how right she is. Yet, she goes on, as if she needs to prove herself to Sasza. And he allows her—it's how she thinks, even if she sometimes has to write down the last thing she thought before derailing herself.

"I kept Father in the council chamber long enough that they had to deliver dinner. I cannot believe he genuinely thinks that the resolution to the Jackiewicz Incident is to declare war. *War*, Sasza! The last one practically ruined our family's reputation. I know you and Ilya worked hard on reforms to help us retain any fragment of respect, but it's too little too late. But Father won't listen. I showed him our numbers, our facts. Nothing. It's like he's possessed. There's no getting through to him."

"I should have stayed behind with you."

"No, it would've ended terribly. He thinks Lord Czarnolaski's death is a vampire conspiracy. I immediately refuted that because it makes no sense. Especially in the context of the truth—why would the Vermilion Envoy attack their own like that?"

Sasza keeps his mouth still. Because there had been a tacit agreement between the Empire and the States that one would not interfere in the affairs of the other. It was a resolution that should have been codified, but Władysław Czarnolaski considered himself an exception, especially once he re-emerged as a human magician instead of a vampiric charlatan.

Władysław collected many enemies, vampire and human alike. Any one of the scorned lovers or betrayed former allies could have pushed him to the brink of harming himself through his own vices. But the culprit behind the murder sits not two meters from Her Highness. The greatest danger came from Władysław's own seed, living inside his own home. This truth Sasza keeps to himself; there's no reason otherwise for Świetlana to mistrust him.

"I need something drastic, Sasza. And I do have an idea, it's just..." She chokes back a sob. It's the most vulnerable he's seen her. Despite the pedigree and responsibility, Her Highness Świetlana sits with Sasza on the threshold of adulthood. No longer children, not quite adult enough to know better. It's the elders around them that are failing. "I do not think I can ask you for more than you've already given me."

He closes the gap between them, crossing the carpet and kneeling at Lady Świetlana's feet. "I'm not sure what I've given you so far, Your Highness, but I need you to know that there's not much I wouldn't do for you." He doesn't know how to infuse sincerity into his voice, only that he knows to look directly at Świetlana, to make sure her purple eyes see into the depths of his amber gaze. "My hand is yours to command. I will be *your* sword, *your* magician, whatever you need, Your Highness."

Sasza places his head in her lap, bowing. Begging for permission. The details of the permission have not formed in his mind yet.

"What I need is for you to be my vampire," she whispers.

The words strike as much fear in Sasza as they do love. She sees him for what he is, not the perfect image he's crafted for others' comfort. "Świetlana..."

"I'm not going to tell anyone, don't worry. It's best if we keep it a secret." She lifts his chin with her fingertips. "I've received information that the Emperor's Chosen who are trained with undead blades will not be the security detail the night of the Solstice Ball. If my father cannot be stopped with words, he should be stopped with violence."

He pulls away from her touch. "You want me to assassinate him?"

"That is what I am asking you to do, yes." She squeezes her eyes shut, freeing the tears at last. "Actually, no. That's not all. I want them *all* gone. The rot doesn't stop with him. It's that entire fucking council. They're all the problem. But the thing is, there are some I want to keep. Like the Jackiewiczes—they've done nothing wrong. They're not even in Korona anyway. And the servants too. I don't want them harmed. *Fuck.*" She grunts. "There's a whole list of people I don't want caught in the bloodbath...this is why I need your help as my friend, my advisor...as someone who also loves this Empire as much as I do."

That's where Lady Świetlana stumbles, but Sasza doesn't have the heart to correct her. If loving her as much as he does means loving the Empire, then perhaps he can preserve some of that affection. He loves the Odonic Empire as much as she needs him to. But an Empire cannot endure without people to live in its lands and guarantee their own prosperity. They don't necessarily need rulers and aristocrats for that.

It's then Sasza realizes he's starting to sound a lot like Ilya. The lingering taste of his seed feels bitter in his mouth, and Sasza would light a cigarette if Lady Świetlana didn't hate it so much.

When Świetlana doesn't seem to have more to say, he leans back onto his palms and raises his head, getting lost in the swirling clouds painted along the ceiling of this imperial bedroom. The splattered mess resembles a sunset, complete with cherubs and soft, dying flames. Its discord swirls in his eyes as if guiding the meandering trail of his thoughts.

Much like how killing Ilya will not stop the Flock and will not resolve the very real danger of impending war, murdering the emperor alone will not stay the madness. Sasza regrets not having more of an eye into the Military's inner workings—an entire battalion must have assembled the report. Someone must have manipulated the findings to blame the Vermilion Envoy instead of working harder to identify the true culprits. Simple solutions with an easy scapegoat sound about right for a hierarchy more interested in preventing its own destruction than preserving anything for anyone else aside from their own legacy.

Every idea that winks into his mind falls apart when he considers that there is nothing he can do without spawning more panic than already guaranteed by the initial declaration of war. The Military belongs to the emperor. Lady Lewońska belongs to the emperor and her own cruelty. The Emperor's Chosen, though they work for the Empire, will answer to the emperor before they answer to him. Ilya has proved himself unreliable.

Sasza is quickly learning that if he wants anything done at all, he must do it himself.

He lets his head fall forward, looking at Świetlana once again. She has the far-off daze of someone completely lost in the mire of her own panic. He's also seen her this way before.

"Your Highness," he says, soft but firmly.

She shakes her head, breaking her own trance. "Yes, Sasza?"

"I think I have a solution. But I have to ask before I share it with you: where is Ute in all this?" Lady Świetlana has not once mentioned her own aide. "She wasn't at the meeting."

She forms her lips in a thin line. "It's not that I don't trust her; I do. But I kept her away because the less she knows, the better. I told her that Father didn't want someone so new to attend."

"You lied to her?"

"I'm not proud of it."

Sasza snorts an exhale. "I've taught you at least one thing, it seems."

"I've learned so much from you, you dolt. So, what is your plan?"

"I'll orchestrate a massacre. Eliminate everyone in attendance. There will be no war to declare if there is no one to declare it. Or if there is no one to hear the declaration."

"All by yourself? You can do that?"

Sasza looks at his pale hands, rotating them in his lap. "I *am* the Imperial Magician, aren't I? I have a few tricks up my sleeve."

"You did graduate top of our class in magical arts."

There are methods of casting magic deemed too dangerous for any one magician, far too advanced for someone at the age of twenty-three to have mastered. Casting at a distance, chaining incantations and curses, turning single spells into a deluge, knowing several magical dialects in the protolanguage—all of these are advanced skills Sasza's collected during his itinerant years. It's how he's kept his secrets, kept so much quiet. He hasn't tried any of the techniques to end lives, but if there was ever a moment to experiment, it would be at the Solstice Ball.

His casting ability does not stretch as far as the dozens if not hundreds of people in attendance, plus staff, plus guards. Repeated uses of the silencing ward is one thing; offensive spells are another, and he lacks the combat training.

Lady Świetlana notices his silence. "There's more to it, isn't there?"

"There is." *Drinking my own blood and becoming a bestiapir.* Years have passed. He doesn't know how long he could maintain his insectoid form. Siphoning blood through his needle, drenching his body in it might make the transformation sustainable. There are ways bestiapiry fight that no human untrained against them can withstand. He is an arsenal all his own.

As Sasza opens his mouth to mention it, Świetlana lifts a finger. "I'd rather not know. And it's not because I am sincerely worried you'll fail—you won't—but I'd rather not have insight into my father's destruction."

"Very well then."

Her face softens into the saddest grin. "Does it make me a fool if I don't think I can witness my parents' deaths? Does that make me a coward?"

Shattered glass, a crackling fire, and the pinch of a needle in his neck assault Sasza's senses as if he's back at the night he killed Władysław. The way his father didn't scream or beg for mercy. Echoes he wouldn't wish on another person. "No, not at all. Your sole survival would be suspicious, however. It's best if we keep you away from the ball altogether. Ute as well."

"Do *you* not trust her?"

"Trust requires some familiarity, and I simply do not know her. Moreover, if she's with you, it's less likely that anyone would suspect your absence. You can fake an illness."

This makes Świetlana laugh. "Sasza, I haven't even had a cold in several years, even while the city suffered a plague. Isn't that just cruel?"

Sasza nods. "But it doesn't have to be a cold. After all, do your parents know that you've had your womb removed?"

She crosses her arm and brings her opposite knuckle to her lips. "You know, they don't. Oh...I see where you're going. The Solstice unfortunately lines up with the worst days of the cycle, and there's nothing anyone can do about it. You really do consider everything."

"Anything can be made an advantage, Your Highness."

"I don't know what I'd do without you, Sasza." She sighs, wistful. "A good imperial servant, and an even better friend."

Sasza swallows hard, because this all-encompassing treason will either stave off a war or launch a conflict more violent than anyone could have anticipated. "In exchange for the weaponization of my monstrosity, I want you to swear that your army will never raise a weapon against the vampires—Envoy or otherwise—unless they pose an immediate threat to the Empire, Your Majesty."

She exhales a chuckles and smooths her skirts. "Come here, Sasza."

He shuffles on his knees towards her again and places his hands on her dress's soft fabric, almost as if praying. "What is it, Świetlana?"

"Lay your head in my lap."

He obeys.

She gently places her hand on the back of his head. "I swear that the only place my army will be is at your command or against your enemies, Aleksander Czarnolaski."

Świetlana bends and presses her lips against the top of his head, sealing the pledge with ancient ritual.

No papers.

No ink.

No blood.

Only a promise of bloodshed to prevent bloodshed, of violence to stay other violence, stamped with friendship's kiss.

EIGHT

I.

Trunks line the back and roof of the large autobus while all Iwona's belongings fit into a single sack easily hoisted over her shoulder. She tucks it among her fellow Chosen's belongings in the undercarriage. It strikes her as odd that they are leaving the same night as the Emperor's Solstice Ball. It sounds like the kind of event that they should be present for, keeping a watchful eye over the imperial family and the rest of the aristocracy. The political unease at Władysław Czarnolaski's funeral and the conversations overheard at the dinner have echoed within her mind during idle times—like the precipice of sleep when she least needs her thoughts spinning. There hadn't been much else to note in the days between, but much like with pets and toddlers, quiet usually means trouble.

The air of serenity of Korona's streets is no different. In previous years, Iwona had read, the proletariat would organize their own festivities, the city alight in drink, rich foods, song, and dance, with other revelry taking place in the more clandestine parts of the city. Here, she stands on the outskirts, near the city's walls with the rest of the Ninety-Second Regiment, overlooking a city in repose, a populace dormant.

Undulating hills of shingled rooftops interrupted by parks and squares stare back at Iwona. Despite shedding her family name and climbing the ranks of the Military's elite, she fits in neither with the aristocrats on the other side of the city nor with the working class who make their lives in its outskirts. This is the life she trained for—one where travel away from the people she's supposedly protecting would be the norm. It confuses her. Given the misgivings and strife she's overheard, she's unsure who needs her protection most.

"Are you all right, Ogrodnik?" Captain Łukasiewicz's voice snaps Iwona out of her reflection.

"Captain, was there a festival scheduled for this evening?" She pushes on her sack one last time as she packs it into the autobus; it does nothing except serve as a ritual for good luck.

"No, the Iwanowiczes did not plan for it. Moreover, whatever falls upon Korona once we depart is neither our problem nor our purview."

Iwona has no evidence for why the city's countenance feels all wrong tonight, but she learned long ago to trust the doubt simmering deep in her gut. "That's a shame. It feels like there's something we should be doing, but I'm not sure what."

"We have our orders, handed down from General Kwiatkowski themself. We need to maintain an element of surprise, Ogrodnik, and keep to the schedule before anyone else finds out about our departure from the capital." Captain Łukasiewicz softly puts her hand on Iwona's shoulder. "We will have wasted an opportunity if we stay here and act as security."

The glare the captain gives her leaves no room for discussion. It saps whatever warmth and camaraderie Iwona might have felt beneath the layers protecting her from winter's chill and enemy blades alike.

Iwona remembers their commitment is to the Empire itself, not its rulers. It suits her lack of loyalty to the aristocracy. She drops her uncertainty and makes her way towards the autobus's open door. One of her fellow Chosen takes her hands and pulls her inside.

The only light within the autobus is from the city's streetlamps. Each crushed velvet seat is filled with a seasoned warrior sitting beside another. Once Captain Łukasiewicz takes her spot upfront, there is no more room for anyone else. In this transition, sadness strikes Iwona. During the few days they were both in Korona, she hadn't even attempted to contact the Imperial household to schedule an appointment with Ute, especially now that rumors say she serves Her Highness Świetlana Iwanowicz in the same capacity that Czarnolaski serves His Majesty. It's the kind of achievement Iwona would have loved to hear from her friend's own lips. An irrational worry sparks that her friend might not want to have seen Iwona, either due to embarrassment or jealousy because of their professional separation. Neither makes sense, as they are on equal footing: both girls are servants in positions more powerful than the average aristocrat or citizen.

Iwona wonders if Ute spends the same amount of time thinking of her—Iwona doubts it; she's always been the one to get more attached.

Snow falls off the autobus's roof as it pulls away from the waystation. The vehicle's conductor honks twice for the border wall to be opened. They wait a few moments. Upon a shout of all-clear and the screech of the gates' opening, the autobus's engines whir as the magic fueling it activates. The vehicle bounces ever so slightly as its terrain-appropriate wheels crunch along the snow-buried cobbled streets. It rocks almost like a crib, with some of the Chosen having already fallen asleep given the dark hour and the long road ahead.

Iwona takes a deep breath and leans her forehead against the ice-cold window. The views will be spectacular. She will see more of the continent than she's ever seen in her lifetime. Her heart flutters at the concept of her first job coming so soon after her appointment. The autobus's gentle rocking pulls Iwona into a peace she hasn't experienced in years. There's trepidation, of course, but the more she thinks about the work ahead, the more calm settles upon her mind.

As the Emperor's Chosen embarks into parts unknown, the citizens of Korona awaken. In the city's Pewter Square, far away from the departing autobus, torches blaze and voices shriek chants. The crowd's demands are fueled by desperation and the harsh truth that the aristocracy sworn to protect them would much rather spend their unearned wealth in decadent, undeserving luxury.

II.

Ute's never been one for taking care of another person. The only nursing she's done is escorting a fellow trainee to the infirmary to get proper care. But this seems to be one of her duties as Imperial Magician—ensuring Świetlana has the comfort she needs. She comes in with rags and a tray of herbal tea warm enough to ease any aches but without the caffeine to inhibit sleep. It guarantees the requisite rest which Ute understands all too well. An injured muscle is not one that will get stronger without adequate recovery. She witnessed more foolish students learn this the hard way, often sent back home or transitioned to more secretarial roles because they are no longer of use.

Ute refuses to be useless.

She walks into Her Highness's bedchambers, let in by a servant. Ute doesn't know how to ask if she's spending the night or if she should request an autocar to take her back to her apartment in Korona, across the street from the outskirts of the Imperial Grounds. These logistics had not been discussed.

If Her Highness has ideas for Ute's lodging, she hasn't shared them. This makes her nervous, as so many best practices and tenets revolve around the utmost preparedness. The only preparation Ute performed was her outfit, a small bag with a change of small clothes and toiletries.

She doesn't know how many hours she'll spend—could be the whole duration of the event or however long it takes for Świetlana to feel better. Perhaps she'll attend the ball, while Ute sneaks back home in deepest night to her apartment, her appointment as Świetlana's Magical Advisor having come too late to be invited.

The cavernous room is definitely that of a young adult's—an untidy mess whose purpose is convenience rather than order. Nothing looks as if it needs to be for the public's gaze, from the untucked chair at her desk, to the missing books, to the piles and piles of notebooks.

"Sorry about the mess," Świetlana says. "It's been a stressful few days, and I didn't want any staff seeing me like this. Come have a seat, Ute." She pats the empty space on the windowsill. The padding sits right atop the radiator embedded in the half wall.

It's the perfect spot for someone seeking warmth to relieve menstrual aches and contractions. Like a cat with its limbs all tucked in, Świetlana hugs her left leg close while her bare right leg dangles. Ute focuses so intently on Her Highness's exposed skin that she misses the fine fabric barely covering the bits it needs to.

Ute obeys, dropping her bag next to the door, and crossing the room to sit beside her liege sidesaddle with her hands neatly folded in her lap. The heat hisses beneath them as another blizzard rages outside. She sweats beneath her many layers, an outfit consisting of several knits and sweaters in anticipation of another snowstorm hitting the capital for the third week in a row. Winter is brutal like that, and preparedness is a necessity.

It relieved Ute to not have to dress up, but the comfort of her outfit reminds her of this strange social isolation. Most of the staff and so many dignitaries from across the Odonic Empire are in the downstairs ballrooms, being served and pampered in their fanciest dress. Ute's heard her classmates talk about the balls and galas, events she had never attended because of her aggressive lack of interest, but, more importantly, her lack of invitation.

Daughters of her lowly stature rarely get to share space with decision makers.

But here, Ute sits a few feet away from the person who holds her employment and her affection wound around her own power and status.

Ute glances first at Świetlana's face but then her eyes fall to folds between Świetlana's legs. She sees not the crimson flood supposedly making her ill but the glistening slick of yonic arousal. She swallows, nervous. She's been close with women before; Świetlana would not be her first. But it's the evidence of the lie that makes her uncomfortable. Ute's had her own menses fairly recently. It came in globs neat in their structure but bloody and inconsiderate of her clothing, the pain of expulsion having no regard for the trauma that had already befallen her body. For Ute, it also comes with sweating, paleness, and nigh constant urination.

Świetlana, however, looks radiant. Not quite as if she had done her makeup for the party she is missing, but lacking the exhaustion of a body's disappointment that it will not be a vessel for a potential new life.

"What's wrong, Ute?" she asks, unaware that her position sets Ute's eyeline directly at the soft hair between her legs. Or perhaps she is aware and wants to ensure Ute knows it.

"Nothing, Your Highness." Heat creeps across Ute's cheeks, and there's no hiding it. "That's not true, you're looking quite well tonight."

"Thank you, I've recovered some since before you arrived. It's amazing what rest can do for a person." She flips her hair from her face. "Though I am sad to be missing the ball."

"Do you think there's time enough for you to get ready and join the others? I'm sure Sasza would love to see you."

Świetlana shakes her head. "No, I'm...tired. So much of my schedule had been spent organizing and making sure the invitations were correct, and, honestly, that party is not for me. It's a different sort of pain, Ute."

"What is?"

"That kind of service. One where you're not sure who it's benefiting." Świetlana turns her head to Ute. "Speaking of pain and illness, does your arm hurt?"

"My...arm?"

"Yes. The metal one." She doesn't look at her magician.

Reflexively, Ute rotates her arm. "It's getting there, I suppose. Sometimes I feel sensations when I have the arm off, but otherwise, it's another limb."

"Can I see how it's attached?"

The question is innocent. The intention, perhaps, is less so. Ute doesn't know how to conduct herself. Does she remove her garments and indulge Her Highness's curiosity? Does she refuse because showing off her flesh to the woman she serves would ruin the propriety of their professional relationship?

The Military did not prepare her for this.

So, Ute consults her heart's wants. She gave up the Emperor's Chosen for the Emperor's heir; it's only fair she acquiesces to her every whim. The last thing she wants is any rift between herself and Świetlana; clothing and the barriers of what's considered proper and professional be damned.

She removes her thickest sweater, followed by the long-sleeved thermal beneath, leaving on the camisole keeping her breasts from brushing up against the coarse fabric designed more for utility than comfort. Though her own nudity is still concealed, Ute feels a vulnerability which she hasn't experienced since the first time someone had wanted to conduct such intimate exploration.

Everything about Ute's body is new to her too. There is the hard wall of a seam between where her flesh ends and the metal begins—the puckered skin where a web of nerves screeches whenever she removes the prosthetic. Idly, she draws her fingers along it, glancing as Świetlana follows the movement.

"Is this what you wanted to see, Your Highness?" Ute asks, throat dry. Something childish smolders between them, a curiosity untampered by years of absence.

"It is. I hope you didn't get injured for my sake. May I?" Świetlana raises a hand. "Or wait. This is inappropriate, I apologize. I shouldn't be taking my privileges as your employer and liege so frivolously."

Ute smirks. "It's all right, Your Highness. You can touch the metal if you want." She extends her metal arm towards Świetlana.

Her Highness grabs it tenderly with her fingertips, much like a lord does a lady upon first greeting and brings the hand to her lips. "Can you feel that, Ute?"

Ute shakes her head. She knows something is touching her prosthetic hand, but that cognizance comes from her eyes and her limb's change in position. Świetlana's touch is too delicate to register as a change in pressure. Even with all the magic and medical technology the world offers, she's not sure she'll ever feel such subtle contact ever again.

Softly, Świetlana glides her thumb against the smooth metal. "I'm...my sympathies for what may have transpired. If I recall correctly, this happened sometime at the Academy."

Ute doesn't want to voice just how recently, but the red rawness of the skin around the creases gives away the wound's freshness. "It was an accident, yes. I got too careless and...some injuries can't be reversed or repaired, Your Highness."

"I know what you mean." Świetlana's gaze sweeps over Ute's face. "Can I trust you with something, Ute?"

Her Highness hops off the windowsill, her feet hitting the plush, midnight-blue carpet. It envelops her trimmed toenails shining with black lacquer. With her back to Ute, Świetlana pulls off her nightie with one motion. The fine silk sails, landing gently on the floor, discarded.

Ute's clit swells as all the warmth drains from her face. Świetlana is naked. Soft, dewy skin blankets a hardened landscape of muscle. The definition of her shoulder and back muscles should be kept in an anatomy textbook as the epitome of form.

Świetlana turns around, presenting the enormous breasts which the meat of Her Highness's back works so hard to uphold. Large nipples stare back at Ute and all thoughts crash to a halt. The tingling in her face relaxes her cheeks. Ute grits her teeth to keep her salivating mouth from dropping like a starving animal. This ruler is on the second rung of the imperial ladder. Ute at once feels privileged and like a charlatan, as if someone had reached deep under the dampest corners of her mind and pulled this perverted yearning out. It's possible that Świetlana is like this with all her staff, a lonely person seeking companionship whose a status keeps others away. Ute wants to believe, given their shared schooling, that her exhibition might be different. That it's something she wants to share with Ute for a relationship's sake, not to satisfy a vessel which will never be full.

"Can you see it, Ute?" Her Highness's gentle tone snaps Ute out of her distraction. She lifts her breasts, raising shadows from her stomach's squishy planes.

She softly grunts and blinks, forcing her eyes to look at a different part of Her Highness naked flesh. Four points almost like a diamond surround her belly button. "May I ask what happened there?"

"Only if you swear to not tell anyone else."

"I swear it." Ute's head swims as if clouded with smoke.

"The last thing I want is to continue the Iwanowicz lineage. They have no sons. They have what they think is a daughter, an offspring who dreams not of parenthood. I want the titles, but that crosshair of feminine expectation never sat well with me. So, I had an operation done to remove the mechanism."

Świetlana closes the distance between them, taking Ute's left hand and presses it against the skin, tender where the scalpels made their mark however long ago. What tightens the heated air around them is the fact that Ute cannot see past Świetlana's bosom, losing most thoughts.

"Does...does Sasza know?"

"About me? About this?" Świetlana exhales a laugh. "He enjoys men too much to be privy to such secrets. In fact, that's why I specifically sought someone with my anatomy for a companion. Someone else who might understand."

It explains the lack of blood. This secret explains why the staff and her parents simply accepted that Her Highness cannot attend the Ball. It explains why Sasza isn't her Magical Advisor. Ute has the pride of being among the top of her Academy class and her own gamble and sacrifice of the Emperor's Chosen to thank for putting her in this position. But it's too tit-brained to admit, even though Świetlana shared a secret which might as well be treason, depending on how much one subscribes to the notion of the divine right of emperors.

A destiny which can be made obsolete by the removal of organs which contribute to life itself.

Świetlana straddles Ute, pinning her to the sill. She puts her hands around Ute's jaw, making sure Ute can see nothing beyond Świetlana's rounded face and her high cheekbones. Her manicured nails brush Ute's loose hair shimmering silver in the bedroom's low lights.

"What I truly need, Ute, is someone else I can trust. Sasza works hard for me, but truthfully, I'm sure I can execute my responsibilities without him. If he dies, Ute, there will be a funeral, but I will not mourn him. He's very much like his father, and I simply cannot have that, Ute. And if you can keep another secret." Her Highness lowers her voice.

"I think my father is a fool. I'm not like him. I would rather be in my bedchambers with my new confidant than in a room full of people I don't know who have none of my interests at the core of their agendas. Per your appointment, I want to believe that I have your fealty, Miss Myśliwska."

Ute puts a hand around the curve of Świetlana's ass. "You have whatever you need of me, Your Highness."

"Good." Świetlana tilts her head and brings her lips to Ute's, giving her a gentle kiss before her tongue enters Ute's eager mouth.

The Solstice Ball unfurls in the palace halls below, its lively music unable to penetrate the soft sounds of two mouths lapping and the incredulity shouting through Ute's mind. Her teenaged self would envy her proximity to Świetlana and the way that the emperor's progeny ensnares her adult lips. This kiss is one she's wanted for almost a decade. Though it isn't an unblemished first for both of them, the fact that it came eventually gives Ute a sense of security.

Świetlana rocks back. "It feels silly to ask after the fact, but do you...want to touch me, Ute?"

Does Her Highness ask this of all her servants? She's an Iwanowicz; her needs should be anticipated and met without questioning or needing further clarification. But Ute is honored—it's another sign of the trust entwining between them.

"There's not much I would like more, Świetlana."

Her Highness angles her crotch forward, the dark hairs glistening with her own desire and yearning. Ute forgets how to move. Her hands stay in the same position until Świetlana takes the prosthetic and gently drags her tongue against the metal. Ute's rehabilitation doctors and specialists told her that it's weatherproofed with the latest in materials science and technology. While the arm itself doesn't register the pliable muscle contorting around the metal, Ute sees it and loses her mind.

This is Świetlana Iwanowicz, offspring of Emperor Iwan, fellating Ute's prosthetic fingers. With utmost dexterity, Świetlana guides the prepared digits in between her own folds, sighing as they brush against her lower lips and clit. It's the only cunt Ute's ever wanted to feel, but there's no sensation. The feelings come as ghosts of muscle contractions and wetness, the curling of her own metal fingers more mimicking her lost muscle memory than responding to present sensations. The encouraging yips and yelps coming lewdly from Her Highness's mouth are the most input she'll receive. Despite her melancholy over the loss of her arm, Ute wouldn't be here with it, working Świetlana up into a release she deserves.

She executes the motions as if rehearsed, slipping in one finger then two, hoping she's causing Świetlana no pain, even with her whimpering suggesting otherwise. Świetlana grabs Ute's tiny tits, grinding the heels of her palms into her nipples. The swelling of Ute's own nub is impossible to ignore, the wetness defeating the purpose of Ute's winter-optimized hosiery. She will not be able to return home in them, especially not with the drip spreading from Świetlana's pussy as Her Highness bucks against Ute's metal hand.

Ute's back hits the cold window. Świetlana curls over her, panting while swallowing Ute's lips and tongue in a fervor contrary to all formal propriety. And while she loves the mess she's making of Her Highness, it stings that she can't feel it in that hand. At the same time, this sexualization of Ute's offering makes the ache and dampness between her own legs increasingly impossible to ignore.

She grabs Świetlana's smaller frame with her right arm and lifts her up. The laugh that sputters from within Her Highness's throat is so girlish that Ute forgets both their statuses. Not liege and servant but something more carnal—simple, even—as it should have been in their youth. Indecently fascinated with Her Highness, Ute deposits her on the bed then removes her thick leggings and socks to match Świetlana's nudity. Her skin isn't as smooth, with the full history of her scars and training etched upon the pale expanse, but Świetlana grants her a hunger that erases any insecurity. The scars, the puckered wounds, the stretch marks—they all melt under the same heavy-lidded gaze.

Her Highness spreads her legs wide, her flushed folds a tempting invitation. As much as Ute wants to dive mouth first, she suspects there will be another tasting opportunity later. Instead, she crawls on top of Świetlana, angling her cunt perfectly such that their bottom lips caress and touch. One clit slides against the other, black and gray pussy hairs mixing and mingling. Ute holds Świetlana's straightened leg close to her chest, embracing the muscle and running her tongue along those honed curves. Her Highness mimics the embrace against Ute's own thick thigh, pressing it against her chest's fullness.

Ute bounces, unable to hear anything over their heavy breaths and smacking skin. She chases her own release while making sure Her Highness gets hers as well. Ute grinds into her liege as if her declared servitude isn't enough evidence of her devotion. There's a possibility that climaxing together might erode all barriers between personal and political, the force of their attraction melding their skin as one. It's what she sought in her pursuit of Military excellence.

This erotic journey cannot only have one end.

Their synching cries compete in desperation. They switch positions, dampening the elegant, thick sheets, getting completely lost in the intoxicating scent and taste of sex and sweat and the tangle of limbs and hair. It's all-consuming and distracting.

Orgasm after orgasm helps them both forget the Solstice Ball in the halls downstairs and ignore the disaster only one of them has any inkling is coming.

III.

Sasza dons the formal wear he is least likely to mourn. The shirt belonged to his father, the slacks and the fitted jacket are his that he should have discarded last season. Though years have passed since his previous transformation, he remembers its violence leaving none of those clothes intact. Sasza doesn't know if his parents kept those tatters and attempted to mend them or if they burned the evidence of their child's monstrosity.

He coifs his hair such that it's neat and tidy but forgoes the jewelry that aristocracy of all genders flaunt at overly indulgent events like the Solstice Ball. He wouldn't want to leave behind evidence. Moreover, if this entire plan he concocted goes to shit, he needs collateral for cash to skip town. He'd studied Władysław's methods of quick currency exchange; though his father isn't around to make disappearance as seamless as possible, Sasza knows enough to make it work for himself.

As he ties his cravat, a knock comes at the townhouse door. His shoulders snap up to his ears. No one should be receiving him. He was going to be taking his own autocar to the Palace, parking, and letting the night unfold.

The knocks come again. Sasza checks himself one more time in his bedroom mirror and goes downstairs.

On the other side of the door is Ilya. For a simple ride to and from the Palace, his outfit is far too seasonal. His head bears an uszanka for the cold and his body carries a large coat. The heavy boots on his feet are made for the snowpack, not for a night of dancing and feasting. There is nothing elegant about his dress, nothing that suggests preparation for a party. Sasza didn't even plan to bring a jacket if he was just going out from one door to the autocar and through another set of doors. He has not even put on his dress shoes yet.

"To what do I owe the visit, Ilya?" Sasza says.

"May I come in? I have some things I must tell you."

Sasza swallows. He hadn't spoken to Ilya since the day of the meeting where Emperor Iwan declared war on the Vampire States. Sluggish days of silence, of shame, of embarrassment. In Sasza's mind, it had been over between them because of the betrayal. But he doesn't know how to voice it.

He lets the older man in.

Ilya has the decency to remove his snow-stained boots, but only unbuttons his coat. "Have I mentioned that you clean up quite nicely?"

He doesn't come closer to kiss Sasza's cheek, but a slight glowing blush graces Sasza's face. "I wouldn't want to disappoint Her Highness by not putting my best foot forward."

"Indeed." Ilya drops his head forward with a sigh, then straightens. "I apologize, Aleksander, but I will not be attending tonight's Ball. In fact, I'm resigning my post and leaving Korona. It was a last-minute decision, and I'm sure it would have been mentioned at the New Year's meeting. But I thought you should know first."

"And you're not inviting me to go with you?" A heaviness grips Sasza's chest. He cannot claim surprise, especially not with the truth in his heart. But Ilya suggesting abandonment first feels like a trick. It should have been a silent agreement between the two of them, not something spoken.

"That depends on you, Sasza. Are you going to abandon Her Highness and join the Flock?"

Sasza scratches his cheek, careful not to upset the powder evening his skin tone. "Regrettably, I cannot do that."

"That's what I thought you'd say."

"I should have seen this coming." Aristocrats only fell in love through the cracks of political marriages. Neither of them had any such commitments. But clearly Ilya has some other more serious obligation if he needs to leave so abruptly. "In fact, I probably should not have gotten my hopes up." For what, Sasza himself isn't sure.

Ilya gives him the lop-sided grin that ensnared Sasza the first time they met behind closed doors, in close quarters. "Oh, you are *far* too young to be speaking like that. The heart wants what the heart wants. It's not a weakness. In fact, I'd even say it's a good quality to have."

"I am still disappointed that you didn't speak up against the Emperor." Sasza feels too proud of himself for stating his true feelings.

"I know you are. I have to admit that I am a coward, and while I cannot condone the declaration of civil war, there is truly nothing I can do to stop it. Think of my departure as a kind of self-imposed exile."

Sasza crosses his arms. "That's a little dramatic, don't you think?"

"Not to me, no. I've organized a rally with the members of the Flock who are infuriated that there is a Ball but no Festival. Consider it a feeble attempt at an apology."

Another detail Sasza had somehow overlooked—typically, the Solstice Ball coincides with a grand Solstice Festival for the proletariat throughout the outskirts of Korona. It had never been mentioned, and it's not something Sasza thinks Świetlana would have forgotten about without a purpose. It slipped Sasza's mind as well, but he has several excuses.

"I'll accept it." He does not, but he's beyond arguing and pleading.

Ilya reaches down to hold each of Sasza's hands in his. "Please think of me, from time to time?"

"Can you at least tell me where you're going? I'd like to send you letters, if you'll have them." Sasza resents how much his chest hurts. Ilya still has principles; it would be much easier to think he had abandoned them for some short-sighted selfishness.

"That is charming of you, but for your safety and mine, I cannot share that information. What I can offer, however, is a ride to the Palace. For old time's sake."

Sasza's stomach warms at the memories of the mornings after late nights spent in Ilya's apartment. He hates already feeling nostalgia for the person standing right in front of him.

Despite his own plan, Sasza purses his lips. "I would like that very much, yes."

"Do you need more time to get ready?"

"I do not, no."

Ilya lets one hand go, but Sasza tightly grips the other, holding it for a few breaths. He hates how he doesn't want to let go. But they do, if only to help each other get their shoes back on. They leave the townhouse. Like a chauffeur, Ilya opens the passenger-side door and lets Sasza inside his sleek, modest autocoupe. Luggage lines the entire back seat, leaving a small window with which to see the back.

Sasza does not lock his front door.

BEFORE PULLING OVER TO the Palace, Ilya takes the autocoupe down a more secluded road where Ilya sucks Sasza off one last time. They share a final, cum-soaked kiss in the shadows of trees elongated by a too-early sunset. It's the secrecy of it that makes Sasza's heart race, and the care Ilya takes to make sure Sasza looks presentable afterwards. It's the service of their relationship that made Sasza want it more than most others. It saddens him to permanently let it go.

When Ilya stops at the Palace to drop him off, Sasza kisses Ilya one last time and exits the car. They gave each other a small salute as a formal farewell. Sasza swears Ilya mouthed the words, "Good-bye, comrade," but it could have been his imagination.

Escaping from the cold, a guard lets Sasza in. He notes the exposed line of muscle tight in their neck and draws his eyes along the taut flesh. To assign the spell's activation point, Sasza pinches his wrist with his index finger and thumb. With a whisper like an inhale, he casts with a syllable from the Odonic dialect of the protolanguage, pricking himself. The guard shudders, slapping his neck as if bitten by an insect. This advanced technique that should be far beyond Sasza's youth connects injuries to other injuries. As long as Sasza has a means to hurt himself, he can eliminate all the guards—and there is plenty of glass to be shattered at a Ball such as this one.

This violent spellcraft works with the same swiftness of a cat extending its claws. Sasza connects all the guards, planting invisible crystals between them to spur forth in a chain not unlike thorns on a vine. It only takes one trigger to activate each subsequent prick. Assigning his wrist as that activation serves another purpose too, in that his own blood spills as the substrate for his own vicious transformation.

The darkest of magical arts are those in which injury begets other injuries without the afflicted party knowing what hit them.

Worries hang on his shoulders like a cloak. Before Władysław, Sasza had never killed another person. Here, he is preparing a spell to eliminate several dozen, with more lives to be claimed through his transformation.

For a moment, he pities the guards. Some had no say in their service. He hopes their lives were worth the years given to a crown most ungrateful.

After ensuring he has marked each guard for death, he makes a final stop at the doors to Lady Świetlana's bedroom. He should greet her and check on her status. But him being the last person she talks to would raise suspicions that she knows something about the forthcoming massacre, that she's connected to him in a violent conspiracy in addition to a rumored romance.

Instead of knocking, he casts the most powerful version of the silencing ward he can muster A headache swarms his head—he hasn't used this much magic since his university days. It takes a sequence of snaps before he feels the spell's weight, a strange warmth that can be attributed to the pipes going through the walls and floors. He knows better but hopes no one else notices the temperature difference.

As if they had interacted, Sasza bows to Her Soon-to-be-Majesty's door and departs.

Night falls shortly after. In what the days before the Solstice would be considered the early afternoon, aristocrats from across the Odonic Empire occupy the Palace like an infestation. Though he knows he should restrain his baser urges, he thinks of them as potential meals. There will be hundreds of pockets of fresh blood flitting past him. With each greeting and introduction, all Sasza knows is how he will drink in excess—and how feeding begets lust, and that lust begets more feeding. For his own conscience, it's best he makes his way through the crowds of attendees like a specter, hyper aware of the meals flowing through the aristocracy's veins.

Music flourishes throughout the main ballroom. The band plays stately dance numbers meant to liven the spirits of the Ball's attendees. Instead, it drowns out the worst of their banal commentary and trivial gossip. Each conversation seems to flit between upcoming marriages, art sales, festivals—nothing about the plight of the people they claim to protect in their inaugural vows or in the creeds held as sacred among each family. None of the last names whose crests decorate entire mansions have a thing to say about the people starving in their streets, constantly striking, in so much strife that their own Emperor decided that war will cure their ills.

Sasza passes through the crowd like a ghost made of pleasantries, weaving his way through aristocracy fluttering amongst each other with the same irritating singular focus as a swarm of insects. He searches across this elegant rabble, making sure he knows precisely where Lady Lewońska will be. She's the next in terms of his slaughter priority. It's a shame she attends the Ball with the youth who ran into him at Laurencja's clinic. He doesn't know their name and isn't sure if that rotten branch spawned from the same trunk. The only aristocracy to be spared are those not attending, either because they declined invitations early or Her Highness Świetlana worked the sorcery of social niceties to steer them away from the event altogether.

The ghouls here would rather wage a war to ease their own paranoia and jealousy instead of addressing the sources of unrest directly.

The bell tolls nine times. Sasza finds Emperor Iwan and Empress Gita and follows them up the double staircase. Thick trains of crimson lace snake along the railings, reflecting the chandeliers lit like starlight. The ceiling mirror brightens the room like day, warming the space with pale orange lights from the candelabras nestled between the columns.

In perfect elegance, the emperor has his hair slicked back, his mustache curled to high heaven. Like a man who earned his place by birth and not by merit, he wears the form fitting Odonic general's uniform, seen as the general of the entire country. The man botched one civil war already—he doesn't deserve the regalia.

Emperor Iwan angles his chin towards the microphone at his podium. Though his voice booms across the ballroom, Sasza doesn't pay attention to the address. The only details he catches are how Emperor Iwan will save the Odonic Empire from itself, declaring the New Year 1918 as the Year of Reunification. Applause erupts as thunderously as possible through silk gloves and elegant hands holding delicate wine flutes. He goes on about the potential for recovering national pride, but all Sasza thinks about is the imperial ignominy. So many lives and resources wasted, and for what? Though humans can fight back against vampires, they are largely outclassed in weaponry. He tries not to shudder at the concept of the mass development of undead blades for regular soldier use. It's not how it should be.

When the applause dies down from some other declaration, Emperor Iwan turns to Sasza and places a ringed hand low on his back. "Come, Sasza, let us rejoin the others."

Sasza leads them downstairs, trying to keep his shoulders squared and head held high despite the shame. A servant approaches Emperor Iwan as soon as they land among the crowd. His Majesty takes two flutes of bubbling wine while Empress Gita declines.

"Please, my dear Sasza Czarnolaski," Emperor Iwan says, offering a flute. "Join me in a toast."

"Your Majesty, I would be honored." Sasza lies, pinching the delicate crystal between his fingers.

"I realize I neglected to honor the son of my late Magician, Władysław Czarnolaski." He raises the glass to cheek-level. "To friends and partnerships, old and new."

Sasza had not noticed the omission, but he is grateful for it. He nods. Their glasses clink. As Sasza sips, the bubbles feel grainy going down his throat. So much blood around him, and not a drop to drink.

"It is a shame that Lady Świetlana could not join us tonight, Your Majesty."

"Ah, yes. Well, she isn't alone—she has her Magical Advisor, Ute, keeping her company. I remember her telling me about that girl when she was younger. Familiar old faces have a calming effect, or so I've found."

Sasza nods, finding nothing calming about all the annual faces present in this ballroom glittering red and gold. "Here's to hoping she does not regret her lack of attendance. She worked very hard on the decorations and invitations, Your Majesty."

"Oh, I'm sure she would much rather be clear headed tomorrow morning, unlike some of her peers." Their eyes look at the aristocrats ruddy from alcoholic excess, guffawing at some nicety or rumor, Sasza doesn't care which.

"Be sure to remember to supplement your drink with water, Your Majesty."

The emperor laughs, though Sasza doesn't know the joke he made. The music swells, but deep beneath the symphony of wintertime gaiety, Sasza hears the faint stomping of feet and the chorus of disgruntled proletarians approaching the Palace. Ilya had promised Sasza a gathering, he didn't think they'd direct their anger so undoubtedly towards the aristocrats drunk on festive cheer and their own opulence.

Gazing upon him, Sasza is aware, for the first time, of just how small Emperor Iwan Iwanowicz is. He barely rises to the height of Sasza's flat chest. Despite his perceived stature and rank, that's all he is: a diminutive collection of flesh, bones, and blood. Chosen by a "divine" right more mass delusion than anything set in stone. That ritual would soon be interrupted—a privilege denied by mortality and sterility.

The shouting grows louder in Sasza's sensitive ears. He looks out of the frosted windows gazing upon the back gardens. In the distance, he sees the dim sparkling lights cast by magic and makeshift torches. The throng might not have proper weaponry. Their rally will not matter if most of them wind up dead at the distant guards' hands.

None of the aristocracy present tonight have any idea the deluge of disappointment and rage coming their way.

Sasza squeezes his flute, hard enough that the glass breaks. Shards shatter and Sasza presses a jagged edge into the designated spot on his wrist. With a snap, the spell activates. A dark, steaming crystal of magic sinks into the spot. His body trembles with the spell working through him, sibling shards of magic penetrating the guards' thick necks.

Someone screams as the guards groan, blood gushing from the wounds. Their hands don't move fast enough to staunch it. Emperor Iwan notices Sasza's own blood loss.

"Aleksander, it seems you have been injured."

Blood seeps into the satin weave of his dress shirt. "I'll be fine."

"Who did this? Guards! Guards!"

There will be no guards to call. Shrieks echo from inside, not before bodies slam into the windows lining the ballroom. Sasza's head aches with their echo rattling the glass. Their weapons are improvised, woven together from homemade objects. Plenty of axes, sure, but also knives strapped to broom handles.

Proletarian shouts and aristocratic screams drown out the interrupted music. The musicians, with a perfect sense of self-preservation, abandon their posts, dashing towards the exit. Frantic aristocrats attempt to follow them, yelling and crying, but it won't be of any use—Sasza had the servants lock all the doors save a few workers' entrances for their own escapes. Other shouts come from deep within the Palace's entryways.

The besieging throng seems much larger than the disenfranchised congregation left out in the snow.

Emperor Iwan grabs onto Sasza's shoulders, shouting, "Please, you must protect us. Save me from them!"

The terror mapped on the older man's wrinkled face hardens Sasza's cock. He doesn't need Ilya's false promises. *This* is faith; *this* is power. He glares down at his former liege and says, "No."

Sasza's lips engulf his wrist, the cloying blood spurting into his own mouth, dribbling down his tongue. The transformation begins.

Sasza's bones burn, breaking and pushing through his skin. His human-looking body explodes in a wash of meat and blood, tearing through fine clothing he will not regret destroying. From this ruin, his form reconfigures. Three pairs of appendages reticulate from the shards of his broken ribs. An exoskeleton envelops his skull, his upper palate cracking and elongating into a tubular proboscis, while his jaw remains human and exposed like any other bestiapir. He groans as his eyes swell and split into the multi-paneled insectoid eyes of a flying bloodsucker.

Color drains from his vision. The darkest colors become deep black as night. The lighter ones feel like staring into a lantern. He can make out the shapes of those around him.

Along his back, the skin flays, stretched thin like crepe dough, the veins expanding and connecting to each other, a pair of ribs siphoned to form the sturdy outline of a mosquito's wings. The remaining bones grow and bend into the scaffolding of his thorax and abdomen, his human muscles and organs melting and meshing into something more appropriate to the female of that bestiapir species—including the small restructuring of Sasza's chest to be softer and rounder. His hands clutch his small breasts, despite the familiar weight of his human cock heavy against his new dipteran lack of skeletal structure. It swells with lust—for blood, for self-preservation.

The destruction of his human form leaves Sasza ravenous.

Sasza no longer hears the screams. Sound escapes him entirely, replaced by warmth and the change in air pressure, rising as the guests' terror intensifies. His head drowns in the scent of blood, sweet and bitter, meaty and sharp like vodka.

There is even more to feed on beyond the windows. He must have access to it. He bends forward and calls upon the strength in his nascent wings. They flap violently, unleashing a buzzing howl that has the remaining aristocrats bent over, covering their ears. The giant membranes flutter, cutting through the air, until the deafening buzz blows out the pane of glass. It breaks into glitter splintering and sprinkling upon those outside like a blessing.

Boots stomping on glass, they rush inside like a flood with the same roar and natural fervor.

Sasza ignores the violence happening elsewhere in the room and focuses on his first dish: Emperor Iwan.

His pale, aristocratic skin glistens with Sasza's gore like the aftermath of back-alley fellatio. Emperor Iwan's fear radiates from him, though he can already detect the briny blood which promises to sate Sasza.

His front legs have claws like fingers. He bends forward, grabbing the emperor by the shoulders. The old man, the supposed father of the Odonic Emperor, does not fight. He remains as still as he had been standing. A disappointing end to a disappointment of a despot.

Sasza plunges his insect's feeding needle between Emperor Iwan's slacked jaw, forcing it deep into his bowels. It pierces muscles, organs, and veins. A slurry of smashed foodstuff and acid irritate his tip, but he pokes, and he prods until blood surges up his rivulets and into his belly. For Sasza's hollow stomach long deprived of a feast or indulgence, this well-fed man is but an aperitif.

Sasza tosses aside the Emperor's drained body. He cannot see enough features to determine where Empress Gita might have gone off to. He reaches for the next closest person. He teeters on his newly formed limbs, entangled in bodies crushed in the bestiapir's sudden appearance. So much blood spilled in carelessness.

Once he drains his second mouthful, he lowers his nose to slop up the mess. He drinks like he's never drunk before, sucking up more food. He feels nothing in his stomach yet; this monstrous form has gone decades without any sustenance. For the first time in its existence, it feeds.

And feeds.

And feeds.

The buzzing from his wings stuns prey as he grabs for them. His insect appendages catch on other people, crushing skulls, severing spines. Sasza eats like the vampiric equivalent of a starving man at a salon, stuffing his mouth with snacks in lieu of a proper meal. It's a degenerate sort of hunger. Pleasure blooms through overconsumption.

Magic pops and flashes against his body, but it's no use. He leaves alone the figures wearing tattered clothing carrying sharp objects. It's the overdressed he wants. The proletariat raise their arms and once again the pressure mounts. They think the monstrous creature in their midst has their interests at heart.

All Sasza knows is to follow the rhythm of his feasting. The snatch, the pierce, the ingest, followed by another buzz to grab, to stab, to devour. This gluttony belongs to a bestiapir.

Frenzied proletarians smash the tables and some even squirrel away the treats baked for people who have appointed themselves as betters. They have no respect for the bodies. They yank out viscera and decorate the shiny wood floor with this butchery. Sasza's own delirium pulls them into his all-encompassing spell. It's the effect some bestiapiry have on others, and Sasza relishes this control.

Enough blood and wine have sunk into the flora's soil and vase water to drown the petals, forcing these unnatural blooms to wilt like they should have given the winter. It's only righteous. It's revenge in its purest form.

The beast's instinct lifts its hold on Sasza when he recognizes the vague form of Lady Lewońska. She hadn't had a chance to escape with her last remaining child—they brawl with a member of the rally. She casts magic at the people she claims to want to elevate with war. Pathetic.

Her skinny hand tightly grips her offspring's, who seeks another way out despite the other aristocracy bumping into them. With enough pressure the doors burst open, and the air expands. They dart out, only to be met with the proletarians who had infiltrated this deep into the Palace. Lady Lewońska runs out into the opposite hallway. The one leading directly outside.

She *cannot* escape.

Stomping on the ground, unsure how to fly, he chases after them. His enlarged exoskeleton pummels through bodies, knocking them over, perhaps killing them. The wasted blood no longer matters—there's no room in his body for more. His humanity reaches for him, passing a baton inflamed in vengeance.

If any aristocrat survives the night, it will *not* be Lady Lewońska.

They reach the entryway with the fountain—she's not far away enough to make a successful exit. With his remaining strength, Sasza buzzes his wings one final time. He's weakening, sluggish with the blood flowing through his body. The vibrations, however, have their intended effect. Lady Lewońska trips forward, skirts flying up and exposing now-bloodstained white hosiery. She slides down the room, her head almost colliding with the fountain's basin. Her progeny doesn't tumble after her, but crouches and tugs at her arm. Their mouth moves, trying to get their mother up with their waning strength. Fear bleaches their face as Sasza approaches.

Excess blood flushes all the other liquids out of his body. Piss drips from his insect's abdomen. His legs puncture the bodies littering the hallways prevent him from slipping. He's not sure who is crushed under his legs.

The need to feed abates, slowly. Sasza feels the enclosure of the insect's body slipping away. One more dish; one more meal and he can let go.

"Run!" She shouts at her child. She flips over and stares up at Sasza, the fear on her face almost as delicious as the blood splattered on his jaw and sluicing down his gullet. "Guards! Guards!"

There are no guards, not anymore. No hope of rescue.

Color returns slowly to Sasza's vision. He sees the red hair the same shade as the blood soiling Lady Lewońska's clothes. The youth's words come out muffled, still under pressure, which squeezes into Sasza's head—he's had too much. Lethargy burrows deeper and deeper, fatigue replacing the intensity and inertia of transformation. The articulated appendages crack and snap, chitin flaking like winter snow.

Harnessing the last of his control over the bestiapir body, he lifts his heavy head and plunges the proboscis directly into Lady Lewońska. It punctures her sternum, rupturing the meat of her heart. Her blood tastes foulest of all, even worse than Laurencja's dying patient. Regardless of the awful taste resulting from a lifetime of prejudice, he drinks. And drinks. And drinks.

His neck goes slack as her skin turns draining's ashy pale. Her warmongering at rest finally. As is the bestiapir body. It collapses. The opposite of starving, but wanting to take advantage of the free, flowing blood, Sasza darts his humanoid tongue along the ground. One last taste for the memory of this gluttonous indulgence. Urine's salt mixes with the darkening, squishy clots.

It's the most degenerate Sasza has ever felt.

The offspring only now releases their mother's hand. The long-sleeved, floor-length gown in some dark color does not suit them at all. Their pink-stained lips open and close, unsure what sound to unleash.

Sasza angles his head towards them, showing them his human-like chin. His larynx has not returned from the transformation. He lost access to his own voice. Even if he could speak, his head spins too much to contemplate the shapes of words and syllables. He lies on the ground, his reticulated legs flattened and splayed like a star. Even if he wanted to, he cannot lift himself. Silently, he begs this child of Lewoński to run away. Sasza definitely did not kill all the aristocrats—the proletarians helped, but some might have gotten away.

He eliminated those who mattered. There's no more work for him to do.

The youth stands on trembling legs. A small trickle of blood comes out of both their ears. They pick up their skirt and run out the Palace's unguarded main entrance into the solstice's deepest night.

Sasza feels like he's going to burst. Too much blood in his stomach. Too much blood flowing through this body much larger than his humanoid form. He has no sense of how much time has passed. He doesn't remember how long the transformations lasted in his own childhood.

The exoskeleton slips off him like a damp cloak, sliding off him like shower grime. He falls hard on his stomach and cock now engorged with too much blood and not enough lust. Ligaments rewind to his two hundred and six expected bones. His chitin cracks and molds itself once again into his familiar, lean musculature. The wings wrap around him like skin, enveloping his more familiar, bipedal shape.

Sasza returns to himself naked, covered in filth. Shouts, screams, and a drunken rendition of an old Odonic anthem echo somewhere far off. He doesn't know if anyone is coming for him, either to murder him or collect him and send him for healing. He feels pathetic for not being sure which one he'd prefer.

Sasza begs his body to move. His muscles are stiff from destruction and momentary disuse. His skin bulges as he attempts to bend his joints. Gore and filth cake him. He needs to leave, but he cannot leave a trail.

The three heads of the Iwanowicz eagle stare down at him as water pours from their beaks. The fountain's trickling liquid sounds like a waterfall. At the fountain's base lay the cored figure of Lady Lewońska. It gives him weak satisfaction to see her finally put down.

He crawls around her, wanting to cry from the balloon-like pressure squeezing his bones and muscles. He worries if he hits a sharp edge, he will pop. This thought escapes him as he pulls himself over the fountain's rim and plunges himself in the freezing pool. He gently spins, submerged, staining the water with blood, salt, and other excrement. Rubbing his hands, the filth leaves his skin. The makeup he put on earlier in the day definitely stains his face, but there's no one around to see it.

Having bathed like a bird after a springtime shower, he sits on the rim, staring at his bloated stomach and distended cock. There's an obvious solution to that one. Swallowing his pride, Sasza tugs at his prick, finding only some personal relief, but the erection remains.

His seed adds to the fountain's fetid cocktail for unfortunate housekeepers and staff to clean later.

Sasza's head throbs and looking at the water makes him sick. Blood mixed with stomach acid squirts into the back of his throat. He looks at his wrist, now healed through consumption, but stained with the reminder of the first of his crimes tonight. There's either no more magic in him or no more energy to summon it—the outcome looks the same. Sasza lacks the strength to cast himself away from the Palace.

He cranes his neck to see that Lewońska's last offspring left the main entrance open. Sasza reaches for a clear patch of water and splashes it onto his face, enough to wake himself up. One leg lifts over the other, and he stands, impressing even himself. He forces himself to walk. His feet drag beneath him, struggling to carry his satisfied, swollen body.

He never remembered this front atrium being so far from the door.

Snow greets him eventually, slowed to a gentle dusting. Emergency bells toll. The Iwanowicz ruling class lies in ruin at the hands of citizens who know that they deserve so much better. Far in the distance, the Military rallies, racing to the Palace with the urgency of having mobilized too late.

Sasza's head swims in a fog of satiety, exhaustion, and excess as he stumbles off into the night, in search of his own bed and the one place he can remotely consider home.

NINE

UTE WAKES UP IN what must be a dream, sprawled atop the only person she's ever wanted. Świetlana's chest rests on top of her head while Ute's arm is draped over Her Highness's soft stomach like a cat. Both are naked and wrapped in sheets gently smelling of yonic musk and diffuse sweat. It's cozy. It's unprofessional.

It being the first morning after the solstice, Ute awakens with her body's natural rhythms instead of with sunlight peeking through soft drapes. There is none. It is as dark as night. There is no sound coming from the other side of the door—the Ball must have come to an end. Ute shivers.

"If you're cold," Świetlana mumbles. "Feel free to take any of my sweaters. Top drawer."

Ute cannot tell if Her Highness had fallen asleep at all or if her not-so-gentle stirring awakened Świetlana. She slides out from beneath Świetlana's ample breasts. She ruffles her short hair to undo the previous night's nest. Her smallclothes lay on the floor where she had left them; she steps into them and grabs the first piece of warm wool she can find. Despite Her Highness's small frame being similar to Ute's, the clothing hangs off her. It's a not-so-subtle reminder of the difference in their breast size. Her face burns at the thought.

One-handed, she ties the sleeve into a knot—her flesh is still sore from wearing the arm when she didn't need to. She doesn't know what she needs. Her Highness has her own bathroom, but that's not it. Ute's stomach makes no indication of hunger. The absolute quiet of that bedroom feels strange. Even in Korona, there are ravens and crows screaming at each other all through the night and into the dawn. But not on the Palace grounds this morning. It's unnerving; she'd seen wildlife flying around before.

Her eyes catch on the door. Something must have been done to manifest such disquieting serenity.

Not putting on pants or tights, Ute approaches the entrance. The preternatural silence could just be her imagination.

But when the lock clicks, she's met with the haggard face of General Oktawia Kwiatkowski. The lights have not come all the way on in the Palace halls, but even then, deep shadows carve beneath their bloodshot eyes. Exhaustion or crying, Ute cannot tell the difference. The general isn't even in their proper uniform. Their trousers suggest a long night at home, and the coat is not buttoned. No regalia. No decorum.

"Finally, we got that door open." General Kwiatkowski straightens. "Miss Myśliwska, is Świetlana Iwanowicz with you?"

Ute tilts her head to the side. "Indeed, why wouldn't she be?"

"Thank the heavens." They lean back to shout at someone out of view. "We have the first born."

"What is going—" Świetlana groans upon sitting up and flicks the switch on her bedside lamp. She gasps upon realizing her bare breasts hang out on display for the Director of the Secret Service. She yanks her blanket to cover herself. "Pardon my nakedness, General. Whatever is going on?"

"Please get dressed, Your Highness." The general blushes red as wine. "There has been a terrible accident."

"Accident?"

"I'll explain everything after you're decent." The door closes quickly, leaving Ute and Świetlana alone.

Her Highness's amethyst eyes go wide, her lips kept in a tight straight line. It's an expression Ute cannot read—she's never seen it on herself or on anyone else. It's either fear, horror, or something else entirely. As advisor—as friend—Ute should help Her Highness dress and collect herself.

"Can I get you anything, Your Highness?" Ute says, deferring to formality.

Świetlana nods, barely perceptibly.

"Where can I find your small clothes? Do you want a robe?"

Her fingers run through her tangled, tousled black hair. "Just...pass me my nightie from the floor. Any sweater is fine."

Ute does as she's told. Clothes get tossed onto the bed, and Świetlana dresses in the dim light. Neither one of them says a word to the other. Ute briefly debates asking Her Highness to help her reattach the prosthetic, but decides on leaving it behind. She doesn't think her metal arm will be of much use in whatever the general wants to discuss. Instead, she puts on her shoes while Świetlana slides her socked feet into a pair of boots more suited for tromping around snow-laden grounds than exploring her own home. Ute reserves her judgment. Whatever emotion courses through Her Highness is either a performance or conceals something darker.

"Let them back in, Ute," Świetlana says, sitting on the floor against the side of her bed, hugging her knees, ankles crossed to preserve her own modesty.

Ute lets the general into the room. Their cheeks glisten as if from crying. Fear cinches their shoulders so they become like earrings.

"I'm not even sure where to begin, Your Highness," General Kwiatkowski says.

"Something clearly went wrong with the Ball," Her Highness responds, eyes staring straight at the highest ranking person within the Odonic Military.

"How do you—"

"It's all over your face, General Kwiatkowski. I'd appreciate it if you got straight to the point. All I'm imagining is the worst."

"It…it is, the worst. Your parents are dead. As are most of the people who attended. And many of the civilians who stormed the Palace last night."

"Many *what*?" The question comes as sharply as her inhale. "What do you mean by civilians? Shouldn't they have been kept far away from here? Didn't they have their own event?" It's then she gasps. "They did not…"

Ute doesn't understand. "Were you supposed to organize that?"

"No, it wasn't my responsibility. At least…no one *told me* it was my responsibility."

"Did you organize it in years' past?"

Świetlana shakes her head. "I had only been in charge of the Solstice Ball. Not the Citizen's Winter Festival as well. That had been my mother's charge. In the wake of Lord Czarnolaski's passing, she must have forgotten." She lowers her shoulders in a measured exhale. "Are you telling me they got revenge for a canceled party, General Kwiatkowski?"

"It might look that way, though I would like to give our citizens more credit than that." The general swallows hard, a lump bouncing in their throat. "The Ball can only be described as a massacre, Your Highness."

"Has there been any cleaning done?"

"No, Your Highness. We…don't even know where to start."

Świetlana sits back low and stands. "I need to see it." Before General Kwiatkowski protests, she adds, "You're not stopping me. I must witness whatever ills befall the ones I'm meant to rule, whether aristocrat or proletariat."

Mere minutes from hearing about her parents' deaths, and Świetlana already conducts herself as a leader. Ute fears for her. Surely, Her

Highness's own perception of stalwart grace will crumble the moment she sees the bodies. Many can hardly handle reading about it, let alone witness it.

General Kwiatkowski concedes. "It's best to do this on an empty stomach, Your Highness."

Świetlana rises, shoulders pulled back. She looks brave and determined, but Ute cannot help but admit this posturing serves as a stark reminder of just how petite Her Highness is. Ute could never be described as tall, but she's taller than her liege. General Kwiatkowski angles their head down to speak to them. They are the true adult among the three of them. They had witnessed what became of the Empire after the civil war with the full maturity of someone who had seen enough and can apply the proper context.

Ute cannot say the same for either herself or Świetlana.

General Kwiatkowski escorts them down the hall. The eerie quiet pervades. No staff shuffle about. No aristocrats wander the corridors, discussing diplomacy and politics in whispers others can hear but whose specifics are impossible to decipher. There is not a single other person until they stop at the fallen body of a guard at the top of the stairs leading to the residences.

They lie on their back, eyes rolled back, and discolored sclera pointed up at the molded ceiling. The pool of blood around their head has seeped deep into the carpet, poured out from a hole on the side of their neck. The wound is precise and measured. The work of an expert, someone who knows human anatomy.

"Every guard stationed last night has been found like this."

"*Every*?" Świetlana's breath comes shallow. She likely has not seen a dead body before.

Neither has Ute, but the Military Academy tries to prepare their students and future soldiers for that inevitability. The first of their courses are readings of memoirs and accounts of famous battles. Not the versions censored and defanged in order to entice the gentler youth to matriculate into the military. These promises of grace and heroism all in the name of protecting the Empire worked on Ute. Even though the Academy had a pragmatic approach to death, discussion of it still came framed in glory. Those who survived had made a virtuous sacrifice of their own sanity. Some of the accounts of those afflicted with soldier's distress still haunt Ute.

The way dead bodies blurred together after a battle, forming a rotting heap under which there might still be survivors.

The way one feared approaching mangled corpses due to an irrational concern of their rising again.

The way sometimes the seemingly-deceased were abandoned because no one knew they were hanging on to life by a frayed thread.

The way it was never advised to fight a war in the winter, for the rivers carry icebergs of decomposed bodies throughout the land once spring's thaw arrives, poisoning fields and streams far away.

She understands those feelings of acute disgust and duress as she stares down at the murdered guard. Who had they been? Did they know that they paid the highest price for their service, keeping watch over an aristocracy who had no knowledge of even their name? Who may have also lost their lives that evening? Thankless work that will at least warrant them a state funeral for a sacrifice they did not knowingly make.

"Before we can continue, Your Highness, I implore you to reconsider wanting to see what remains of the Solstice Ball."

Świetlana glances at General Kwiatkowski and then goes back to staring at the dead. "What kind of Emperor would I be if I feared death?"

"It might be too soon to speak ill of the fallen, but you'd be just like any other Iwanowicz, Your Highness, if you went back to your room right now and let the Military take care of it." There is nothing respectful about the frankness in their tone. Ute's heart pounds thinking of the unequivocal way that the Iwanowiczes ruined their own legacy through their haphazard rule. It's not a truth she ever wanted to confront, considering she had pledged her entire life and body to their service. But it's neither for the family nor for the Empire itself that she gave up her arm. It's for the heir, who is the only thing stopping the Empire from falling to utter political ruin.

"Then I'll be someone worthy of more respect," Świetlana replies. "Let's go on."

They reach the main stairwell and make their descent. The silence continues. The Palace's hollowness makes Ute shiver despite the heat hissing through the pipes. Without any noise to latch onto, aside from the steady patting of their soles against the carpeted floor, the smell that permeates the stairwell infects their heads. Putrid, festering, malodorous vapors weave their way into their mouths and noses. General Kwiatkowski produces kerchiefs for themself and Świetlana to cover their noses. Not for Ute. She presses the back of her wrist into her mouth. Ute had read descriptions of death's decay, but this stench of unfiltered rot is not something she should ever become accustomed to.

Świetlana steps onto the final landing. General Kwiatkowski catches her as she slips on slick blood. Ute clutches the wooden banister as if it's the only thing that will keep her upright. No description or verified account could have prepared her for the nightmare that is the Palace's main entrance.

The chandelier lights shine bright on the massacre. Red floods the floor and splatters against the unnaturally blooming plants lining the walls and benches. There are bodies—a half dozen, Ute reckons, but the gore makes it hard to tell where one person ends and another begins. Ripped clothes and cored abdomens turn organs out on the skin's wrong side. There's not much hope for any survivors, not with the way sinews and flesh have been torn apart.

Ute's memory of having a right arm burns, as if seeing these injuries reminds her of the day she lost her own limb. Despite the rush of light-headedness, she stays standing.

Świetlana's breaths come heavy. Her shoulders rise with much effort between her inhales. Her Highness was not prepared; there was no way *to* prepare.

Without saying a word, Her Highness steps further into the antechamber, sliding one foot over the other against the stained marble floor as slippery as the ice covering the Żyła. The streaks suggest violent death and panic while the victims bled out. Ute does not want to identify the smears of blood mixed with brackish brown.

What puzzles Ute is the filth in the waters of the otherwise pristine fountain. Its three beaks are not spilling water. "Was there a body in the fountain? Or has it been removed?"

General Kwiatkowski coughs. "No, there has never been a body. Not one recovered or otherwise."

One of the culprits of this massacre must have bathed in the water. That's the only explanation. But who? There is too much blood and the splatters have been too disturbed to make heads or tails of who passed through this space. Ute purses her lips, unsure if she should say anything.

Świetlana pays no heed to keeping the blood undisturbed. She glides along, looking at the bodies. Yelps come with each frantic inhale of air. Ute knows that Świetlana isn't ready to witness carnage. If these aristocrats passed peacefully through poison, that would be one experience, but this is something else entirely.

She pauses in front of a woman laying on her side. This corpse's arm is draped over her stomach, blond hair stained red with blood. Ute knows she shouldn't, but she wants to cover her exposed breast. The flimsy fabric will do nothing to obscure the hole torn through her bones and her heart. Swords do not rend flesh and bone like this. Neither should magic, but some combat magicians are more aggressive than others. Ute resorted to cleverness and trust in her own swordsmanship, not magical tricks like these.

Staring at this fallen aristocrat, Świetlana's eyes go glassy, brows turning towards contempt.

"Who is this, Your Highness?" Ute asks.

The simple question breaks her trance. "This is Lady Bianka Lewońska, the Minister of the Interior. *Former* Minister of the Interior." Ute knows nothing of the woman. "Let's continue."

All down the hallways, corpses lie with largely the same wounds. Chests gape with the same puncture as on Lady Lewońska, completely impossible by any human-sized weaponry, and with the fallen lying so close together, it can't have been the work of a single being. But given the city's security that night and the lack of news of a siege, there can't have been a battalion here. A siege so violent and so unnoticed is impossible, though Ute admits she had never trained to be a strategist.

There are too many corpses donning civilian clothes and not enough military uniforms. Did the aristocracy cast some magic? Ute assumes some of them might have trained with the Military before, but nothing about the heaps they lie in suggest anything like a defensive.

The silence comes heaviest from the grand ballroom. General Kwiatkowski blocks the entrance with their slumped, broad-shouldered frame. "Are you *sure* you want to see it, Your Highness?"

"Surely, it cannot be worse."

"This is where your parents lie."

"Take me to them."

General Kwiatkowski exhales loudly and steps inside.

The desecration and bloodshed in this room makes the desolation in the hallways seem tame, tidy. The fallen lie among the ruins of a party. The dimmed lights do not show the extent of the damage, but what little the scant glow illuminates makes Ute's stomach churn. These corpses are the descriptions from the memoirs she studied made real. The bodies lay like meat discarded at the butcher's. There is so much blood, both carmine and sticky, and black and caked like tar. And the *smell*. She tucks her face into her sweater's cowl, hoping her own bad morning breath will mask it. No such luck.

Snow wafts through the shattered windows in the faintly rising dawn. Corvids hop on the patio leading to the back gardens, unsure if they should enter or leave. Neither the birds nor the soldiers inside make a sound as they go through the bodies.

It looks like every attendee and every intruder had fallen the night before. What makes bile rise in Ute's throat is how Świetlana's bedroom sits several floors above, and yet the sounds of violence and suffering had not reached them. She wonders how that could have been. As a magician—as *Her Highness's* magician—she should learn how to capture the whispers and echoes of magic long cast. She didn't feel anything in Świetlana's bedroom upon entering last night or leaving this morning. Someone must have warded the bedroom, though it's a forethought too tidy and neat for this slaughter.

What disturbs her more is how little magical residue there is in the ballroom's air. Perhaps the breeze coming in through the windows washed it all away. Ute refuses to believe that no one among the aristocracy fought back. Whatever attacked, there should have been a fight against it.

Instead, corpses lay fallen like columns and broken statues. Blood stains trickle from their ears. Shattered plates and broken glass cascaded into the circular lesions and lacerations marking each of the dead. As the three of them follow General Kwiatkowski to presumably where the Iwanowicz parents lay, Ute notices makeshift weaponry in the hands of some of the civilians. She looks at the windows, and then back at the bodies so she doesn't lose her footing.

The same jagged edges and circular wounds in people's chests and stomachs appear among the severed limbs and through fractured joints.

It doesn't seem mechanical, not to her—there is no system to this violence. It's all haphazard and unintentional. How can carelessness leave this much debris in its wake?

"Here he is, Your Highness," General Kwiatkowski says, listless. "We found your mother's body down another hallway."

"I'll see to her later." Świetlana crouches low to look upon her father's face.

Or, what remains of it. His jaw hangs off his cheeks, connected by flaps of skin. Something had gone down his throat, puncturing his lower stomach. Dark brown mingles with the deep purple. The smell intrudes Ute's nose the second she notices the injury.

His Majesty, Iwan Iwanowicz, lies skewered among his citizens, both aristocratic and civilian. He did not die as he lived—surrounded exclusively by wealth and family. He bled like the rest of them.

Ute cannot read whatever might be going through Świetlana's mind as she inspects her father's remains. Her bottom lip quivers in what could be a sob or what could be self-soothing muttering. There is much to learn about how Her Highness reacts to the unnerving. She doesn't dare reach out for comfort—only if commanded will Ute lay her hand on Świetlana.

The sight of the destroyed ruler breaks Ute's heart. He should have been celebrating the turning of a final season. This ball should have been one of joy, not one that ended in lives ruined. She swallows back rising sick as she thinks of the staff who will have to clean the mess afterwards. It might be easier to sequester the ballroom and simply leave it as a memorial for the emperor and his allies rather than attempt to bring it back to its former sparkle.

None of these decisions are hers to make, but this grim reality hurts to acknowledge. For all they know, there is no longer anyone left to rule the Empire, except for Iwanowicz's only child.

"Are you going to blame the Vampire States for this as well?" Świetlana's eyes are the size of raw gemstones as she glares at General Kwiatkowski. "Are you *positive* this violence didn't come from within the Empire?"

Ute had read the reports of the aftermath of the Jackiewicz Incident. Charred bodies, disemboweled, dismembered, decapitated, and strewn about throughout Daszek like the refuse the morning after a riotous festival. She had heard rumors of who was to blame. Some whispered about the Kingdom, others murmured that somehow it had been the aristocrats themselves, and some shouted that it must be something else entirely. Not a single person, rag, or outlet mentioned vampires or their States. She didn't form her own opinion—that was for the version of her that would have confidently joined the Emperor's Chosen. Her job now is and has been to protect Her Highness. It unsettles Ute to her core that she has no direction on what to protect Her Highness from and how.

A faked malady and a night spent responding to lust's throes had spared them both from suffering this same fate.

"Your Highness, what are you talking about?" General Kwiatkowski asks, brows knit in concern.

"My father wanted to reunite the Empire." Świetlana's voice quakes as she speaks, getting louder and louder with each subsequent declaration. "In 1918, he was going to lead a campaign against the Vampire States. Vengeance for the Jackiewicz Incident, he said. Against an unknown enemy. War will not bring them out of hiding. War will not bring us peace."

"Świetlana..."

"These things are happening everywhere across the Empire. I refuse to believe a simple answer that is more bandage than healing."

"Świetlana...did you—"

"I *dare* you to make that accusation, General."

Ute had never imagined this sort of ferocity from Świetlana. It could be grief, it could be something more nefarious, but either way, it introduces an ache deep in her belly that she will need to find a better venue for relieving.

Świetlana does not break her terrible gaze at General Kwiatkowski as she stands. "It's antithetical to everything this Empire had been founded on to think, for a second, that I would betray my father like that, General. He might have been an incompetent ruler and exhibited the worst leadership we had seen in generations, but I will not desecrate his memory so blatantly."

"You're...you're absolutely right, Your Highness. Forgive my transgression."

"Where is Sasza?" Świetlana murmurs as she looks around the bodies, as if any of them can be distinguished without closer inspection. "Did he...did he survive the night?"

It takes General Kwiatkowski a beat to remember the name and title. They clear their throat. "Ah, the Imperial Magician. No, we haven't seen any sign of him. But we reckon a handful of the aristocracy in attendance might have escaped. We did find some survivors."

"Did you now?" Świetlana closes her eyes, squeezing them tightly to let tears roll freely down her cheeks. "Can you leave us for a moment? I would like to be alone with Ute."

The general bows, whistles for the other soldiers and members of the Military Police to exit the destroyed ballroom. The two of them are left among the gore, the twisted bodies, the putrescent smell, and the shattered glass. Ute turns to face Her Highness, who falls forward and grabs onto Ute's shoulders. She tucks her head beneath Ute's chin.

"They're gone, they're all gone," she repeats breathlessly into Ute's chest.

"I know, Świetlana, I know." Ute presses her lips to her barely combed hair. "Whatever you need, Your Highness, that is what I will be."

"I think it's Your Majesty, now." Świetlana hiccups through her new title as she looks at her Magical Advisor.

Most aristocrats would be ecstatic to be granted the highest position in all the Empire. Ute will protect the ruler she gave up the Emperor's Chosen for. "Whatever you need, Your Majesty, that is the role I will take."

"Until we find Sasza, you're my Imperial Magician. Can you do that?"

Ute reaches a hand up to Świetlana's cheek and brushes a tear away with her thumb. "I can do that."

She will serve, just as she intended. She gave up her own flesh to be in service—and fealty—to Emperor Świetlana Iwanowicz, first of her name.

TEN

Since leaving Korona on the evening of the Solstice ball, the Emperor's Chosen traveled several days by carriage to the eastern part of the Empire, a day's train ride from Daszek. The veritable fortress that is their destination had once been the seat of a Vampire State, but the lands had long been relinquished to the Empire. It sat silent, until recent reports came of its shell becoming a music box of blood-curdling screams and crashing magic. No one had investigated, for there was no crime or activity to investigate. The lack of answers after the Jackiewicz Incident, however, made it a job for the Emperor's Chosen.

Captain Łukasiewicz mentions the emperor coming to his own conclusions about the perpetrators of the attack, but she never states those specifics. It's not for Iwona and the others to know. The only instructions for their mission had been to memorize their target's internal layout and to heed the captain's orders.

As night falls on New Year's Eve, the Ninety-Second Regiment of the Emperor's Chosen is to infiltrate a castle. Despite the thick layers of fleece and armor, and the way her nerves set her skin aflame, Iwona shivers. The year's final full moon hangs like a lantern in that crisp, cold, cloudless night, veiling the stars and casting long shadows. Much like this night, the objective is clear: investigate. Return to Korona with any information on the new residents.

The castle rises atop a rocky hill, high above sweeping moors. Trees gnarled and weighed down by snow bend against its thick walls. Two wings embrace a courtyard, connecting to an iron gate several stories high. The Emperor's Chosen forgoes that approach and enters via a gaping maw of jagged stone and broken iron. No one had bothered to repair the damage from battles past. A siege had torn it open, and open it remained.

Captain Łukasiewicz climbs through the opening and extends her hand to Iwona. She takes a step up with the captain's help and offers the same courtesy to the person entering behind her. Only half the Chosen enter this way—the others go through dried out pipes from a sewer system unmaintained. Much like this entrance, Iwona hopes that no surprises greet them either.

The fortress's interior is a similar ruin to the exterior. Worn, decayed carpeting in faded colors cover the stone floors. Cobwebs hang from corners. Dust piles in the angles of the lantern lights and floats in the bright moonlight like glitter. Some form of vermin has chewed holes in the planks and rafters holding up the ceiling. No one can possibly live here. Stale air tickles Iwona's nose. From beneath her mask, she mashes her tongue against the roof of her mouth. The sneeze never comes.

Wordlessly, the group follows Captain Łukasiewicz through these abandoned corridors. Their footfalls and labored, scratchy breathing are the only noises. There are no signs of life, no words, no voices, no screams. Iwona cannot tell if this vacated serenity comforts or disturbs her. Her stomach curdles regardless. Eventually, they find stairs leading a long way down in a spiral. Their feet pat against more threadbare carpeting. Lights appear in equal intervals and high mirrors cast the illumination across the dry, stone walls. They go down and down and down, passing below what could reasonably be the ground floor and into the castle's foundations.

Captain Łukasiewicz stops them, however, with a raised fist. At the very bottom stands a lone soldier in armor Iwona does not recognize. It neither has the deep red of the Empire's tapestries nor the cerulean elegance of the Kingdom. The covering reminds Iwona of the makeshift armor peasants scrape together out of discarded wood and unused wicker. It's not made professionally; she doubts it offers much protection, especially with how tightly it binds to its wearer. Muscles bulge through uneven sections. Skin protrudes, blistering like a wound.

An arrow whizzes past Iwona's ear. It finds its mark in the back of the guard's skull. The force of her fellow Chosen's projectile shoves them into the opposite wall. Iwona's breath hitches. Eliminating potential threats and obstacles is part of the job. She exhales deeply, counting, just like the captain taught them to do on their way out of Korona.

They tip-toe past the body and enter this subterranean dungeon in its pale, candle-glow. Iwona doesn't dare touch the lights—they might be traps. An atrium almost like a reception area with its rows upon rows of matching, broken benches extends before them. Shadows settle in the corners. Water drips and plops. The air reeks of mildew. They make their way across the bumpy, shattered floor under several more archways, descending shorter sets of stairs. It reminds Iwona of the highways cutting through the mountainous sections of the Empire. Especially its length. Iwona has never heard of tombs or dungeons like this one—visitors and mourners are not meant to get lost, and she worries that the Chosen are not likely to find their way back out. Not easily, anyway.

After what feels like an hour, the group stops. Captain Łukasiewicz raises her fist again. The Chosen have reached a blank, stone door with two archways flanking it to the left and the right. Iwona sees shadows dance through the stone rail. This is not music she recognizes. Metal clanging against metal provides a steady, jovial beat. Stomps, growls, and feral shouts echo from below, almost like a party, appropriate for the New Year.

With a sequence of gestures, the captain assigns half the group to go down each archway. Iwona follows her captain, crouching to muffle her footfalls, assuming her thundering heart doesn't give away their location first. No amount of breathing will steady it. Her instructors had warned about the jitters of the first assignment, and Iwona hoped she would be immune. She's only human, and with so much unknown, it's only natural that fear becomes the thing keeping her alive.

No guards stand to overlook the rectangular hall marked with cylindrical columns and dozens of candelabras. The Chosen flatten themselves against the wall and observe. Long, wide steps slope down from the other side of the closed door. At the room's center is a circular panel of light beaming sickly orange rays like a pale dawn against the ceiling. Its glow spreads like a fountain along the walls. Much like the moonlight in the Empire above, it too casts protracted shadows against those revelers flailing and thrashing about with the abandon of small children.

No amount of studying or eavesdropping, however, could have prepared Iwona for these dancing creatures.

She refuses to see humanity despite the familiarity of the limbs. There's definitely a person somewhere at each monster's center—bestiapiry have human-like torsos and jaws, after all. But this is something novel and grotesque. Too many arms connect to too many sets of shoulders and elbows. Not all of them are the same size either. Flesh has also been grafted to create a large bipedal thing, looming and swaying. Each footfall might be their last.

Iwona has never seen anything like these things. The steadier creations resemble neither humans nor bestiapiry, but are, instead, new quadrupedal creatures, piloted by what looks like a single body slotted within the greater flesh construct's back. Their bare chests hunch forward, their hands and forearms molding into the planes of meat into which their hips and legs disappear. Canvas sacks obscure what would be their faces, much like executioners.

The revelers that make Iwona sickest resemble failures of the studier beings. Their chunks of flesh have been spackled on like clay. Multiple heads and sightless eyes make it difficult to determine if each body has a single consciousness. Large, tattered drapes cover the quilt of flesh and sinew that make up each torso. Blood leaks from vessels connected incorrectly and stitches not sewn tightly enough. The masses splatter and hiss against the light's warmth. The smell of sweat and sweetness rises and falls and like a wave.

These are no bestiapiry. These are no vampires. These are not humans. No one present can possibly explain what the fuck it is they're looking at.

One of the Chosen lets out a scream. Iwona lurches silently. It wasn't her, not with how tightly her teeth grind against each other.

The ruckus and revelry stop at once. They did not expect guests. The creatures shriek in unison, chilling bone and shaking the masonry. Their calls come out like a discordant chorus.

"Run," Captain Łukasiewicz groans. There's no time to reprimand. Punishment comes after survival.

Iwona's feet move before her mind has a chance to absorb the situation. Her boots fall upon the ground with loud pattering like heavy rain. Gone is the need for stealth. The primary focus is escape. Iwona almost wants to lose her weapon and its unwieldy weight.

The gnashing of teeth and tearing of flesh suggests the beasts have gotten to someone behind her. It's not Captain Łukasiewicz, and it's not the arrow wielding Chosen chasing close behind them. In fact, they crouch, their bow glowing with the blood activation. They fire off arrow after arrow as they jog backwards. Only a handful of giants lumber after them, unimpeded by the undead weaponry. It breaks something within Iwona that there don't seem to be others like her.

No humans, only unfamiliar beasts.

The long halls become short passageways in their haste. Iwona swallows hard, mustering the stamina necessary to climb all those stairs again. There must be another exit.

Captain Łukasiewicz whistles, finding a side path they had missed on their way in. They round that corner, fly down another set of matching halls with even lower ceilings. Those monsters are too big to crawl through, not without destroying themselves and rendering their forms stiff like the defiled flesh attached to them.

The three survivors pause, bending over and catching their breath. Safe at last. The archer—Mariola—vomits.

Iwona looks away, not wanting to be sick herself. "What was that?" She whimpers. "Captain? What *was* that?"

"A surgeon's attempt at immortality." The three wince as shrieks pierce the hall. It lacks the disarming effect of bestiapiry hollers, much to Iwona's slim relief. "I would promise to tell you everything I know, but my knowledge ends there."

"So, they sent us to check it out for ourselves?" Mariola yells. "Write a report in our comrades' blood?"

"The report is my responsibility and not an immediate one." Captain Łukasiewicz glowers at what remains of the Ninety-Second Regiment. Just the two soldiers, fresh from the Academy. "I refuse to believe this path does not connect to the sewers. Let's hope the others found less violence than we did."

After a few more steadying breaths, the trio collects themselves. They move at a steady clip while the howls die behind them. Iwona has always been steadfast, and never once cried. The pressure around her eyes begs her to, but grief and mourning can happen after survival. The job matters more than sentimentality.

The winding tunnel ends at a singular stone door. Captain Łukasiewicz pushes against it. It doesn't move. Mariola then spots a lever and pulls on it, commanding the slab to open. Captain Łukasiewicz enters the barren hall first.

A set of claws attached to a chain rips through her open mouth and pulls her inside. Iwona chases after her but stops abruptly upon seeing what had taken the captain.

This beast sits on six legs like a malformed spider, swinging several other claw-like weapons held within its many hands. Captain Łukasiewicz's still attached body flaps like a flag. Her skin and armor come apart like stewed meat. Bones slap and snap against the excess flesh. Blood spurts like paint. Other fluids burst, freed from their vessels.

The last death Iwona had witnessed before tonight was quiet: an old relative passing in his sleep surrounded by wilted flowers in his unkempt personal garden. The opposite of this violence.

Iwona gulps. The grief of missing Captain Łukasiewicz's company and counsel will come later. What ignites her terror more than the monstrosity before her is the fact that all the plans and ledgers lived within Captain Łukasiewicz's head. That's gone now. The true purpose for infiltrating this death trap died along with her.

Iwona is no use to anyone dead. Her career with the Emperor's Chosen will not end here.

The enemy flings Captain Łukasiewicz's corpse off its weapon, sending the curved claws towards Iwona. She dodges them. The curved, metal fingers stick in the stone floor. The archer fires an arrow into the extraneous hands like fingers gripping the weapon's handle. Thinking quickly, Iwona scouts the larger atrium for a side entrance. There must be more than one.

An opening with faint orange lights catches her eye. With her captain gone and Mariola trapped behind, engaged in combat, this is Iwona's only chance. Iwona had always been one of singular focus, but she had never been this selfish. Her survival, however, would be the opposite: someone else would find out about these monsters. It's not just about protecting her flesh, but saving the Empire from whatever monstrosities lurk in its abandoned places.

She takes off. Mariola's skirmish ends in squelching followed by silence.

Down this dimmed corridor stands what looks like a regular human guard in that strange wicker armor. They notice Iwona's approach and clumsily jog, swinging their rusted sword. Iwona side-steps away from the feeble attack. Her halberd clips it right through the stomach, breaking the threads and opening its guts. This enemy falls over, dead.

Facing forward, determined, Iwona keeps her eye on the opposite end of this tunnel. There could be side passages; she does not see them. There's barely any time to think. With boots digging into the dusty floor, she books it down the widening corridor. Sweat pours down her face and terror chokes all thoughts that aren't for making it out of here as the last remaining member of the Emperor's Chosen.

Another room identical to the party space appears before her. Instead of continuing on, she skids to a halt. She glances around the upper rafters filled with guards and more abominations. None of them wear recognizable regalia. They all look like peasants and workers; none of the decorum of the Military or any militia. Their weapons are either broken or too big for the wielder. If one drops down, Iwona can maneuver around it. At the Academy, they trained for getting around obstacles and enemies. They trained against each other and veterans; none of the things here have had the same experience.

She sees bows and arrows trained on her. At the Academy, she and her cohort practiced avoiding artillery. She doesn't dally long; her feet pound the ground as she takes off again. Instead of running straight for the exit at the far side, she swerves into a zigzag.

Despite her coordination and her vigilance, an arrow pierces Iwona's stomach. She trips, her toes sliding against the mosaic floor. Careful not to plunge the shaft deeper into her, she falls on her side. The pain sends white flashes in front of her eyes. Her muscles contract to hold her blood in, though her layers grow damp with its spill.

Another arrow clips her cheek, breaking the skin. She rises on shocked, trembling limbs, only then realizing that her halberd flew from her hand. She has no idea when she lost it or where it went. The only thing she has is the pain and the fear of her not making it out alive to warn someone, anyone.

An upright abomination wielding a blade that looks far too large for its singular pair of human arms to swing blocks the escape. Reluctant tears flow. If Iwona is going to go down, it won't be in a way that shames her training. She takes a deep breath. The pain radiates from the wound, but the searing, infected heat melts the tightness in her muscles. She channels her focus into running.

The abomination slices at her. She ducks under it, losing a few split ends in the maneuver, and takes off again, fighting the tightness in her muscles. She sways as she moves, avoiding more arrows as her vision tunnels. Too much terror, not enough strength.

If she's to die, the Odonic Empire's wilderness feels preferable to these dungeons.

Weakening, her gait becomes sloppy. She doesn't lift her leg high enough. Pain shoots through her calf as another arrowhead punctures the strong muscle. She tumbles forward, slapping the ground face-first. She yells as the arrow pushes further inside and the wooden shaft breaks. Mewling groans come out of her lips. Try as she might, she cannot get up. Pain and panic pin her in place. Her arms have lost all control, lying limp at her side.

Metallic blood rising from her throat soaks her teeth and lips. Her body's only movements are violent twitches as arrows enter her legs with the same succession as a mallet tenderizing a chop or a loin. She wants them to stop firing at her—it's obvious she's done for. Sadness born of failure blankets her. Tears pour onto the dusty ground as her vision darkens.

All that will be left of her for the Ogrodnik family is a letter of her disappearance and perhaps a death certificate if enough time passes. No body to bury, no report to send to the Military's highest-ranking officers. All that remains is to find another cohort of students to replace the short-lived Ninety-Second Regiment of the Emperor's Chosen.

ELEVEN

Sasza awakens a week into the new year naked and staring up at the mottled ceiling of his residence. The coarse carpet presses roughly against his bare skin. His head throbs and sloshes like an overfilled pitcher.

Slowly, counting his breaths in and out, he sits up, holding the sides of his head as if his neck is going to snap under its own weight. Pressure builds up in his sternum and erupts from his lips. A sticky, red mass spills out, splashing between his legs. Another carpet will need discarding, and Laurencja can't even help him this time—she must have left Korona by now to take her new post.

He vomits again. It's acrid, gooey, and, most distressingly, still enticing in its flavors. The scant electric lights prove too strong for Sasza's photosensitive eyes, still inflamed by the blood coursing through his vampire body. But he catches his reflection in the mess. He's frightened by how engorged he looks. The puffiness around his eyes reminds him that the aftermath of blood drunkenness is not much different from his understanding of the human hangover. He's taken care of Świetlana the morning after long nights out while at university together. There's no opportunity for her to return the favor.

All three of the adults he'd ask for such assistance are long gone. His father, dead. Ilya, departed Korona. Laurencja, off to the Institute.

The rumbling deep in his stomach comes and goes like ocean waves, part hunger, part nausea. He doesn't want to waste the blood piled before him, like a dog sopping up its own sick. The bestiapir body requires far more blood than his wiry human frame. His stomach stays swollen like a man menstruating. He's afraid to find out how much more vomiting lies ahead of him.

Shaking, he rises to his feet and curses that the bathrooms are upstairs. He wants to shed the blanket of grime and filth from his skin, scrub the evidence of his crimes and make it a problem for Korona's sewers. Unfortunately, he has just about the same balance as a toddler. He lifts one foot, then another, teetering to the bottom of the steps. He makes it up on the first two all right, but then falls forward, scraping his forearms against the coarse carpeting. His delicate, blood-filled skin pops almost like a blister. He shouts as the liquid sprays and drips down the wood. If he continues like this, Sasza will have to burn the entire townhouse down because this level of biohazard raises too many questions.

It takes an eternity, but he makes it into his bathroom. Sasza had forgotten that he had drawn a bath before attending the Solstice Ball. Through the darkness, he sees the still, frigid water and carefully lowers himself. It feels like the pins and needles he's heard from others. He tries casting a warming spell. The stress and strain of casting make him vomit once again. The water stays cold.

Never before had he ever been so drained of magic. He isn't sure if he should build up his stamina for a faster recovery from his bestiapir transformations or if he should vow never to do it again.

Sasza turns on the tap, shoves his hands under the steaming water, and splashes his face. The crusts around his eyes are a jarring texture. Had he been crying? Perhaps from feeling so physically undone, not due to grief. The ones he slaughtered are not worth his tears. His upset towards Emperor Iwan's betrayal has dulled to a simmer. The anger remains enough that it stirs the sickness in his belly. The specific sadness that accompanies loss, however, doesn't come.

Disappointment arrives instead. He spent so many years assimilating to the humans' penchant for quiet violence, he forgot that vampire upbringing encourages bodily harm. The skirmishes between his peers never ended in anything close to death, even under arguments considered heated for childish grudges. Still, bloodshed was to be expected, even for minor slights.

Even Ilya warned of righteous violence, but those words seem wrong to describe Sasza's massacre. What befell the emperor and his closest allies is on a different tier of personal injustice. He meted out appropriate punishment for the major slight that is declaring unnecessary war. It would have caused irreparable harm to the Empire and forced Sasza to choose between vampires and humans. Blood spilled here spared the Odonic Empire's terrain from turning toxic and crimson, unfit for any form of life.

Guilt still nags at him, but it might be nausea and thirst. Sasza sinks below the ice-cold water's surface and sips. Chunks of blood and hardened clots make their way into his throat despite his attempts at filtering them out with his teeth. They taste bitter, like the flavor he's heard attributed to over-steeped tea.

The polluted waters leave similar deposits on his scratched-up knees as he drinks from his cupped hands and creates gentle waves.

As his eyes float shut, a pounding at the door shakes his head with a ferocity that should be reserved for wanted criminals. Technically, that means Sasza—if Świetlana has forgotten to lie, then his life is forfeit. He's too weak to panic, accepting whatever fate comes his way. The pounding stops. Sasza realizes he never locked the front door after passing out.

"Sasza? Are you here?"

Świetlana has come for him. This does not make him any less nervous.

"Oh, fuck!" She must have seen the blood in the entryway. "Are you all right?"

He hears her perfectly despite the cotton in his head. "I'm in the bathroom," he shouts, the effort straining his sticky, clogged throat.

Another lifetime goes by the time Świetlana enters his little, sanguineous sanctuary. Drinking blood enhances his ability to see through the dark; in excess, even more so. He can see the pits that are her eyes and the way winter's winds have wounded her face as clearly as on a sunny day.

"Do you want the light on?" Her hand hovers at the switch.

"No…" His throat is thick and raspy. "I'd love a smoke if you have one."

"Though I don't approve of it, you deserve it."

"Watch out for—"

"It's sticky, what the fuck?" She jumps, disgusted at the red jammy blood now stuck to her imperial stockings. He'll have to offer to clean it for her later.

"I'm…incredibly ill, Your Majesty." He flops his hand over the porcelain lip of the bath. She lights him a cigarette and places it between his wet fingers. Nicotine and ashes have never tasted so delicious in his life.

She takes a seat on the closed toilet. "It's been…several days, Sasza. Is there anyone we can call about this?"

He shakes his head, the water sloshing, but remembers she can't see him. "There was one, but she likely left Korona for a new position. I think I just need—" He throws his head to the side and the contents of his stomach splash into the tub instead of on Świetlana.

She swallows hard, keeping her own sick at bay. "How long have you been like this?"

He spits up a wad. "Since I woke up…however long ago." Sasza licks his lips, hating how much he enjoys the taste.

"Is this a hangover? For vampires?"

It's a hangover for hybrids. He takes another puff. Świetlana coughs at the smoke, waving her arm. "Why are you here? Did you come to arrest me?"

"I would only arrest you, Sasza, if you did something wrong." She laughs, and it comes out as a sob. "My parents are dead, as is the rest of their council. The only aristocracy left alive are those who didn't attend. If the aftermath wasn't so gruesome and so destabilizing, I'd applaud you for a job well done."

"If you had something more subtle in mind, you should have shared it with me, Your Majesty."

"I would hit you if you weren't in so much pain already."

He manages a smirk. "Since you're not here to arrest me, how did you explain why I wasn't among the bodies?"

"Well, you see, I paid off one of the servants to believe that he showed you a secret passage out of the castle, whisking you away to safety. I gave him a medal of honor for that."

This is his first time hearing of this. "Does such a passage even exist?"

"Well, now, it wouldn't be a secret if I answered that, would it?" She sighs. "That's the story I've come up with and put in place. Ute believes it. The whole Empire believes it."

He raises his brows. "You lied to Ute? Why?"

"Because I don't know how she feels or what she knows about you. I also don't know if she's some kind of spy from a dissenting faction of the Military. Which, if you must know, is very pissed at me."

"Oh?"

"I should've thought to eliminate them as well, so I could truly start this entire wretched government completely from scratch. But alas. They're mad that I have no response, that there is no rational explanation for the assassination. It's the Jackiewicz Incident all over again, but I think they're calling this one the Solstice Massacre."

"And what are they saying about it?" Sasza had never been around for the birth of a rumor. It gives him a slight thrill.

"There were some survivors. They cannot speak about it, like soldiers haunted from a war. One person mentioned a bestiapir, but the Military has brushed it off as the ravings of the traumatized."

That's how Sasza would describe it as well if he wasn't the one who became that nightmare. "You're not curious at all about the veracity of these ravings?"

"I would…" She hiccups. It surprises Sasza that she might have tears left to shed. No sobs come. "I would prefer not to know, actually. I don't need to be burdened with the knowledge of its execution—that way, no one will suspect me. Or suspect *us*. So, it remains a legend, a mystery. One that isn't mine to solve because we also haven't heard from the Emperor's Chosen since the New Year. Did you have anything to do with that?"

Sasza shakes his head as if she can see him. "I thought they had left Korona on another assignment."

"And you had *nothing* to do with that?"

"Of course not. They barely told me anything about the attack at Daszek—why would they tell me anything about their active missions and assignments?"

"You have a point." Świetlana lets out a shuddering breath. "It's all a mess, Sasza. Rule of the Odonic Empire falls entirely on my shoulders with no support but dozens of conspiracy theories. I need you to understand—I cannot do anything without you at my side."

"Well, with me at your side, you averted a civil crisis." He takes another drag. "Congratulations, Your Majesty." Smoke billows from his lips like a dragon.

"The problems have only just begun, unfortunately. Obviously, not right now, but I'm going to need your help. I need to rebuild the council, but I do not want it to only consist of nepotism-rotted elites who think they have earned spots as decision makers because of their lineage. But I cannot determine their qualifications all on my own. There's where you come in—spymaster."

He can intercept letters, eavesdrop, and threaten. It's familiar work. It's terrible work, but it's what Sasza excels in. The title also suits him much better than Imperial Magician ever could. "Will that be all, Your Majesty?" His eyes close, and he cannot imagine he has more sleep left in him.

"For now, yes. I won't wear you out much further." She stands. "Will you be all right? I'm going to tell everyone that you're on medical leave. I will come collect you when you're well enough. Not when *you think* you are well."

He smirks. He appreciates her concern. He is a glutton for work and performance, and she sees right through it. With the jelly that is his bones and his body, Sasza admits that Her Majesty is correct in that he needs rest. Recovery takes time, even if it feels like they don't have any to spare.

When she leaves, he submerges himself again. Sasza is unsure if vampires can drown, but he's not about to find out. Much work lies ahead of him, and if there's any hope for a reformed Empire, it's on the other side of a very, very long to-do list.

THE STORY CONTINUES IN...

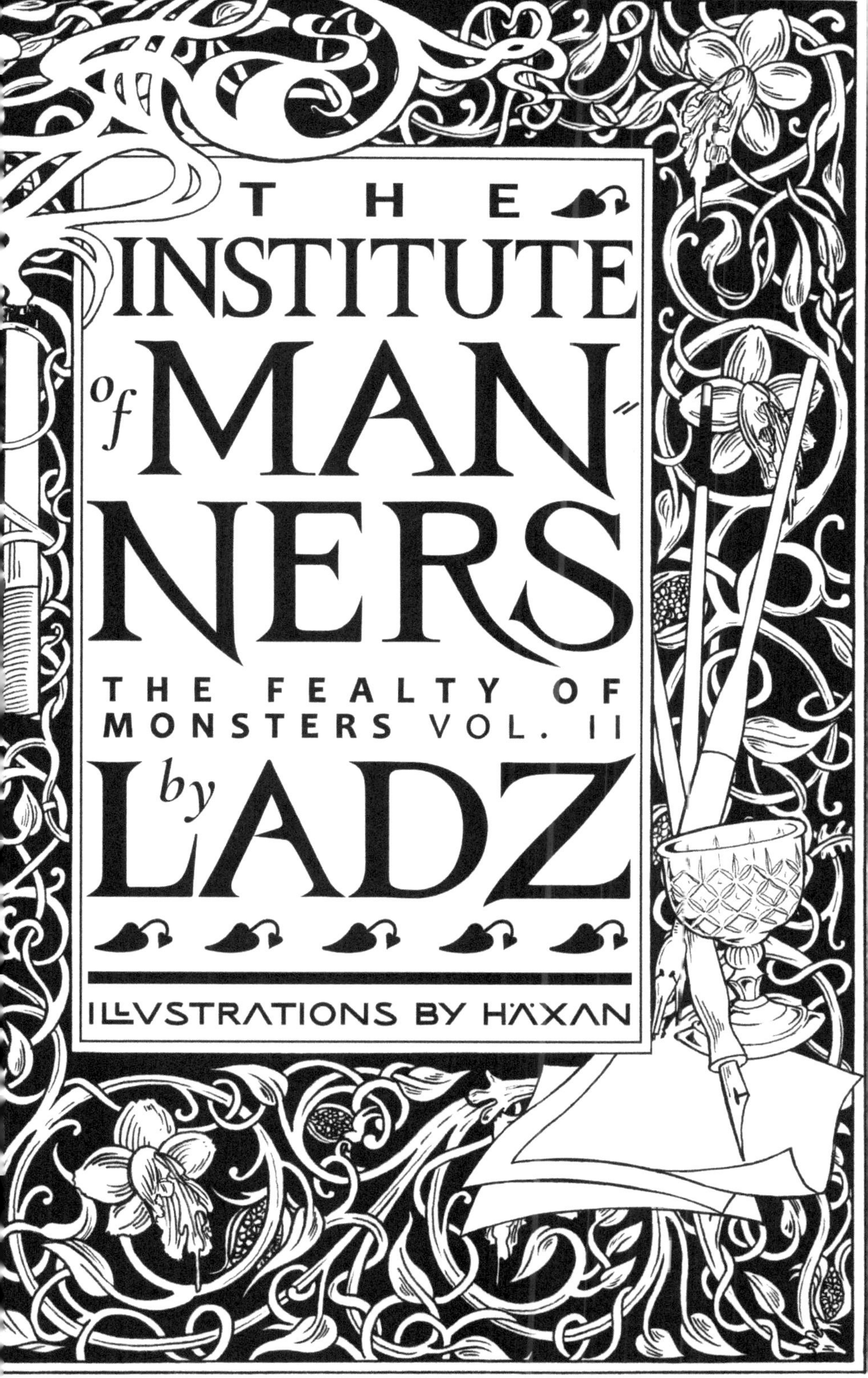

THE
INSTITUTE
of MAN-
NERS
THE FEALTY OF
MONSTERS VOL. II
by LADZ
ILLUSTRATIONS BY HÄXAN

COMPENDIUM

CHARACTERS

Main Characters

Aleksander "Sasza" Czarnolaski (Ah-lek-SAN-der "Sah-sha" Char-noh-LAH-skee): Twenty-three years old. He/him nonbinary hybrid vampire. Son of Władysław and Zofia Czarnolaski. Masquerades as a human among the Odonic Empire's aristocracy.

Iwona Ogrodnik (EE-voh-nah Oh-grod-nick): Twenty-four years old. She/her cis bisexual human. Emancipated daughter of an unnamed aristocratic family. Joined the Emperor's Chosen.

Ute Myśliwska (Ooh-tah Mysh-LEAF-skah): Twenty-four years old. She/her cis lesbian human. Rejected daughter of the Myśliwski family. Should have joined the Emperor's Chosen; becomes Świetlana's Magical Advisor instead.

THE ODONIC EMPIRE

Jan (Yahn): Early twenties. Mechanic in Daszek. Wants to go to an engineering school.

Jan's Father: Mid-fifties. Mechanic in Daszek. Does not want his son to go to an engineer's school.

Empress Gita Iwanowicz (Ghee-TAH Ee-vahn-OH-veetch): Fifty-five years old. She/her cis heterosexual human. Wife of Emperor Iwan. Mother of Świetlana. Władysław's secret lover.

Emperor Iwan Iwanowicz (Ee-VAHN Ee-vahn-OH-veetch): Fifty-five years old. He/him cis heterosexual human. Husband of Empress Gita. Father of Świetlana. Rules the Odonic Empire.

Władysław "Władek" Czarnolaski (Vwah-dys-swahv "Vwah-dek" Char-noh-LAH-skee): Sixty years old. He/him cis bisexual secret vampire. Father of Sasza. Emperor Iwan's Imperial Magician. Gita's secret lover. Masquerades as a human among the Odonic Empire's aristocracy.

Świetlana Iwanowicz (Shvyet-LAH-nah Ee-vahn-OH-veetch): Twenty-three years old. She/her nonbinary lesbian human. Parents are Emperor Iwan and Empress Gita. Best friend of Sasza. First in line for the Odonic Empire's throne.

Bianka Lewoński (Bee-YAHN-kah Leh-VOIN-skee): Early forties. She/her cis heterosexual human. Minister of the Interior. Had four children, only one still lives.

Ilya Górniak (Eel-YAH GOOR-nee-ahk): Fifty-two years old. He/him cis gay human. Finance Minister. Not originally of the aristocracy. Sasza's lover.

Laurencja Wielkodomska (La-oor-EHN-see-yah Viel-KOH-dom-skah): Forty years old. She/her cis lesbian vampire. Former songstress; works as a medic in Korona.

Captain Teodora Łukasiewicz (Teh-oh-DOH-rah Woo-kah-SHYEH-veetch): Late thirties. She/her cis human. Captain of the Nine-Second Regiment of the Emperor's Chosen.

General Oktawia Kwiatkowski (Ock-TAH-vee-ah Kvee-aht-KOHV-skee): Sixty-four years old. They/them nonbinary human. Director of the Emperor's Secret Service, which includes the Emperor's Chosen.

Mariola (Mah-ree-OH-lah): Twenty-four years old. She/her human. Archer within the Emperor's Chosen.

THE VAMPIRE STATES

Zofia Czarnolaska (Zoh-FEE-yah Char-noh-LAH-skah): Forty-five years old. She/her cis bisexual vampire. Mother of Sasza. Ex-spouse of Władysław.

Sylwia Kapuśniak (Sill-VEE-ah Kah-POOSH-nee-ahk): Thirty-two years old. She/her cis lesbian vampire. Sister of Sasza. Daughter of Władysław but not Zofia. Lives in Castle Otto and is a secretary of the Vermilion Envoy.

PLACES AND LOCATIONS

Mokosza (Mo-KOH-shah): Name of the continent where *The Fealty of Monsters* takes place.

THE ODONIC EMPIRE

Odonic Empire / Empire of Odon (Oh-DON-ick / Oh-DON): A large empire spanning eleven time zones and several terrains. Ruled by the Iwanowiczes. Home to dozens of autonomous political zones called The Vampire States.

Żyła River (ZSHY-wah): A large river separating the Kingdom of Waza from the Empire of Odon.

Daszek (Dah-SHEK): Port city renowned for scholarship far in the eastern Odonic Empire. Home of House Jackiewicz. Recovering from a firebombing during the summer of 1917.

Korona (Koh-ROH-nah): Capital of the Odonic Empire, home of the Iwanowiczes.

Imperial Military Academy: Rigorous training academy for elite soldiers. No one beyond the upper ranks knows its location.

The Institute of Manners: Elite university in the Empire's central steppe. Specializes in multi-disciplinary studies for aristocracy but has recently started accepting students from the proletariat.

THE VAMPIRE STATES

Castle Dytryk (Dih-TRICK): A state in the northeastern corridor. Where Sasza was born.

Castle Otto (Oht-toh): A state in the Empire's central steppe. Where Sasza's sister Sylwia lives.

Castle Wanda (Vahn-DAH): A state close to Korona. Sasza goes on trips to this one often.

GLOSSARY

Abyssal Flock: Collective; objectives and identity unclear

Aristocrat: Member of the elite within the Odonic Empire

Autobattery: Battery that stores magic instead of electricity

Autobus: Public transit. Large vehicle that can carry multiple passengers and runs on magic

Autocar: Car that runs on magic rather than coal

Autocell: Like a light bulb, but runs on magic

Autocoupe: Two-door vehicle for four passengers that runs on magic

Autocarriage: Larger vehicle that runs on magic rather than coal or drawn by steed

Bestiapir (Beh-stee-AH-peer): Beast vampire; come in two species—bat-form and mosquito-form

Blood tobacco: A more potent species of tobacco grown in the Vampire States; not safe for human consumption

Centrum: The middle of a city, usually a commercial district

The Emperor's Chosen: Secret service branch within the Military; not even the Emperor knows of their activities

Grosze (Groh-SHEH): pennies, singular is grosz

House Jackiewicz (Yatz-KYEH-veetch): Ruling family of Daszek

Hybrid vampire: Vampire which can transform into a bestiapir with the consumption of one's own blood; exceedingly rare

Inventors' Fair: Annual gathering of scholars, inventors, and other intellectuals taking place in Daszek

Imperial Magician: Role assigned to Władysław in service of Emperor Iwan; there is no consensus on what this role entails

Imperial Palace: Primary residence of the Iwanowiczes

Jackiewicz Incident: Title given to the massacre in Daszek during the summer of 1917

Kaszanka (kah-SHAHN-kah): Blood sausage, usually made with boiling buckwheat groats in pig's blood

Magical Advisor: Role assigned to a magician who isn't the Emperor, e.g. Ute's role under Świetlana

Noble: Member of the elite within the Vampire States

The Order of the Flock: Decentralized organization of proletariat working for a more egalitarian society within the Odonic Empire

The Pewter Square: Korona's largest plaza, typically the site of events like state funerals and coronations

Pierogi (pee-yeh-ROH-gee): Potato dumplings that can be filled with whatever filling the cook desires

Przekąska (p-sheh-KOHN-ska): Means appetizer

Proletariat: Member of the working class

Samogon: Home-made grain alcohol; everyone has their own recipe; sometimes infused with fruit

Smacznego (smatch-NEH-go): Roughly means bon apetit, typically said before eating a meal

Smalec (smah-LETS): lard, or poor man's butter

Tata (Tah-tah): Diminutive for "father"

Undead Blade: Weaponry smithed with the flesh and body parts of bestiapiry; feed on wielder's blood; can be swords, bows, shields, etc.

Uszanka (oo-SHAHN-kah): Fur hat with ear-covering flaps

Vampire: Blood-drinking species who looks mostly human

The Vampire States: Autonomous zones within the Odonic Empire where vampires rule

The Vermilion Envoy: Multi-state ruling body of the Vampire States

Winter Solstice Ball: An event for aristocracy to celebrate the ending of the year

Zdrowie (zdroh-VEE-eh): Means "cheers"

BIBLIOGRAPHY

This series is largely brought to you by the following deep dives:

- *The Unwomanly Face of War: An Oral History of Women in World War II* by Svetlana Alexievich (2017, Random House)

- *God's Playground: A History of Poland, Volumes 1 & 2* by Norman Davies (2005, Columbia University Press)

- *Revolutionary Russia, 1891-1991: A History* by Orlando Figes (2015, Picador)

- *Queer Gothic* by George Haggerty (2006, University of Illinois Press)

- *Rasputin: Faith, Power, and the Twilight of the Romanovs* by Douglas Smith (2016, Farrar, Straus and Giroux)

ACKNOWLEDGMENTS

This is my first ever story written without the intention of submitting it for traditional publishing. It was a scary decision to make, being left to my own devices like this, and I cannot thank the following people enough for helping bring *Fealty* into this bookish form.

First, my beta readers—especially those of you who were willing to read this story a second time.

Second, Soren, for being open to taking on this years' long project and for having such an incredible eye for art and design.

Third, Koren, Noah F., Noah M., and Ro who helped with line and copy edits.

Fourth, my writing group chats for being an endless font of support.

And last, but not least, Matthew, for making sure I'm getting enough sleep, water, and food when I'm losing my mind trying to write the exact sort of dark fantasy book I'd like to read.

ABOUT THE AUTHOR

Ladz was born in Poland, raised in New York City, and currently lives in Texas. When they're not a marketing manager for a major digital publisher, they're writing dark fantasy that tends to straddle other genres like true crime and horror.

They can be found online at jowritesfantasy.me or on most social media @ladzwriting.

About the Illustrator

Soren Häxan. Undead artist, author and historian of the gothic, the erotic, and the horrific. Dad to one very large cat.

Website: https://www.thornapple-press.com/

About Robot Dinosaur Press

Robot Dinosaur Press features queer, inclusive science fiction, fantasy, and horror books from a collective of global authors. For an introduction to our work, sign up to our newsletter at robotdinosaurpress.com/newsletter and receive a free anthology of short stories by RDP authors.